THE
COUPLE
BEFORE
US

BOOKS BY DANIEL HURST

The Holiday Home
The Couple's Revenge
The Family Trip
The Husband
The Baby Swap

THE PERFECT NURSE SERIES
The Perfect Nurse
The Nurse's Lie
The Nurse's Mistake

THE DOCTOR'S WIFE SERIES
The Doctor's Wife
The Doctor's Widow
The Doctor's Mistress
The Doctor's Child

THE
COUPLE
BEFORE
US

DANIEL HURST

bookouture

Published by Bookouture in 2025

An imprint of Storyfire Ltd.
Carmelite House
50 Victoria Embankment
London EC4Y 0DZ

www.bookouture.com

The authorised representative in the EEA is Hachette Ireland
8 Castlecourt Centre
Dublin 15 D15 XTP3
Ireland
(email: info@hbgi.ie)

ISBN: 978-1-80550-081-0
eBook ISBN: 978-1-80550-080-3

PROLOGUE

This was meant to be a new chapter in our lives – after all, moving into a new house should be an exciting time, a memorable moment. It's a chance for a fresh start, a new beginning and you want it all to go perfectly.

You certainly don't want any shocking surprises.

So what would be the worst thing to discover just after you've moved into your new home?

As I stare at the note in my hands, I think I might have the answer.

This feels like a warning, and it feels like it was written for me.

The note I have discovered hidden away in an upstairs bedroom of the beautiful house that my husband and I have just moved into was not part of the plan. We came here to be a family. Me, my husband, Christian, our five-year-old son, Kai, and our unborn daughter, who is due to arrive into this world in a few short months.

As one hand rests on my bump, the other continues to clutch the ominous piece of paper while I look out of the bedroom window and down at the large garden where I imagined my two children playing together happily one day. But instead of daydreaming about my family's future, all I can think about now is what I've just read.

Who wrote this? Why was it left here? And why did I have to find it?

I had hoped this to be our new start in these rooms coated in fresh paint. I thought we were going to be the first couple to ever live in this recently built house, and I assumed Christian thought the same, although now I'm not so sure. Either one or both of us has been lied to.

A couple lived here before us.

Their lives were in danger. But what happened to them?

And does this mean my family isn't safe here?

BEFORE

ONE

I anxiously rest my hands on my ever-expanding baby bump as I look around the house and try to imagine if this is the place I should raise my family. In three months, I will welcome a baby girl, to complete my family. My husband and our five-year-old son are both so excited. And if that wasn't life-changing enough, we are in the process of moving house too. We outgrew our previous place and need somewhere bigger. We also need it quickly. Our house sold after we accepted an offer that was too good to refuse. Although we haven't found the perfect house to move into, so we are currently living in a hotel room that is even more cramped than the space we had before.

I'm not quite panicking yet but I will be if we haven't found a home to live before my baby is born. That's why I was pinning my hopes on this viewing. But now I'm here, I'm not so sure.

'What are you thinking?' my husband asks, the sleeves rolled up on his work shirt and his top button undone after he removed his tie. He might be finished in his professional capacity today, but there is still plenty of work to be done in a personal capacity before he gets to lay his head on a pillow tonight.

I turn away from the perfectly polished marble countertop in this kitchen and face Christian, who is standing beside a large sliding glass door that leads out to the huge back garden. When I see his face, I already know what he is thinking. He likes it here. He likes it a lot. But I didn't ask him for his opinion. He asked me for mine.

'I'm not sure,' I say quietly. I don't want to be overheard by the estate agent who is showing us the property. The man in the sharp suit who unlocked the front door and invited us inside to take a look around is in the hallway, giving us a little space after already giving us his best sales pitch. He's done his work, telling us all about the four bedrooms, the three bathrooms and the room downstairs that would make either a perfect office for an adult or a perfect playroom for a child.

The estate agent has also told us all about how we would be the first people to live in this newly built property. In fact, we'd be one of the first people to live on the brand-new luxury housing estate. He assures us that the few residents who are already here are very happy with their decision to buy. Lastly, he mentioned that house prices in the area are sure to soar in the coming years, dropping a not-so-subtle hint that if we don't buy now, we might never be able to buy here ever again. Then, mercifully, he ended his sales pitch and left us alone to talk between ourselves. But I'm still talking quietly because I know he will obviously harbour hopes of getting the sale and earning a commission, so he might not like overhearing that I am not actually sold on the house yet. I glance out of one of the windows to see a large yellow excavator digging a huge hole at the end of the street. While I'm sure it's the foundations for something, I can't help but feel like I'm watching a grave being dug.

Quickly, I try to shake that thought from my mind.

'What's not to like, Di?' Christian asks me, holding out his arms as if I have somehow been blind to the wonders that he seems to have seen in this house. He always calls me Di, which is short for Dionne.

'Well, it's not very homely,' I say, raising my first worry.

'Of course not. We haven't moved in yet and made it our home. But we can do,' Christian replies smartly, but he's missing my point.

'No, I mean, it doesn't feel like a home. It feels a bit plain. Superficial, perhaps. No, what's the word I'm looking for?' I think, searching for the best way to describe it before it arrives. 'Vapid.'

'Vapid?' Christian chuckles. 'Were you reading a dictionary on the way here?'

'I'm just describing how this place makes me feel,' I go on, not joking around. 'It doesn't feel like somewhere I can see myself living. It's too modern. Too neat and perfect. I want somewhere more lived in, somewhere with a bit of history. Somewhere with character.'

'You knew it was a new-build house,' Christian says, finally realising that I'm really not warming to this place at all.

'Yeah, I didn't expect it to feel this new. It's just a bit... soulless.'

'No, it's not. It's amazing. Fresh. Tip-top. Pristine. Look around. This kitchen is a wonder. These smooth surfaces. This gleaming marble. The bifold doors. That immaculate lawn. Then there's the bedrooms. Any one of them could be the master. And the bathrooms. The walk-in showers. The his and hers mirrors. The heated flooring. Don't even get me started on the lounge. There's more than enough space for an L-shaped sofa and you've always said you wanted one of them. We could get two of them if we wanted to, there's so much room. And think of the playroom we could make in that spare room. What a perfect place for our kids to play together with their toys.'

For a second, it feels like the estate agent has taken posses-sion of my husband's body, such is the sales spiel that is coming from his mouth. The thing is, nothing Christian has said is wrong. He is right about all of it. Everything in this house is immaculate, and spacious, and ready and waiting for us to move in and put our mark on it. But I'm right too. Just because this place is big and fresh and ready to go, it doesn't mean we should take it. It might look perfect, but isn't it the imperfections that make a home? The creaky floorboard in the hallway. The shelf with a slight slant. The door handle that squeaks when turned, less annoying and more comforting in its familiarity. Nothing in this house creaks or squeaks. The steps of the stairs don't groan under our weight, nor does anything on the walls look uneven, as if it were a hurried DIY task in between countless other tasks that day. I don't want perfect, I want normal. Most of all, I want the house we viewed yesterday.

'I like the other place better,' I say quietly.

Christian scoffs loudly. 'Are you serious? The one with the overgrown garden and the tiny second bathroom? How can you prefer that to this?'

'I don't know, I just do,' I say, getting irritated that I'm having to defend my preferences so much. Then again, I guess differences of opinions are a part of any relationship, particularly a marriage. We haven't had too many disagreements in our seven years together, but we have had plenty of debates. In fact, the debating started before our first date. We met randomly on a night out with our friends and swapped numbers before arranging to see each other without anyone else around. Planning the date, I wanted to go for a meal while Christian tried to sell me on the virtues of just going for drinks. I won in the end. However, my winning record is no longer one hundred per cent.

I have a right to like what I like, just as Christian does. But when it comes to something as monumental as buying a house, it's imperative that we both agree. I guess that's not the case here, so it would make sense for us to leave and continue to keep looking for something we do agree on. But before I can suggest that we do just that...

'We could move in quickly,' Christian begins pitching to me. 'There's no chain because nobody has ever lived here. We'd be the first to own this incredible house. What an opportunity. Instead of spending our first few months redecorating over the previous owners' terrible wallpaper choices or fixing all the problems they caused, we could just enjoy being in this new place from day one.'

I know my husband hates decorating, so I can see the appeal for him. We really could simply move in and not have to do much, besides getting all our furniture unpacked when the removals company deliver it from storage. I know Christian is really desperate for us to be settled somewhere safe before our daughter arrives. I also know we'll be busy enough with our new baby soon to have time to worry about painting. I can see why Christian would rather focus on dad duties than opening tins of paint and putting shelves up. He's been incredibly attentive to me during my pregnancy so far and I know he will only step up even more after I have given birth. I also appreciate how hard he has been working to give us the chance to afford a bigger place like this. Even so, something about this house feels off to me and I think I know what it is. It's to do with the point Christian just raised. He thinks it's a selling point, but for me, it's a turn-off.

'It makes me nervous that we are the first to live here,' I tell him. 'I'd feel more comfortable buying a house from a couple who raised their children in it and have wonderful stories to tell about the memories they made inside their four walls. But there is no past here. It's a blank canvas. So how do we know this is the kind of home we should be raising our kids in? And it's not just the house, but this estate too. It's still mostly unoccupied, and not even completely finished. I want somewhere that feels neighbourly, not somewhere with big empty houses and a construction site at the bottom of the street.'

'When it is finished, it will be the most desirable estate in town,' Christian counters. 'Although when it's finished, it might be too late for us to get in. It's now or never.'

'But is it right for the kids?' I ask, not caring if I live somewhere desirable. I'm not trying to impress other adults; I'm simply trying to be a good parent.

As always, my main concerns are not for myself but for my children. I dote on my son and soon, I will be doting on my daughter too. This move is more for them than me. All the money we will spend, money that will really stretch us financially, is to ensure that they have the best childhood possible, with space to play in and room for their imaginations to soar. I don't want them to ever feel cramped or restricted because that might limit their happiness and potential. But while this place is big, it is missing something. It's missing what our previous home had and what I want our next house to have. It's missing the seal of approval from the people who lived in it before us. But there are no people. It's just us. We'll be the first to live here. And that makes me uneasy...

'Can we even afford this?' I ask my husband, wondering if a discussion of the finances will bring him back to reality. 'It is above our budget.'

'Don't worry about that. I'm due a bonus and I'll most likely get that promotion next year,' Christian replies, not bragging – he's not that kind of guy. He works hard as a Finance Officer and is proud of the progress he makes while supporting our growing family. If he isn't worried about the money then I shouldn't be because he knows a lot more about managing it than I do, considering his line of work, so I drop that particular argument. Before I can raise any more concerns, Christian sidles up alongside me, drapes an arm over my shoulder and points towards the glass doors.

'Look,' he says quietly and when I do, I see our blond-haired, blue-eyed son quietly staring out at the garden.

'Are you thinking what I'm thinking, Kai?' Christian says. 'Are you thinking that the garden is big enough for some goal-posts for all the games of football we are going to play?'

I watch my son to see his reaction, eager to know if he likes the house or not. When he turns around, I realise he is more on his father's side than mine. He's smiling.

'Yeah,' he says, still grinning, and I guess the garden has sealed it for him. Kai is football-mad, so having as large a space as this to play in is clearly appealing to him. It makes me happy that he's happy, but I'm still undecided. But I can't stay that way for long. Whether it's this house or another one, we have to find somewhere quickly. I can feel my daughter kicking again, a reminder that in just a few short months, she will be in my arms, demanding food and warmth and comfort. When that time comes, I won't have a spare second to think about anything else other than caring for her.

We need to find our new house fast and, judging by the looks on my husband's and son's faces, they feel they have already found it.

Maybe this is the place.

But if it is, why do I have such a bad feeling about it?

TWO

'Don't do that!' I cry as I lunge towards the lamp that my son has just hit with his miniature football. Fortunately, I grab the wobbling lamp before it smashes into a million tiny pieces, which is a relief, and not only because it would take a long time to tidy up. It's a relief because this is not my lamp to break and I'd have to pay for the replacement of it.

The lamp belongs to the hotel we are staying in, though this is no holiday.

This is our current home.

Living in a hotel room quickly humbles you. They're great places for a short break, or during a business trip, but not so great when your entire life is squeezed into the four walls of a very modest area. Christian and I are on the double bed that takes up most of the available space in here, and Kai is on the small, single bed by the wall, while what is left of the carpet is covered by all our bags and belongings. Our furniture items are in storage, but we have most of our clothes with us, and the solitary wardrobe in here is nowhere near big enough to house them all.

Living out of a suitcase in these cramped conditions is far

from ideal at any time, let alone when I'm pregnant. It's a nightmare trying to locate something I want in all the luggage that surrounds the bed. It's even a nightmare just trying to go to the toilet because with space at such a premium, finding a clear path from the bed to the bathroom is tricky. Try doing it in the dark of night while not wanting to disturb the other people in the room. My bladder has been the size of a pea lately, so I'm constantly up and down, stubbing my toes on suitcases and muttering under my breath about how we never should have sold our house before we'd found somewhere else to move into.

Kai initially thought it was cool that we were living in such close quarters to one another, and he certainly liked the fact that he could run around in the hotel corridors and take the elevator up and down to whichever floor he felt like visiting. He also enjoyed the fact that we get a free breakfast with our stay, and there is a view of the cars zooming along the motorway in the distance. But the novelty has worn off and he is now as fed up with our current living situation as I am. As for Christian, he prefers to focus on 'solutions, not problems', and to him, the solution has become very clear as I lie back down on the bed beside him.

'I think we should make an offer on that house,' he says to me. He's watching the television while Kai is now on his own bed engrossed in something on his iPad. 'I can message the agent this minute with our bid, and I think they'll accept. He told me he thinks he could have everything in place within a month, so we could be out of here soon.'

I wish things were a little more romantic between us than the current situation, where we are both tired, living in cramped quarters with our son and half-heartedly watching something on the TV. It's a far cry from our early dating days when time on the bed meant something else entirely. It's certainly very different to when Christian and I would go on holiday together to a hot country, only to forgo sipping cool drinks by the pool for a long, lazy day between the sheets in the spacious hotel room.

I also wish I had the energy to debate this conversation topic or at least had more options available to me in terms of other properties that we could potentially move to. But I don't have either. I'm exhausted, aching and have just finished another online search for available houses on the market only to be disappointed that very little has come on today. Even the property I liked, the older one with plenty of character, has been delisted. It might have sold or the owners might have changed their mind. I don't know, but either way, it's not available anymore, meaning at present, the only potential new home we are looking at is the one we saw today. The one Christian and Kai like. And the one I am still unsure about.

'We can't just buy it because we want to get out of this hotel room,' I reply. 'That's not a good enough reason to make such a big decision.'

'Of course not,' Christian counters. 'We're buying it because in a few months, there will be four of us, not three, and we really need to have a proper home to live in by then. So, what do you say? Shall we go for it?'

'I don't know,' I say with my hands resting on my swollen stomach, and Christian lets out a sigh.

'I sent a link of the house to your parents. They think it's great,' he tells me, and even though it takes me a few seconds to do so with my big bump, I sit up on the bed.

'Why would you do that?' I ask, frustration rising up inside me.

'They wanted to know how the house hunt was going.'

'It's none of their business.'

'It concerns their daughter and grandchildren, so I think they beg to differ,' Christian says, still horizontal on the bed beside me, though he doesn't look very relaxed. 'And they're worried about you. They want you to be comfortable in the last few months of your pregnancy.'

'I'd be more comfortable without having them interfering,' I snap back, feeling my mood worsening and it can't entirely be blamed on my hormones.

'Di, calm down. I'm just saying that—'

'Leave it.'

I decide to get off the bed and visit the bathroom then, making the perilous journey by sidestepping all our luggage, but it's worth it when I close the bathroom door and have a little bit of privacy. I don't want to argue with my husband, especially not in this small space with Kai present, but it's difficult when he does things he knows will annoy me.

He might maintain that my parents, Walter and Loretta, mean well, but I know better. My mum and dad aren't simply caring, they can be controlling too, which is the main reason why I refused the invitation to stay at their house while we were in between homes. I might feel stifled here, but it is nothing compared to what I would have felt like if I were living with my parents now, like the old days, having them constantly checking on me, ultimately, controlling me. I want to be independent, which is why I've always tried to refuse their offers of money ever since I became an adult. The easy thing to do would be to accept their help, and I know they'd like me to, but only because they are used to just throwing money at things and getting what they want.

My mum and dad had good careers, spending decades climbing the corporate ladder in the insurance world and reaping the monetary rewards. I don't pretend to know much about their working lives as my only experience of insurance is getting cover for the house and car, or the occasional holiday, and all I know is that it gets costlier by the year. It must be better to be an insurance employee than a customer, though, as my parents saved a lot over the years and then wisely invested it in various ways, so they are very wealthy in retirement. But with that accumulating pot of money came snobbery and a sense of entitlement. I have tried not to be like them, and I am trying to ensure Kai and my unborn daughter don't grow up to be like that too. Money isn't everything in the world, despite what my parents might think. I've found that I'm much happier when I limit my time around my mum and dad and their influencing ways. I love them, but I want my own life.

Frustratingly, rather than respect me and give me a little space, my parents just message Christian now to get updates on us and like a dutiful son-in-law, he replies to them every time, giving them what they want. It sounds like Mum and Dad want us to move into this new house, but of course they would. It would mean they get to tell all their other rich friends about how their daughter lives on some fancy new estate. I can just imagine Dad at the golf club talking about it with his mates on the fairways or Mum passing on the news to the other ladies in the clubhouse. Maybe I'll say no to this house just to spite them. Although that would be silly and, as I look at myself in the bathroom mirror, I know I am fighting a losing battle. My face is swollen and blotchy, my stomach looks even bigger than it did this morning, and while I can't quite see my legs in my reflection, they are aching and urging me to go and lie down again. Then, as if on cue, I feel another kick. My baby girl is moving around inside me or maybe she is trying to tell me something.

Take the house, Mummy. Get us out of this hotel room.

Do what your family need you to do.

Maybe it is the hormones or maybe it's fatigue, but I find myself listening to what I think are the wise words of my unborn child to the point where, as I leave the bathroom, I can't believe what I am about to say. I wait until I'm back on the bed, lying beside my husband, before I speak the words.

'Okay, let's make an offer on that house.'

Christian's eyes go wide as he processes the instruction I've just given him before it's his turn to sit up on the bed. Then he gives me a kiss on the head while looking like a child who got what he wanted on Christmas morning.

'Are you sure?' he double-checks before getting too carried away.

'Yeah,' I mumble back, not sure at all. 'They might not accept it, but we can see.'

Part of me is hoping they won't accept our offer because then I will have tried to appease my husband, but don't actually have to move into that house. But another part of me knows we are running out of time and life would certainly be a lot easier if we were living there in a month rather than still living here.

As Christian takes out his phone and excitedly tells me he is going to message the agent, I can see how happy he is, so I close my eyes and try to picture myself living on that estate. I try to remove all the elements like the unoccupied new homes and the construction site and instead imagine a bustling community that will be a joy to be a part of. I also try to imagine myself making that house a real home, filling it with our things, adding individual, intricate details that distract a little from the untouched nature of the property as it currently is.

Maybe I can make it work. Maybe living there will be great, after all.

Some family has to be the first one to live in that house and to make precious memories.

It might as well be us.

I just hope we're doing the right thing...

THREE

It is the second time I've stood outside this newly built house on this newly created estate. It's also the second time I have spotted construction work going on in the distance, as well as the second time I have looked around at the vacant homes and imagined the silence inside them.

But it's my first time here as the homeowner.

When Christian gave me the news that our offer had been accepted, I didn't have all the feelings of excitement that should be felt at a moment like that. Instead, I had one overwhelming feeling of panic. And I can't stop wondering if we've made the right choice. Only time will tell but this is day one – moving-in day – and the huge removals van parked behind me is the clearest indicator of that.

'We're going to be so happy here, I just know it,' Christian says to me, rubbing a reassuring hand across my shoulder before he goes to direct one of the removals men who has just taken a kitchen chair from the back of the van.

I smile because I can see how happy my husband is and I am hopeful that I will experience that same level of happiness shortly, once we are properly in this house and everything has settled down. But I'm not quite there yet.

The removals van is also further proof, if I need it, of how quickly the whole process has moved since we decided to make an offer on the house. Buying a house often takes a long time because there is usually a chain of properties being sold and each one depends on the other. But because we're the first ones to live here, we didn't have to wait for any previous owners to find a new place to live. And because we had already sold our place and we were living in temporary accommodation, once our offer was accepted, which it quickly was, we were told we could move in as soon as the paperwork was complete. The whole process was done in just a matter of weeks, which is crazily fast, and as I stand here watching the removals men work, I'm wondering if it was all a little *too* fast.

'Are you sure I can't get either of you a drink?' I ask the two burly men who are moving past me with our dining table, but they refuse my offer for a second time, clearly focused on getting this job done as quickly as possible. I can't grumble about that, so I leave them to it and go and join Kai, who is currently kicking a football around on the front lawn. He isn't too impressed at my attempts to play with him, laughing at me because I can barely kick a ball myself, certainly not in a straight line, but I'm trying to show an interest in my son's passion. His father usually plays football with him but he's busy dealing with the guy who has come to install our Wi-Fi, leaving me to juggle parenting duties with moving-in duties. But it's nice to see my son enjoying the garden space, which is one of the main reasons we wanted to move somewhere bigger, and I can see him really making the most of outdoor playtime here as the years go by.

As Kai runs around in pursuit of the ball I miskicked for the second time, I glance up the street at some of the other houses here. They all look identical to the one we have bought – two-storey, white-stone façade, with exactly the same size lawn and driveway in the same configuration. It's a little too samey for my liking, too cookie-cutter, but I'm sure things will change and these homes will start to look more personalised over time. Holidays are always good for that. People tend to have different tastes when it comes to Christmas or Halloween decorations, so all that seasonal bunting and lighting is sure to add some much-needed individualisation to this area.

From what I can gather, only three of the eight homes on this street are currently occupied, meaning there are five that stand empty, although they are complete and ready for new occupants to buy them and move in. I can see the same estate agent who showed us around taking a couple of prospective buyers into the house at the end of the street, so maybe we'll have more neighbours very shortly. But for now, it would be good to meet the neighbours we do have, so I look towards the house next to ours. There is a car on the driveway, so I presume it's occupied, but I haven't seen who lives there yet. I'm eager to meet whoever it is, though, and not just because it would be nice if somebody could put my mind at ease about our decision to buy here.

I'd love to make a new friend, so I'm hoping there is a woman of a similar age to me next door. Ideally, it would be another relatively new mother in her mid-thirties, who would enjoy long chats about parenting and married life and when that got too heavy for discussion, we'd move onto trashy reality television and celebrity gossip. We'd start by sharing coffee but then, once I've had my baby, we could progress to glasses of wine and eventually, over time, we could become great friends. It would be even more perfect if her partner could become friendly with Christian; my kids could play with her kids, and it could be a nice slice of suburban life. Or, in an alternate reality, I could get unlucky and the person living next door to me is not somebody I will get along with at all and we'll be resigned to

just awkwardly waving at one another whenever we acciden-
tally leave our homes at the same time.

I'm desperate to know which one it will be and suddenly,
when I see the front door of my neighbour's house open, I figure
I'm about to find out.

'Hi, welcome to the neighbourhood!'

The greeting comes from a smart-looking man in his thirties
who leaves his home and walks across his perfectly manicured
lawn with his arm extended by way of greeting.

'I'm Theo. Nice to meet you,' he says as he reaches me.

I quickly shake his hand to ensure I make a positive first
impression.

'I'm Dionne,' I reply before I notice Theo's eyes briefly flit
down from my face to my body. Is he checking me out? Or is it
simply impossible to ignore my bump?

'Looks like there'll be another person to meet soon enough,'
he says with a smile. 'Boy or girl?'

'It's a girl. I'm due in about three months.'

'Congratulations. And who might that energetic young boy
be?' Theo asks, looking over at my son who is now kicking his
football against the side of our house.

'That's Kai. And my husband's name is Christian. He's
inside.'

'I look forward to meeting him,' Theo says, sounding like he
means it, and while he glances at my house, I look over his
shoulder at his own. That's because I'm wondering if anybody
else lives with him or if he's the only person I'll get to meet.

'Oh, my partner is inside too,' he says then, seemingly
figuring out what I'm thinking. 'Her name is Hayley. I'm sure
you'll meet her shortly, although she can be quite a private
person, so don't be offended if she doesn't come out to introduce
herself right away.'

'Of course not,' I say, eager to meet Hayley but not wanting
her to feel any pressure about meeting me before she's ready to.

'So, I guess you fell for the same sales pitch that we did,' Theo says then.

'I'm sorry?'

'The whole spiel about why this is a great place to live and how we'd be crazy not to buy before the estate is full. You know, all that nonsense we were given by the estate agent.'

'Nonsense?' I repeat tentatively, worried that this is Theo's way of telling me that living here isn't as great as it's advertised to be.

'Oh yeah. It's all lies, believe me. Big mistake moving here. We'd move out as soon as we could, but we'd lose so much money, we can't afford to do it. So we're stuck here. Just like you are now.'

I stare at this man I've just met as my stomach sinks and my heart flutters. I knew it. It was a mistake to move here. This is the first day and my neighbour is already warning me. But it's too late. We've committed.

Why couldn't I have met Theo sooner and I would never have told Christian to make an offer on this house? But then I notice the wide grin spreading across Theo's face and realise he is just jesting with me.

'Got you,' he says, laughing and seemingly enjoying the brief period of panic I endured.

It's such a relief to realise that he wasn't telling the truth that I start laughing too.

'You had me worried for a minute there,' I confess, feeling a little embarrassed to have been tricked so easily. 'So this place is actually okay then?'

'Yeah, it's great. You'll love it here,' Theo tells me rather confidently. 'It might seem weird that most of the houses are still empty but it's really peaceful. I think I'll miss that once all the homes are full and there are noisy children running around everywhere.'

By that last remark, I get the impression Theo might not

have children and maybe it's because he doesn't like them, but then he smiles again.

'Don't worry, I love kids,' he says then adds, 'I'm not a father yet, but hopefully soon. In the meantime, don't worry about your son kicking his ball over our garden fence or anything like that. I won't mind. And don't worry about your baby crying whenever it is that she gets here. Don't worry at all.'

That's good to hear because I'm sure that even if I warned Kai not to disrupt the neighbours with his games, he'd most likely fail to stick to that agreement. What five-year-old plays quietly? As for the baby I'm soon to have, all the will in the world can't stop a newborn from making noise.

'I better get back inside, but it was a pleasure to meet you, and you know where I am if you or your family need anything while you get settled in,' Theo says before he turns and heads back to his house.

That was a nice introduction for him to make, but I make a mental note to be on my guard around him, at least until I have spent a little more time with him and got to know him better. That's because he's obviously the type of person who likes to joke around and be teasing in conversations rather than give the safe, honest answer. Those types of people usually make me feel on edge because you never know where you stand with them and it's hard to know if they are being serious or not. Hopefully, I'll get used to him and his ways and relax around him as time goes by. I also hope I get to know Hayley too, even if she is private like Theo says. For now, I return my focus to my family.

After telling Kai to come inside our house, I enter my new home to check on the progress of the removals men. Thankfully, they have put everything where I politely asked them to, so it's all looking good there. Progress seems to be made with the Wi-Fi installation too which is good and, as Kai goes to join his father, I'm momentarily free to have a little time to myself. I decide to go upstairs and have another look around the rooms up here, visualising what I am going to do with each one and how soon, hopefully very soon, this place will feel like our home and not some house that essentially came off a conveyor belt of other houses just like it on this estate.

I wander from room to room, imagining all the possibilities while simultaneously quieting the nagging voice at the back of my mind that is still telling me we should have waited for a property I preferred to come on the market. Just before I leave the third bedroom, I absentmindedly open the built-in wardrobe in here, and when I do, I notice something.

I was just checking to get a visual reminder of how much I can fit in this wardrobe, but now I have noticed something wedged in the bottom corner. It's a small folded piece of paper, which I presume is just a little bit of paperwork from when this wardrobe was installed, like the manufacturer's instructions on how to fit it or something like that.

Picking it up to clear it away, I unfold the piece of paper to see there is something written on it.

It's a short, simple statement and when I read it, I realise that we were lied to.

We are not the first people to live in this house after all.

FOUR

'I need to talk to you,' I say to Christian, eager to get him away from all the people helping us move in so I can speak with him urgently about the disturbing note I just found. I also need to have this conversation out of earshot of our son. I think I can manage that because Kai is now following the removals men around and that should keep him occupied for the next few minutes at least.

'Just one minute,' Christian says before turning back to check on a box of books that have been placed on the hallway floor.

'No, now!' I say, raising my voice a little more than I intended to, which draws the attention of one of the removals men, though he quickly averts his eyes from mine and carries on with his tasks. He probably thinks I'm stressed and struggling to cope with the pressures of a big move, but that's not it. I'm a stressed housewife who has just found something very concerning.

My husband knows better than to ignore me when my tone of voice is so curt, so he follows me into the kitchen. I thrust the note I found into his hand before he even has time to lean against the marble countertop and get comfortable.

'What's this?' he asks me.

'Read it,' I tell him, waiting the extra few seconds it will take for him to do that.

Christian lets out a deep sigh and does as I ask.

'"This house is not safe. Something terrible happened to the couple who lived here before you,"' he reads out loud before looking up at me with a puzzled expression on his face. 'What's this? Did you write it?'

'No, of course I didn't. I found it in the wardrobe.'

'You found it?' Christian replies sceptically. 'You mean to tell me this was just lying around?'

'Yes.'

'Who wrote it?'

'I have no idea, but somebody obviously left it here, maybe as a warning, and I found it and now I'm freaking out because it doesn't make sense. We're supposed to be the first people to live here, right?'

'Yeah, we are the first people.'

'That note suggests otherwise. It sounds like somebody was here before us. And they know something terrible happened. Who wrote this? And why have we been lied to about being the first people here?'

'Okay, first of all, calm down, because you're letting your mind run away with itself and that's not going to help matters,' Christian says smoothly, which only frustrates me more.

'I'm worried, Christian—'

'There's nothing to be worried about; you're reading too much into it.'

'No, I'm not. I'm just responding to the facts, and the fact is this note is very disturbing and suggests that we may have been lied to about our new house.'

'Nobody has lied. You're building it into something bigger when it doesn't need to be.'

'Stop talking to me like I'm a kid with an overactive imagination,' I snap. 'I'm an adult, just like you, so take this seriously or we are leaving here right this minute.'

'Woah, slow down. We're not going anywhere,' Christian cries.

'Then explain what that is,' I urge him, desperate for him to have some simple explanation as to what the note could mean that doesn't equal to us all being in danger.

'Well, erm,' Christian says, looking back at the note. 'Maybe it's a prank.'

'A prank?'

'Yeah, maybe one of the builders left it.'

'What? Why would they do that?'

'Because they probably thought it was funny,' Christian says, sniggering a little before remembering that he's supposed to be taking this seriously. 'Not that it is funny. Not at all.'

'What if it wasn't a builder? What if it was a previous homeowner?'

'Di, please. You're overreacting to this. It's just a scrap of paper. It's nothing.'

'But it shouldn't be here, should it? We're supposed to be the first owners, but that suggests otherwise.'

'It could be from anywhere. Maybe someone who lives in one of the other houses here snuck in and left it as a joke. Maybe some kids broke in and did it. This estate is still being built. I bet it's a great place for bored teenagers to hang around and get up to mischief. That's probably all this is.'

'Mischief? Really? That's what you're calling this.'

Why is my husband not listening to my concern? I wish this was the first time it had happened, but he's been like this ever since I got pregnant again, like he thinks any worries I have about anything can just be put down to my changing hormones.

To be fair, a lot of them probably can be. But not this. This is real and this could be serious.

'We don't have time for whatever this is,' Christian says then. 'We need to get all our stuff out of that van and get it unpacked. Are you helping or not?'

Christian tosses the note onto the kitchen counter then before leaving the kitchen. I guess this conversation is over, but I don't ever remember a time when Christian just stormed out of a room before we had finished our discussion. He would also listen to whatever I had to say, and he has always alleviated any fears I might have had in the past. But not this time. Something is different, which makes me second guess myself and worry that the problem here is me.

I think about what my husband said. Could he be right? Could that note just have been left by some kids messing around? Or a builder with a strange sense of humour? I suppose it is possible. We must be the first ones here. This place is brand new.

Now I'm doubting everything.

I know what I'll do. I'll ask the neighbours because they'll know, won't they? They'll know if anyone was here before us. I've already met Theo so I could just ask him, and he'll tell me the truth. At least I presume he will, assuming he doesn't make a teasing joke first. Then I wonder if his jokes could extend to this note. Could he have left this? He clearly likes to try and inject some humour into his daily life. Is that what this is? Being so close to next door, he could potentially have got in here when the house was unoccupied and left the note as a prank. Would he do that? If he has, it's not funny. But I don't know until I ask him. Until then, there's not much I can do about this. If we leave, we have to go back to that hotel. The removals company would charge us a fortune to pack all our things away again and return them to storage. And I'd have to somehow explain to Kai why we aren't actually staying in this big house with the big garden for playing football. He wouldn't be happy about that. He'd probably hate me for it. I'm sure Christian would too. I really don't want that to happen. So I guess we're staying.

I'm going to look out for more signs that someone might have been here before us, and I'll be asking the neighbours too. For now, though, all I can do is pick up that note and put it in my pocket. It's not that I want to keep it. It's just that I don't want to lose it. If I do, I'll end up thinking I imagined it and I definitely haven't.

I leave the kitchen a minute after my husband and go in search of Kai. If this note was just a bit of mischief like Christian thinks it was then I don't need my son adding any more mischief to our day. I can't see him in the hallway, nor is he with the removals men when I step outside to check the van.

'Where's Kai?' I ask Christian as I see him carrying a box into our garage.

'I don't know; I thought he was inside,' Christian replies with a shrug.

I shake my head but before I can say anything, we both hear a loud cry, and it definitely came from our son.

'Kai!' I call out as I turn and rush in the direction of the howl of pain. It sounded like it came from down the side of the house, so I race around the corner of our new property, but I still can't see him. I do hear another sound, however, though it's more a whimper than a cry this time.

I keep running as best I can with my bump weighing me down until I reach the back garden and that's when I see him. My son, lying on the grass, with blood pouring from his knee.

'What happened? Are you okay?' I ask him desperately as I reach him and drop to my knees on the grass to try and offer my assistance. But no sooner have I done that than I feel pain myself and when I look at my knee, I see blood too.

That's when I notice the sprinkler hidden in the grass. I

must have knelt on it by accident, then my son explains what happened to him.

'I fell on it,' Kai moans, pointing at the sprinkler with a pained look.

'Is everyone okay?' Christian says as he comes running around the corner of the house to find his wife and child on the floor with bloody knees.

'No, we hurt ourselves on that,' I cry, pointing at the damn sprinkler. 'Why is that there?'

'I don't know. I guess it must be fixed in,' Christian says. 'That's pretty helpful for summer, actually. Saves me having to water the grass.'

He quickly realises he has said the wrong thing and goes back to trying to help us both up, but I push his hands away. I'm mad at him. First, the note, now my son and I have hurt ourselves and we've not even been here an hour yet. I know my pregnancy hormones have something to do with how I'm feeling too, but in that moment, I lose control of my emotions.

'We should never have bought this house!' I cry, loud enough for not only my husband to hear me but the man who enters our back garden then. He's a handsome man in a sharp suit. I feel so embarrassed; this isn't my usual behaviour. He's clearly heard my outburst and he looks offended.

I soon find out why.

'Who are you?' I ask the random intruder into our garden.

'I'm Cesar,' he says, surveying the chaotic scene of a pregnant mother in distress, a child lying on the ground with a bloodied knee and a husband looking on gormlessly. 'I'm the owner of this estate and I've just come to welcome you to the neighbourhood.'

FIVE

'A good cup of coffee makes everything better, doesn't it?' Cesar says before taking a sip from the hot drink he just had one of his assistants fetch him.

That assistant brought back coffees for Christian and myself too, although I've barely touched mine because, despite Cesar's assertion, coffee does not make everything better. I also have to be careful about how much caffeine I consume while pregnant. Sure, the scrapes on mine and my son's knees caused by the hidden sprinkler will heal. Kai is already feeling better and is back to running around so I'm not too worried about him anymore. Although I am still worried about the note I found and now that I have the owner of this estate in front of me, it seems like the perfect time to ask him about it.

'I found this upstairs,' I say to Cesar, interrupting his latest sip of coffee by handing him the note from my pocket.

Cesar, a cool character who seems unflappable in the short time I have known him, takes the piece of paper from my hand. I expect this will be the moment he starts to lose his cool like I have already lost mine. But that doesn't happen. Instead, he reads what is written on the note before smiling.

'What's this?' he asks with a grin.

'I want you to tell me,' I fire back.

'Well, I have no idea,' Cesar replies, and I see him give Christian a look as if to ask him if I'm this difficult all the time. Although he's smart enough to not ask that question out loud. If he did, Cesar would be the next person with blood leaking from their body and it wouldn't just be from a small cut on his knee, that's for sure.

'Are we the first people to live in this house?' I ask Cesar firmly.

'Of course you are. This is a brand-new property, just like all the others on this estate.'

'Yes, that's what we were told. But that note seems to suggest otherwise.'

'I told her it was probably a prank,' Christian cuts in. 'A builder, maybe. Or some bored kids who snuck in.'

I study Cesar's face, but he doesn't give much away to let me know if he agrees with my husband's assertion.

'A prank from a builder? It's possible, although that would not be very professional and I've been sure to hire the best,' Cesar replies. 'As for kids or other intruders, no, this estate is very safe and that would not happen.'

'What about one of your staff here on the estate?' I ask him then. I have already seen that he has an assistant and maybe there are more staff here. I presume there are groundskeepers based on the fact that there are lots of green areas surrounding this estate that seem to be well maintained.

'No, absolutely not,' Cesar says, looking offended that I would suggest he might employ somebody who would play a prank.

'So it was the builders then?'

Cesar seems uncertain but eventually concedes.

'That must be the case,' he says quietly. 'I apologise.'

That's something, I suppose, but my paranoid brain needs more.

'Do we have your word that no one lived in this house before us?' I ask Cesar, staring him in the eyes.

'Yes, absolutely,' Cesar replies, totally unflinching, so he must be telling the truth. Or he's an excellent liar, one of the best I've ever encountered.

'I apologise about this,' he says again. 'I have no idea how it got here, but it shouldn't have been left by whoever thought it was funny to do so. And I apologise about the incident with yourself and your son with the sprinkler. The sprinklers are mentioned in the details of the home, but we could do more to make our buyers aware, so I'm sorry for that. Is there anything else that has caused you any trouble so far?'

Considering we've only been here a short time, I'd say that should be more than enough, so even though I shake my head, it's hardly a win for Cesar. But he looks to have quickly regained the confidence that he first appeared here with because he sets his coffee down on our kitchen countertop and begins a very impassioned speech.

'I came here to welcome you to this estate and thank you for putting your trust in us that this is the best place for you and your family. You have made an excellent choice, and I am absolutely certain that you are going to enjoy being a resident here. I understand that life is unpredictable and circumstances change, but all being well, you will live here for many, many years and, who knows, maybe you will pass this house down to the next generation of your family and they will continue to live here after you have gone.'

'Let's hope so,' Christian says with a smile, but I choose to remain quiet.

'Now, I appreciate that you have lots to do around here as you settle in and make yourselves comfortable,' Cesar goes on and I get the impression he is more of a talker than a listener.

'Before I leave you to it, I'd like to highlight what makes this estate extra special. You see, this isn't just a place to live. You have bought so much more than a house. You have bought into a community. It might seem quiet as we continue to build and sell the other houses, but there is already a strong sense of community and that is most on show during our monthly neighbourhood get-togethers.'

'Get-togethers?' I repeat, looking at Christian because I didn't know about this, but he just shrugs.

'That's right,' Cesar says. 'On the first Saturday of every month, all residents are invited to a lunch at our estate main office, although we will have the event outdoors if the weather is nice. And while it is just an invitation, I really do encourage you all to attend as it really is the best way of not only getting to know your neighbours but to really embed yourselves in this community and make yourselves an integral part of it.'

There's that C-word again. *Community.* I guess it's Cesar's buzzword.

'There will be food and drinks and music, as well as fun games for the little ones,' he goes on. 'Last month, we had a puppeteer. The kids loved that. Plus, a couple of beer kegs, which went down well with the men.'

He winks at my husband.

'That sounds great,' Christian says, easily sold by the prospect of drinking alcohol with like-minded men. 'We'll be there.'

There goes my husband, once again committing us to something I am not sure about yet, but Cesar has the answer he obviously came for, and he is now ready to leave.

'Excellent. I'll leave you to finish getting moved in but if you need anything, do come by the office. And if it's outside of office hours, I live on the estate myself, so I'm always around. That's how I can give you my personal guarantee that you will love it. It's because I love it so much that I choose to live here too.'

With that, Cesar departs with a flamboyant wave, marching out of our kitchen, and the only sign that he was here is his empty coffee cup sitting on the countertop. I pick it up to dispose of it and notice that it hasn't left a circular coffee ring on the counter. Of course it hasn't. There are no imperfections here, and that continues to irritate me. The house is so pristine that I feel like throwing the coffee at the wall just to add a little life and colour to this room. I only have to look at all the boxes piled up on the other side of the counter to remind myself that soon, the house will be full of things that make it feel a little more normal. I just need to unpack them all first.

I should get started on that but I'm still mulling over my first encounter with Cesar, the charismatic, albeit cocky, man behind our house and all the others on this sprawling development. He must be a very wealthy man, and he certainly dresses like one, but he did seem keen to stress that he is here to help. He was also keen to stress that people love living on the estate. A little too keen, if you ask me. But of course he would say that. His profit margins depend on it.

It's interesting that he lives here too, but then that could just be because it's where he works and it saves him time off his commute. He'll probably leave as soon as the last house is sold and retire to the Caribbean with all the money the residents made him. The real answer as to how good this place is to live in should come from the other people like us, outsiders who purchased property like we have, so I will be sure to ask them. If I have to go to those get-togethers on the first Saturday of every month, I won't just be going for the free food and drinks. I'll be going to ask questions of my neighbours. I can even ask them about my house and if anyone knew about anything that might have happened before we moved in.

Yes, I'm still thinking about that note, and I realise that Cesar never handed it back to me. He must still have it and he might have disposed of it already. Getting rid of the evidence, perhaps? If he has been lying to us then that would certainly be the right way to go for him. But why would he lie? What possible thing could he be trying to hide? Something about another couple before us, or something about this estate as a whole?

But it doesn't matter if he does destroy that note because it's too late.

I already saw it.

And I won't forget it.

SIX

It's quiet out here. *Too quiet.*

It's nine o'clock in the evening and I've just left my new house to go for a walk. An evening stroll is something I committed to in the early stages of my pregnancy in an attempt to avoid the rather rapid weight gain I experienced during my first time as an expectant mum. So far, it seems to have helped. I'm definitely not as large as I was at this stage when carrying Kai, although that may be less to do with my daily exercise and more to do with the fact I haven't been craving cheese and biscuits like I was last time. But while these nightly walks have been regular over the past several months, this is my first time walking here.

My new neighbourhood.
My new home.

It feels weird calling it that, but that's what it is. It feels even weirder to be outside on a street full of houses and not hear a single sound. It might be getting late but there are usually some suburban sounds around to disturb the peace, sounds that are surely common in all neighbourhoods. Like a front door being opened and shut or a car trundling down the road. Maybe something being emptied into a bin or the sound of a dog barking. A little music drifting out from an open window, perhaps, or even just a piece of litter blowing along the pavement before getting stuck in a gutter. Anything that indicates signs of life. But no, it's deadly quiet out here, as any half-populated estate in the middle of the countryside would be, I suppose. The location, surrounded on all sides by sprawling fields, is supposed to be another one of its selling points, but right now, it just makes me feel incredibly isolated.

Adding to that feeling, I can barely see any lights on in the other houses. There's the light from the front room of our home behind me, which is where Christian is currently unwinding on the sofa with a glass of red wine while Kai sleeps in his new room upstairs. And I can see a light on next door at Theo's, though I cannot see him or his partner, who I still haven't met yet. But that's it. All the other houses on this street are dark. I thought there was another couple who had already moved in. If they have, they must have gone to bed early. Or they are out. Either way, they aren't helping make the area seem any more lived in.

I start walking, not a fast pace, just enough to get my legs moving and my blood pumping and like any doctor would say it will, the fresh air and exercise do start to boost my mood. But only slightly because I'm still feeling a little uneasy as I make my way along the eerie street, wishing a car would pass by or a light would turn on in a window, giving me the opportunity to wave and see a friendly face smile back at me. But nope. It's just me out here.

I keep walking down my street, passing houses that look exactly like mine, before I turn onto the next street and see that all the houses are the same too. That's the case on the third street I go down and very quickly, I'm starting to feel like my nightly walks will be extremely tedious if the scenery doesn't change at all. But then I reach a street where the houses are different. Not only are they bigger, but the design is different. These houses look more rustic, and as such, they appeal to me a lot more than the one we have. But I can't regret choosing the wrong house. Given how big these properties are, there's no way we would have been able to afford one of them.

Suddenly, the fact the neighbourhood is so quiet is to my advantage because it means I have the time and space to walk slowly and have a good snoop at these impressive houses. There are a couple of driveways with cars on them, so I guess they are occupied, but many are still empty. I'm surprised they haven't been taken off the market yet by people with boatloads of cash because these homes look lovely, but I'm sure they'll all be full soon and when they are, I won't be able to stare at them so much without being seen myself.

I keep walking until I realise that the street is a cul-de-sac and there is no way for me to exit it from this end. I'll have to turn around and walk back the way I came, but just before I do that, I get a good look at the house at the end of the cul-de-sac. It's dark but it stands out. While the homes on here are huge, this one is even bigger.

'Wow,' I actually say out loud as I stare at the imposing property and try to imagine how much it must cost to buy. But I can't even think of a figure that could be correct, which is only a reminder that I don't have the kind of money to even think about making a purchase like this myself.

I want to get closer and have a better look, and I have a feeling I could because there are no lights on inside, so the house might be unoccupied too. But I hold back, feeling like it would be wrong of me to just go up to it and start looking through the windows, even if there is no one inside and no one's privacy to invade. Maybe I'm too polite but I should just walk away and leave the street and the massive mansion behind, before trying to shake the feelings of envy I have for whoever will own this place one day.

Then I see movement in one of the windows and, a second later, I find myself staring at someone I know.

It's Cesar.

I guess I was wrong. This house is not unoccupied. It must be where he lives, and he's just caught me staring right into his home.

I don't know whether to wave or just turn and walk away and pretend I haven't seen him, but before I can do either, he waves at me. I guess I should wave back to be polite, so I do that before rushing away in the opposite direction. I can't help but glance back and when I do, I see that Cesar is still watching me.

I hurry along but think about him and the note I handed to him earlier. Did he take it back to that house? Does he still have it? Or did he dispose of it?

One thing is for sure; he has a lovely home. He's clearly done well for himself, but I suppose I can't dislike him for being a smart businessman. But I can dislike him for potentially lying to me.

Is that what he did earlier?

That's the problem with the truth.

You don't always know if you've heard it.

I walk for ten more minutes in what I thought was the way back to my house before I realise I have actually gone the wrong way. It's easily done when it's dark and the houses look so samey, but that's not going to help me find the right way home. I try another street and think I'm on the right track now.

I finally reach my house after that unplanned detour and let out a deep sigh as I walk up the driveway. That's because I know how much work is waiting for me when I go inside. I'd like to say we've made progress on the unpacking, but it doesn't feel like it. It certainly doesn't look like it. There are boxes everywhere and while I won't continue the laborious process of emptying them tonight, I'll have to be right back at it tomorrow morning if we are to make any headway. Just before I can open my door and be greeted by all those boxes, I freeze because I hear a very distinctive sound.

It's the sound of someone crying.

I turn to my left, as that's where it's coming from, and now I'm looking at the house next door. It's Theo's house, but I don't think he is sobbing. That's because the noises sound like they are coming from a female. Is it his partner? Is it Hayley? Was that her name? It must be her, though I can't see her. But I can hear her and she is definitely in distress.

What should I do? Knock on the door and ask if everything is okay? What if Theo answers instead of her? That might make things worse. I decide to leave it but another sob, this one louder, makes me realise why I can hear the sounds so clearly.

They are coming from the back garden.

I tiptoe to the rear of my property before pausing by the fence and listening to the other side of it and now I can hear the crying is louder. Yep, Hayley is right on the other side of this fence and that means if I was to whisper to her, she would surely hear me like I can hear her.

So I go for it.

'Hey, is everything okay?'

My voice is low but loud enough to be heard and no sooner have I spoken than the sobbing stops. But I don't get a response, so I speak again.

'It's Dionne. I've just moved in next door. We haven't met yet, but I met Theo, and I just heard you, so I wanted to check that—'

I stop whispering when I hear the sound of a door slamming.

I listen out but hear nothing else and that's when I realise Hayley must have gone back into her home. She obviously didn't want to talk to me and tell me what was upsetting her. She might have been embarrassed that she had been overheard, but she shouldn't be. I just want to make sure she is okay.

Is she?

I guess I've lost my chance to find out.

I decide to give up and go inside my own home, but as I do, I am only feeling more unsettled.

This place has me on edge. And Hayley is crying, so what has happened to cause that?

Is it something Theo did to her, or is it something else?

I want to know. *I need to know.* While I'm in a relationship with a good guy now, I suffered through my fair share of bad boyfriends in the past, so I know what it is like to not be happy with your partner. Theo does certainly give off an unsettling vibe, so is he the source of Hayley's suffering?

I've only been here a day but already the questions are starting to rack up, questions concerning both my house and the neighbour's house.

One thing is clear.

Cesar is not the man to answer them. I'm not sure I trust him. He has a vested interest in keeping anything negative about the estate quiet. But I have my own vested interest, and it is one that is far stronger than his concerns for future profit. I have to ensure the safety of my family.

That means one thing.

I'm going to have to get the answers myself.

SEVEN

I slept poorly and while it would be easy to blame it on being my first night in a new house, the truth is there were lots of things swirling around my brain, not least of which is why the woman next door was in tears in her back garden. I didn't mention it to Christian last night when I got in because he'd fallen asleep on the sofa, clearly exhausted from a day of moving furniture. I just gently woke him, and we both went up to bed. But I will mention it now we're both properly awake.

'I heard something strange on my walk last night,' I say as I watch Christian fastening the blue tie that sits on top of his crisp white shirt. 'The woman next door was crying.'

'Crying?' Christian says while checking his reflection in the mirror.

'Yeah, she sounded really upset. I spoke to her through the fence and asked her what was wrong.'

'You don't even know her.'

'I know that, but it seemed like the kind thing to do.'

'So what did she say?'

'She didn't say anything. She just went back into her house.'

'Maybe it's nothing then,' Christian says with a shrug before he brushes a speck of lint off his shirt.

'It obviously is something if she was so upset.'

'Okay. Then maybe it's none of our business.'

He must know that's not what I want to hear, but before I can reply, he walks out of the room. I know he'll be going to wake up Kai and get him ready for school, and I don't want to make him run late this morning. But I also want to talk about this. That's because I am worried that the tears I heard being shed last night might also be connected to the note I found. What if my neighbour Hayley is upset because of something terrible that's happened in my house?

I get out of bed and get dressed, throwing on an oversized hoody and a pair of loose leggings, comfortable pregnancy attire that will provide me with enough manoeuvrability to manage both my bump and bending over to take things out of boxes all day. Then I go and check on my husband and son. When I do, I find Kai resisting the start of a new day, which is common for him since he turned five. Before that, he used to be up at dawn, seven days a week, but like all kids, just when you think you have them figured out, they change their ways. Now, Kai seems to be someone who wants a lie-in, which is great on a weekend, but not so great on the days of the week where he is required to get up and get to classes.

'Come on, Kai, get moving. I won't ask you again,' Christian says, and I know he doesn't have the patience for being held up when he has work to get to. He'll be dropping our son at school on his way into the office, so on top of dealing with other road users on his commute, he also has a sleepy schoolkid to contend with. Our son is still at the same school, which, thanks to the move, is now a further fifteen minutes away, so time really is of the essence in the mornings, more so than ever.

Not for the first time, I feel a little guilty about the fact that I'm pretty useless at this time of the day. The reason for that is because I don't drive. I never have. I never even took a lesson. I just decided as a teenager that driving wasn't for me and that was that. Christian laughed during our first date when I told him I didn't have my licence. He thought I was joking. Then, when he realised I wasn't, he was worried I had experienced something terrible on the roads that had put me off ever getting behind the wheel myself. But I told him that wasn't it. I just didn't want to do it. Maybe there is a fear there deep down somewhere, or maybe it's just because I genuinely do prefer to walk everywhere I can. Whatever it is, I can't drive my son to school, so Christian has to fit it into his morning schedule instead, which is something that I really appreciate him doing.

Christian said that me not driving wasn't a dealbreaker if we were to get together as a couple, though he may have just been saying anything he thought I might want to hear as he hoped to woo me into bed during our early dates. I have to imagine he has become more than irritated by it now, although, bless him, he has never actually explicitly asked me to start taking driving lessons. Nor has he ever told me to think about a possible career change. His understanding of me is one of the reasons I love him so much.

In terms of work, I have a small online business. I sell fridge magnets and other household decorations that I design and make myself. I've always been into arts and crafts since I was a child. I'm a 'tinkerer', as my dear grandmother used to say, which means that I like to make things with my hands and express myself creatively, turning small, seemingly banal items into something pretty and hopefully useful. I have plenty of positive reviews from people who have bought my items online over the years, and while the price they pay for them is often small, the pride I get from such feedback is huge. I don't earn us a fortune, even less once parenting became my main focus and I had less time to 'tinker', but I like it as an occupation, and Christian earns more than enough in his job to allow me to do it.

I guess I'd have had to do something else if I'd still been single, unless I wanted to live with my parents forever, but having dual incomes helps, even if it is massively weighted towards one person. But again, Christian has never expressed frustration with that. He knows parenting is what I enjoy the most rather than chasing a lucrative career, so between raising Kai and his future sister, making my household decorations plus doing whatever needs doing around the house, I contribute more than my fair share in our relationship and maintaining our household. Our relationship works well and I'm excited for our growing family. But I'm still not driving. *No thank you.*

'A guy is coming to fix the landline connection this morning,' I tell Christian as we're in the kitchen tucking into our bowls of cereal. Thankfully, Kai is with us, his uniform on, just like his grumpy frown is on too.

'Do we really need that doing?' Christian asks me with a chuckle. 'This is the mobile era, if you hadn't noticed.'

'Our mobiles aren't much good without a decent signal,' I reply easily. 'And we don't seem to have that here, *if you hadn't noticed.*'

I just love it when I can tease my husband with his own words, and he rolls his eyes to show I have him beat.

'Yeah, the signal is pretty lousy,' Christian agrees, glancing at his phone and giving up easily. 'I guess we need to get the Wi-Fi installed sooner rather than later.'

'I thought this house was supposed to come with the connection already installed,' I say, remembering something the estate agent said while he was showing us around. 'Like an additional selling point they had to offer.'

'I can't remember now,' Christian replies with a shrug. 'Either way, I'm sure it won't take long to resolve.

'What else have you got planned today?'

It's a safe, sensible question and despite all the upheaval recently, I find some comfort in the fact that in this moment, we are just talking through our upcoming day like any other married couple would be doing.

'Unpacking, unpacking and more unpacking,' I reply, looking around at all the boxes and that sounds like a pretty simple, if not a boring daily plan. But there is something else I intend to do, although I won't tell my husband about it yet. That's because I know he'll try and talk me out of it. I plan to go next door and see if I can speak to Hayley. I want to see if she is okay and give her another chance to open up to me. One, I want to be a good neighbour, but two, I have a feeling there are some things about our house she might have to say that Cesar never would. I'll have to wait for my husband to be out of the house before I try anything, though, but fortunately, I don't have to wait long.

'Right, come on, kid, let's get going,' Christian says as he picks up his empty bowl and carries it to the sink.

Kai tries to protest but he knows it's futile, so he begrudgingly gets up and follows his father into the hallway, where shoes and coats are put on before the two males in my life are ready to be waved goodbye.

'Have a good day, I love you,' I say, mainly to Kai, but the message is just as relevant to my husband, and he gives me a kiss before he opens the front door.

Christian looks good in his suit, just like Kai looks cute in his school uniform, and I admire the pair of them as they go to the car and get inside. Then I wave them off before closing the door and enjoying that first moment of peace that always occurs this time of day, ever since Kai started school and I felt like I was starting to get back some time for myself.

I'll certainly miss a quiet house when this little one is born.

I stroll into the kitchen with one hand resting on my bump and decide to unpack a couple of boxes, as it's a little too early to go next door and try and talk to Hayley yet. I'll wait until mid-morning because that feels like a more respectable time to knock on a person's door. With a bit of luck, Theo will have gone out to work, although Hayley might have done the same. I don't know what they do for jobs – I don't really know them yet. I just know that Hayley was upset about something, and I want to find out what it is.

A personal issue? Maybe.

A neighbourhood issue? *I really hope not.*

I've just opened the first box and reached inside to grab a carefully wrapped salad bowl when I hear a knock at the door.

'What have they left behind now?' I say out loud to myself as I head for the door, wondering whether it's my husband or son who has forgotten to take something with them. I expect it's Kai who has been absentminded, but when I open the door, I don't see him or Christian.

I see Theo.

'Oh, hello,' I say, caught off guard.

'Hey, good morning,' Theo says with a big smile, one that looks a little forced and I find myself worrying that Hayley told him about me calling to her through the fence last night and now he has come around here to tell me to keep my nose out of their business.

'I just wanted to check if you were settling in okay and to offer my assistance if you need any help with anything,' Theo says, which doesn't sound like him telling me off at all. It just sounds like him being very nice. But maybe a little too nice? I notice his eyes lowering again as he looks at me, plus there's the fact that he seems to have appeared the second my husband left. Is he being neighbourly? Or a bit of a creep?

'Everything's fine, thank you, and that's very kind of you to offer to help but I'll manage. Thanks.'

'Are you sure?' Theo says. 'I'm very flexible with work so I can come in and help move anything that might be a bit heavy.'

'Erm, I'm sure, thank you.'

'Okay, well if not today then maybe some other day. I'm just next door.'

'Right. Of course, thank you.'

I don't really know what else to say other than to keep thanking him, but just before Theo leaves, I blurt out something that I probably should have kept to myself.

'Is everything okay with Hayley?'

Theo pauses.

'It's absolutely fine. Why wouldn't it be?'

Should I mention the crying? Would Hayley have told him that I heard her? Or would me bringing it up with him potentially get her into trouble if he is the cause of her suffering?

'I was just asking,' I say as casually as I can, and I think Theo buys it.

'Cool. Well, I'll catch you later,' he says before pausing to add something. 'This estate is really quiet during the day. If you ever need any company, just give me a shout.'

Theo winks then before departing, and I decide that he is flirtier than he should be considering he has a partner. I also decide that him being overly nice with me might be masking a very different personality behind closed doors and that Hayley's tears could be a sign of that. I will be wary of Theo, just like I'm choosing to be wary of Cesar. But as I close my front door and walk through my home, I realise that I'm wary of it too. That damn note won't leave my mind and between that and the Hayley mystery, I have more than enough to keep me occupied before I even start any more unpacking.

So much for suburban housewives being bored all day.

I *wish*.

EIGHT

It wasn't my idea to host a dinner party while my home is still in such a dishevelled state. It wasn't my husband's either, nor was it my son's. Nope, that idea belonged to my parents. Walter and Loretta, aka Mum and Dad, are on their way here after not only inviting themselves around this evening but insisting that we all sit down and share a homecooked meal together.

It's understandable that my parents want to see my new house, but it's not very understanding of them to neglect the fact that half my kitchen was still packed away in boxes before their 'brilliant suggestion of dinner'. I tried to suggest a take-away instead, or maybe even going out for a meal, but Mum and Dad insisted on coming here and they said it would be nice if we all sat down to eat a 'proper meal' on plates rather than out of cardboard containers, so here we are. I've spent the last two hours trying to make a lasagne and getting increasingly frustrated because I couldn't locate half of the cooking utensils required to make such a dish. It's taking me way longer than it usually would to cook, and I've felt like giving up several times and just phoning the nearest pizza place instead, but I've always been prevented from doing so by Christian.

'It'll be worth it,' he said. 'It'll be nice. Your parents mean well, you know they do. Kai will love seeing them too.'

I should have known Christian would be on their side rather than mine. He'd do anything that my parents wanted, always keen to make a good impression with them, and I can see that is evident again this evening. He's put on a very smart shirt and is currently opening a bottle of red wine that he picked up on his way home from work. Two minutes ago, he was trying to locate our speakers so he could have a little background music playing during our dinner. As if we have time for any of this. But it's too late now because there's a knock at the door and I guess that means our guests are here.

'I'll get it,' Christian says, instantly smoothing out his shirt and running a hand through his hair before heading for the door. I wish he wouldn't be so nervous around my parents. It was cute at first, but we've been together years now and they've already accepted him into the family. Even if they hadn't, at this point, I wouldn't care as long as I was happy, but he still acts like he's constantly meeting them for the first time.

If I had to guess, I'd say it's because of their money. I might not care about it but I think Christian does, or rather, he cares about staying close with my parents up until the point when they have made their wills and there is a large inheritance to be gained. But I'm sure Mum and Dad made their wills many years ago and as an only child, I stand to inherit it all, so there really is no need for him to be rolling out the proverbial red carpet every time they are in our vicinity. But here he goes again...

'Come in, welcome!' I hear my husband cry from the hall-way. 'You're looking lovely, Loretta. Is that a new coat? It is? Well, I love it!'

I roll my eyes as I continue preparing dinner while I listen to Christian go on.

'Good to see you, Walter. Are you well? Found time for any

golf this week? You're looking in good shape. I'll have to play nine holes with you again sometime. It's been a while.'

I hear Kai coming down the stairs to greet his grandparents, and I know he'll be pleased to see them, so that just leaves me as the only one who has to go and give my greetings. As I reluctantly leave the kitchen, I notice the bottle of wine Christian opened sitting on the side ready to be poured and, not for the first time during my pregnancy, I rue the fact I can't temporarily boost my mood with something to drink that is stronger than green tea.

'Hi, Mum. Hi, Dad,' I say with a decent enough effort as I see them greeting Kai. 'Welcome to our new place. What do you think?'

I hug my parents before receiving their opinion on the house they are seeing for the first time.

'It's very nice,' Mum says as she looks around the hallway, and I suppose that's a good start. I see that she has plenty of make-up on as always, and is wearing a lovely green blouse, which might be new, and knowing how often she shops, I'm sure it is.

'You've done well to get a property here. I believe they're selling like hotcakes,' Dad says then and that sounds just as promising.

'Shame there's no phone signal,' I lament with a roll of my eyes but also as a good way of giving an excuse as to why I might not answer their calls in the near future.

'That's easily sorted. Just get a signal booster,' Dad says casually before looking around and nodding approvingly.

Maybe it's my experience from years of my parents always judging me, pushing me and living vicariously through my achievements that made me think they would have wanted me to buy a bigger house than this, but they actually seem quite impressed. I also thought that, having turned down their money more and more in recent years to gain my independence, they would be annoyed that they hadn't been able to contribute financially to this purchase, but they seem okay with that too. But the night is still young, and the wine has not been drunk yet, so as always with my family, there is plenty of time for the drama to begin and the concealed truths to be aired.

'I just need to finish making dinner but I'm sure Christian and Kai can give you a tour of the house in the meantime,' I say casually, figuring that's a good way of keeping everybody out of the chaotic kitchen for long enough for me to get the food on the plates.

'That's okay, there's plenty of time for a guided tour. I'm sure we'll be visiting a lot,' Mum says, which I am sceptical about as we're now twenty minutes farther away than where we used to live and they weren't always eager to visit then. 'But for now, how about a drink? I'm parched.'

'I've just opened a bottle of red,' Christian says, springing into action as the eager host once again.

'That sounds perfect,' Dad replies, and Christian heads to the kitchen to start pouring as my parents follow him in while Kai trots dutifully behind.

I presumed my parents would be desperate to see every room and make their judgements about whether I could have done better or not, judgements that they may or may not have verbally passed on to me tonight. Instead, they seem more interested in having a drink. Maybe that's their way of showing their disapproval about us buying this house and not somewhere bigger with all the money they could have lent me. *Whatever*. This house is more than big enough for my family. It wasn't my first choice but we're here now and we'll make it work. *I hope*. And sure, if I had accepted my parents' money then maybe I could have afforded to buy a huge house like the one I saw on my walk the other night. But that's not me. I'm not a mansion girl and I'm definitely not my parents. Money is only a part of life, not the best part of it, and maybe Mum and Dad will realise that eventually, probably when they're on their death beds and all their pretentious golfing buddies and overworked house-keepers are nowhere to be seen.

Christian serves the drinks while I focus on serving the food and soon, we're all sat around the dining table tucking into the lasagne that was almost a disaster but has actually turned out okay in the end. For a few blissful but naïve moments, I feel like this evening might actually go okay and being in the company of my parents might not be the arduous ordeal it sometimes can be. Sure, I have to put up with them making a few slightly obnoxious comments about the service they received at a restaurant last week, then there's the snobbish statements about the current unemployment statistics that the government just released. That's their usual fare and I'm old enough to just ignore it now rather than argue it. But then Dad goes and says something that I can't ignore.

'This is a really nice estate,' he says, running a tanned hand over his salt-and-pepper beard, the colour of which amuses me because Dad is actually allergic to pepper. 'Your mother and I were having a drive around before we arrived and we saw some lovely properties that are still on the market. Who knows, maybe we'll end up buying here too.'

'What?' I say, my mouth hanging open but not because I'm about to put more food into it.

'Why not? It could be a great opportunity,' Dad goes on, his slim physique showing what good shape all the games of golf keep him in.

'Like an investment opportunity?' I ask, wondering if he's just thinking about adding another property to his portfolio. He has a few rental properties already, filled with rent-paying tenants who only add to his net worth. But if that's all it is then I suppose that wouldn't be so bad. At least not as bad as—

'No, for us to move into and live in,' Dad replies. 'It could be time for a change. What you do you think, dear?'

Dad turns to Mum, and she doesn't disagree.

'I think it could be nice,' she adds as she fiddles with her gold wristwatch for a moment. 'We'd see a lot more of each other if we lived closer. We could help take Kai to school some days and, of course, spend lots of time with our darling grand-daughter when she is born.'

That all sounds very caring and loving of them as grandparents, but I know Mum and Dad better than that and sure, while they do proclaim to love their family, and I'm sure a part of them does, there is always something else going on. Neither of them do anything unless it will make them money or boost their status, so if they are serious about buying a house here, it's not because they want to be nearer to the grandkids. It's because there's either a profit to be made or bragging rights to be earned.

'That would be great,' Christian says as he picks up his glass of wine. 'I think it's a good idea. What about you, Di?'

Everyone at the table looks at me. Everyone except Kai, who is too busy stuffing his face with lasagne. I wish I could just eat my meal in peace like my son. But I can't. Not now Mum and Dad are threatening to move to this estate too.

I've already got my reservations about this place, reservations that have not yet been settled. The last thing I need is any more.

Damn it, that red wine looks so good right now. But I'll of course refrain for the baby's sake.

Stay inside me for as long as you can, little girl. Life is much easier in there than it is out here.

NINE

The worst thing about last night's dinner party wasn't having to tidy up the kitchen afterwards. Nor was it the heartburn I got shortly after going to bed. The worst thing was finding out my overbearing parents might be about to become my neighbours.

I've spent most of this morning after Christian and Kai left the house telling myself that my parents aren't really serious about moving here. They're always full of grandiose ideas and speculative thoughts, which I guess is just what happens when people have so much money that they can do anything they like on a whim. But I doubt it'll happen. They probably drove past six other houses they 'might like to buy' on the way home last night, and I bet by the time they woke up this morning, something else had captured their attention. Something like share prices, or a vacation idea, or what to wear for the next fancy dinner at the golf club. I doubt they are thinking about me or the grandkids and how nice it would be for them to live closer to us.

At least I hope so, anyway.

As hard as it might be to settle in here, it will be even harder if I have my parents lurking nearby, constantly checking up on me, second guessing whatever I might be doing either as a wife or a parent. As for the extra babysitting help, I know that won't materialise. They'll pretend like they want to do it but it won't be long until they offer to pay for a nanny before telling me that I could do with more space, so why don't I just take their money and move somewhere bigger? I can't face the judgements, the snobbery and, eventually, the arguments. So please, Mum and Dad, live your lives elsewhere and I'll see you whenever you are back from your latest cruise.

I've been unpacking while thinking about all this but while the boxes are starting to reduce and the house is feeling less cluttered, my mind is going in the opposite direction. I consider getting started on making another fridge magnet, not only because it's my job but because being creative always cheers me up. But despite getting out a few of my paints, I realise this isn't going to cut it. I need to get out of the house. Fresh air is what my mind is craving. With that, I put on my shoes and decide it's time for a walk.

It's mid-morning on a weekday, so I expect the estate to be quiet, but then since we moved in it's been quiet, so it doesn't really matter what time it is. Although I did see another removals van drive past earlier so I guess another house has sold. The sooner this place is bustling, the better, because right now, the only thing I can hear are my anxious thoughts.

I decide to walk in the opposite direction to where I go on my evening strolls, and I do that because I plan to walk off this estate and down to the shops that are about twenty minutes away. There is only one road in and out so rather than go deeper into it, I will head for the exit. But before I can get there, I glance at my neighbour's house and that's when I see a woman in the window.

I haven't seen her before, but this must be Hayley, the neighbour who I heard crying the other night. It is my first sighting of her and it's a sorry one because while she looks like she might be pretty if she were smiling, all she is showing at the moment is a sorrowful expression. Her dark hair hangs down alongside a pale, mournful face and while she isn't crying, her eyes look bloodshot.

I decide to wave at her.

She doesn't wave back.

Instead, she moves away from the window and out of view and I guess she doesn't want to be seen. But it's too late for that. I have seen her and now that I know she is home, I am going to go and talk to her and check that she is okay.

Marching to her front door, I knock and wait for her to answer. She has to. She knows I saw her in there, so she can't just ignore me. Can she? But the door remains closed and the longer it does, the more I realise she is doing just that. But she is not just ignoring me, she's hiding. What is going on with her?

I can't see a car on the driveway, so Theo must be out. That means this is a really great opportunity to talk to Hayley without him around and check that she is okay. But I can't do that if she isn't willing to talk to me, and short of breaking and entering her home, I have no way of getting face to face with her.

I know Christian would tell me to mind my own business and leave, but he's not here, so I'm going to keep trying. At least that's the plan until I hear a car parking behind me.

I turn around, fearing that it is Theo returning home, but it's not. It's Cesar. He's just parked on the road in front of the house and now he is lowering the window on the driver's side of his vehicle so he can talk to me.

'Good morning. Is everything okay?' he asks me.

'Good morning. Erm, yeah, fine, thanks,' I say, giving him a dismissive wave which I intend for him to take as a hint to move on, but Cesar doesn't look like he's ready to leave.

'Anything I can help with?'

'No, I don't think so,' I say, not wanting to admit to him that I'm trying to get into a house that doesn't belong to me.

'It's just that I notice that's not your front door,' Cesar goes on. 'That's your neighbour's house, which makes me think you're calling there for help with something. But there's no need for that because I can help with anything. So what is it that you need?'

I realise Cesar isn't going anywhere so I give up on standing by the front door and waiting for it to open and walk over to his car. But maybe this is okay. Perhaps he can give me some information about my neighbours that might help shed some light on what is going on with them.

'Theo and Hayley live here, right?' I say, gesturing to the house behind me, and Cesar nods.

'Yeah, that's right. They're a lovely couple.'

'Are they? I've met him and he seems nice, I suppose. But I haven't met Hayley properly yet. I've only briefly seen her, or heard her. And it's just that...'

'What?'

'She always seems upset. Or sad.' Even just saying that about another person is enough to make me feel exactly the same way. It's in my nature to be empathetic.

'Sad? Hmmm, I wouldn't know anything about that,' Cesar replies. 'I'm sure she's fine. More than fine, actually. Happy. Just like everybody else here.'

Off Cesar goes again, making out like everybody who lives here exists in some perfect bubble of bliss. But he's not living in the real world if he thinks that his residents can't have problems and issues behind the closed doors of these newly built homes.

'Are you sure? I think there might be something wrong, so I'm trying to check on Hayley. I know she's in there, but she isn't answering the door. Is there any way we can go inside and check on her?'

'You want to enter her home without her permission? That's obviously not something I can allow to happen.'

'No, of course not. But it's not as if I'm trying to break in and steal anything. I just want to check if my neighbour is okay.'

'Like I said, I'm sure she's absolutely fine and is enjoying her peace and privacy inside her home. If she wants to talk to her neighbour, I'm sure she will do so in her own time. For now, I'm going to have to ask you to stop bothering her and move on.'

'I'm not bothering her! I'm trying to...'

My voice trails off when I realise this is a waste of time, and also possibly making me appear like I'm succumbing to some raging pregnancy hormones, so rather than argue with Cesar, I call it quits and give him what he wants.

'Okay, fine,' I say before walking away from his car.

He wishes me a good day as I leave him behind but I don't hear his car drive away, so I guess he's still sitting outside Hayley's home and making sure I definitely leave. But I'm going and now it's back to the original plan. I'm going to exit this estate and visit the shops. An hour or two away from this place will do me good.

It takes me ten minutes to get to the exit, during which time a couple of construction lorries rumble past me on their way to the part of the site that is still being developed.

More houses being built.

More money in Cesar's pocket.

More mystery about the people who live here or who may have lived here before me.

I try not to think about that but just before I can leave, another lorry appears, and it stops in the middle of the road before turning and reversing so that it now completely blocks the exit.

I wait a few moments, presuming it will soon be on its way

and I can walk out of here as easily as I intended to, but the lorry doesn't move and then I see the driver lower his window and poke his head out of his huge vehicle.

'Sorry, we've got a concrete delivery scheduled, so we can't have people going in or out of here. Health and safety reasons.'

'What? I can't leave?'

'It won't take long. An hour, tops. Sorry about this.'

I look around but there is really no other way past. Not unless I want to try and scale one of the wooden fences that flank either side of this road and that's not something I could do even if I wasn't pregnant.

I guess I'm stuck here. No, that's not the right word. It's something else. Something stronger.

I'm not just stuck.

I feel trapped.

TEN

The best way to stop feeling trapped is to escape, and thankfully, that's what I was able to do last night. After my attempt at getting off the estate was thwarted by the lorry yesterday morning, I spent the whole afternoon stewing at home, feeling like the walls were closing in on me and my increasingly paranoid thoughts. That was why, when Christian and Kai were home, I told them that we were going out for dinner. Christian said he was tired and Kai said he wanted to play with his toys, but I insisted and, eventually, I got my wish.

I got away from here for a short while and it felt good.

I'm aware that not driving only contributes to my feelings of isolation sometimes, but it is what it is and after a lovely meal at a local restaurant, I was feeling much better. Christian felt good too when our waitress told us that there was a twenty per cent discount for all residents of the new estate nearby, and once we confirmed that we qualified for that, our total bill was reduced. I guess Cesar has been making deals all over this town, but at least that was one I could get behind.

It was good to have some quality family time too, away from all the drudgery of the chores that come with a house move, and for a little while, it felt like we were back in simpler times. Christian, myself and Kai, the terrific trio, as I sometimes call us. I'm excited for us to be a four soon, but there is a lot to be said for the number three.

So that was yesterday but today is a new day and despite the break from this house, my worries about it and the drama with my neighbour, my anxiety about it all is starting to gnaw away at me again. That only grows when Christian reminds me what today is.

'It's the first Saturday of the month,' he says as he enters our bedroom to find me trying to reconfigure the wardrobe space in here.

At first, I don't see what is so special about that but then he reminds me.

'That means there's a social gathering for all residents, right?'

I realise my husband is correct. Cesar told us there was a get-together held on this day every month, so I guess something must be happening this afternoon. But is there?

'We haven't received anything,' I say. 'No invite or reminder in the mail or anything like that.'

'They probably don't send reminders. It's just a regular meet-up.'

'Maybe. But Cesar seems like the type of person who would make a big fuss about something like this. So maybe it's been cancelled. Or maybe we heard wrong and it's not the first Saturday of the month but the third instead.'

'I don't think we misheard,' Christian replies, but I wish he would just humour me so we can get out of going. I've still got lots to sort out around the house and as this is the first day Christian has not been to work since we moved in, it would be great to have my husband's help with all this too.

'I think we should get ourselves smartened up and head over to the estate office,' Christian says. 'That's where Cesar said the get-togethers are held, right? And the weather's nice so maybe they're hosting it outdoors today. That would be good. We could take Kai's football and let him burn off some energy.'

'Do you really want to go?' I ask. 'Or are you just trying to fit in?'

'A bit of both, I suppose,' Christian replies. 'I think it would be nice to meet some of our neighbours. Don't you?'

I suppose he might be right. I also wonder if Hayley is attending because it would really be great to meet her. I am tired – fatigue being another one of the joyous symptoms of pregnancy – which is why I am a little unsure about an afternoon of socialising. But socialising is the best way to get to know my neighbours and that's something I want, and need, to do.

'Okay, let's get ready and head over there,' I say, giving up on this latest bout of chores in favour of potentially getting some answers, either about my house or my neighbour.

As Christian throws on a casual T-shirt before going to tell Kai to get ready, I spend a little more time choosing my outfit. If I am going to go to this event, I want to make a good first impression, so I choose a nice summer dress that complements my baby bump rather than accentuates it before going into the bathroom to apply some make-up. Self-care usually goes out the window in the early years of motherhood, and I admit I don't beautify myself anywhere near as much as I probably could do these days, but I'm making the effort now. I apply lots of concealer and a little lipstick before deciding that I look much better than I did ten minutes ago. Then I leave the bathroom and join my family downstairs as we prepare to leave the house. Kai has his football under his arm while Christian has plucked a bottle of wine from his collection and my boys look ready to go. But I don't have anything to carry.

'Do you think I'm supposed to have prepared something for this?' I suddenly worry. 'A cake or a quiche or something?'

'It's a little late for that,' Christian chuckles. 'But it's our first time, so I'm sure people will understand. We can just go and survey the scene and then we'll have a better idea of what to bring with us the next time we go.'

The fact that Christian is already talking about the next time suggests he thinks this is going to be worth attending, but as we leave our house and start walking, I'm not so sure. This feels like a rather contrived way to try and bring the neighbourhood together. Forcing people to meet on the same day every month rather than just letting them organically mix and mingle over time. I've never known anything like it but then again, I've never lived anywhere like here either. Perhaps the thing that bugs me the most about this is that it feels like a way for Cesar to not only control his residents, but control the narrative. He is clearly eager to talk about how everybody loves being here and how there's such a good community aspect to it, but does it really count if he is pulling all the strings in this way, reducing us to puppets in his play? Telling us what to do on the first Saturday of the month seems a little much, doesn't it? What if we had other plans? A wedding to go to or we simply decided to have a weekend away? Would he mark us down as 'absent' on his attendance sheet and then give us a warning about our future conduct? It seems silly to think it but I actually wouldn't put it past him.

Like I've been doing ever since I got here and discovered that disturbing note, I try to put my doubts about this place to one side, and as we reach the gathering, I see that it does appear as advertised. There is a barbecue underway, long tables full of food and drink are laid out and there is even a guy making animal balloons for the kids.

Kai quickly spots where the action is and runs over to join the six or seven other kids who are watching the balloons being made, while Christian does what he does best and locates himself a beer. He does at least remember to pick up an orange juice for me but before I drink it, I look around because it feels like I should thank somebody for this drink. Who brought it? Who prepared all this? I don't know. It's hard to tell in this sea of faces.

I count about thirty or so people here, which is more than I thought there would be, the estate feels so deserted most of the time. But it is a big development and there must be more houses occupied than I realised. There is certainly a better attendance here than I expected and now I'm glad we came because it looks like everybody else did. Everybody except Hayley; I can't see her anywhere. Theo is here. He's standing over by the barbecue, holding a beer and having a laugh with a couple of other guys around his age. But there's no sign of his partner mingling with some of the ladies. So where is she? Home alone? Did she want to come? Or did Theo tell her to stay away?

'You made it! Fantastic!'

I turn around to see Cesar approaching, a glass of champagne in one of his hands but his other hand is extended out to welcome us. Christian shakes Cesar's hand before I have little choice but to do the same, and then I watch as he takes a large glug from his glass.

'I love it when we get the right weather for these days,' Cesar proclaims. 'It's not that we wouldn't have a good time if we were indoors. But it's so much more fun outside.'

Christian agrees with him before Cesar continues playing the good host.

'Please, help yourself to anything you like. There are some sausages cooking over on the barbecue, and we have vegetarian options if you require those. Plus there's salads and desserts and I can see you have already found the drinks table, so it looks like you're all set!'

Before I can ask Cesar who made which dish and who I can thank if I try them, he waltzes away to talk to somebody else, while an energetic-looking woman in her fifties approaches and welcomes us to the neighbourhood. She's quickly joined by her husband and the pair of them look good together, at ease, comfortable, happy. That sets a few of my nerves about this place at rest, albeit temporarily. But I still have plenty of doubts, including about the man who oversees everything that happens on the estate.

When I look around for Cesar, I see he is talking to a man who is a lot older than us. I'd say he's possibly in his eighties, and I guess while we moved here to begin the next chapter of our lives, he may have chosen to see out the remaining chapters of his life here. I suppose it might be a nice place to retire, and I think this gentleman looks nice, especially in the suit he is wearing, even though it's a little oversized on his skinny frame. I plan to go over and say hello as soon as Cesar is finished talking to him, but as I wait, I notice the man is looking right at me. He has a walking stick so that might be to make sure he doesn't lose his balance, but he doesn't seem too worried about that. He's simply too busy staring at me.

I smile at him, but he doesn't smile back. I'm just about to give Christian a nudge beside me to ask him if he's noticed that we are being eyeballed, when Cesar finishes his conversation with the man and when he does, that man starts approaching us.

He takes his time reaching us, aided by his stick. I notice that he is not smiling as if coming to give us a greeting, which makes me hold off on smiling for a moment too. Then the man speaks and when he does, I doubt I'll be smiling for quite a while yet.

'You live at number fifteen, Evergreen Drive?' the man asks Christian and me, and my husband confirms that is correct. But before we can ask him which number he lives at, the man speaks again.

'What happened to the other couple?'

'Sorry, who?' Christian asks as I frown.

'The couple who lived at number fifteen before you.'

'Excuse me?' I reply as my heart begins to race.

'There wasn't a couple living there before us. We're the first ones in that house,' Christian says confidently before taking a swig of his beer. My husband does look very relaxed, a consequence of the alcohol no doubt, but also his appearance. He looks good in his shirt and denim shorts, as if he's dressed for a holiday and not just a gathering near his house.

'No, I don't think that's correct,' the man replies just as confidently, which disturbs my husband's rhythm. 'There was a couple before you. What were their names again? Let me think...'

I stare at this man and wait for his memory to jog because I'm desperate to know everything he seemingly does about our house. Christian looks a little anxious too and holds off on taking another sip of beer as he waits. But before the man can speak again, Cesar reappears.

'Is everything okay?' he asks us.

'No, I don't think it is actually,' I answer before Christian can. 'This gentleman here has just told us that there was a couple living in our house before us. Is that right?'

I stare at Cesar, thinking there is no way he can lie his way out of this now, not when there is somebody else who seems to know otherwise. The elderly man has not recalled the names of the couple yet, but he clearly believes they existed, and I have no reason to doubt him. Especially not after that note I found that also lends itself to someone having been in that house before us.

'Oh, okay. I see what's happened here,' Cesar says, suddenly looking very apologetic and I wonder if this is when he begs us for our forgiveness for lying to us about the house. But he doesn't do that.

'I think you might have got a little confused, Arthur,' Cesar says to the man. 'How about we go and have a sit down over there?'

Arthur doesn't look too confused, but Cesar quickly wraps his arm under his and escorts Arthur over to one of the plastic chairs that have been set out on the grass. That prevents me from talking to him anymore, but only if I stay where I am. There's nothing stopping me from following Arthur and asking more questions. Unless he really is confused; in which case, I wouldn't want to cause him any distress. But is he? Or has Cesar just tried to cover up the past again?

'What's going on here?' I ask my husband as we watch Cesar seating Arthur before getting him a glass of water.

'Am I going crazy or did something happen in the house we've just bought? Something that we're really not supposed to know about?'

ELEVEN

I want to ask Arthur questions to find out what he was talking about, but I'm hesitant because what if Cesar is telling the truth and the poor man does have memory issues? I don't want to risk upsetting him, which is why I'm still standing here with all my questions unanswered. But then I realise I'm surrounded by all the other people who live here, so maybe one of them knows the truth.

'Excuse me. Hi, I'm Dionne and I live at number fifteen. Do you know if anyone lived there before us?' I abruptly ask the first person within earshot of me. It's a man who was just about to take a bite out of a hotdog but upon hearing my question, he pauses and shakes his head.

'I don't know, sorry. I only moved here this week.'

I ask a couple more people but get similar answers. It seems most of these residents are very new, even newer than we are, which means they won't have been here to learn the history of our house. If there is any history.

Maybe Arthur was just confused. But he's not the only one anymore.

'Hey, relax,' Christian says to me as I look around for the next person to accost. 'I don't want us to make a scene in front of all our new neighbours.'

'I'm not making a scene,' I say, but my voice is a little loud and I notice a couple of people by the barbecue look over in my direction. Christian is worried that we're going to become a piece of neighbourhood gossip, or at least I am. The strange woman at number fifteen who embarrassed herself at the monthly get-together. I don't really want to be labelled with that moniker, but I also don't just want to stay quiet and ignore all these warning signs that are flashing in my face.

This is the last thing I need. I'm a woman with more than enough on her plate. I really don't have time for playing detective or adding any more anxieties to my already-anxiety-ridden life. But how can I ignore this? I can't.

So what can I do?

I want to get away from this gathering, but Kai looks like he is having fun with the other children here, so it would be harsh if I were to drag him away. But he can stay if Christian does. Only I need to leave because it seems like I'm the only one who is struggling with what Arthur just said.

'Watch Kai,' I say to Christian as I leave. 'I'm going back to the house.'

'Why?' he calls after me, but I ignore him and keep walking away from the gathering until the chatter and the music fades into the background.

I walk down the deserted streets all the way back home before going inside and taking a deep breath. I'm better to be on my own when I feel this confused and worried, rather than surrounded by a load of strangers, because at least I can't say or do anything in a public place that I might later regret. I know this because I once made a bit of a fool of myself at a party years ago. I was a little drunk and mistakenly thought Christian was flirting with a work colleague in front of me. It turned out I was overreacting, but not before I had started an argument with him in front of everyone. What would have been better to resolve behind closed doors was played out in public, and that was the only time I've ever seen Christian appear embarrassed by me.

I don't want to see that look in his eyes again if I can help it.

If Arthur was just confused, and if there really was no one in this house before us, I would embarrass myself, as well as my husband, by asking everybody at the barbecue about it. I might even come across as unhinged and that's not really the first impression I want to make. Some people might see my bump and put two and two together to come up with five, figuring my hormones are making me act a little erratically. But I'm not. I'm only trying to find out if I should be concerned about this house and, indeed, this estate that seems too perfect from the outside.

I feel bad for abandoning Christian at the gathering and think about going back in about half an hour when I've had time to compose myself, but before that time can pass, I hear footsteps outside my door. I guess Christian or Kai have got bored, and they have come back to join me here. But if it is them, why are they knocking instead of just coming inside?

I open the door and get a big surprise. It's not a family member on the doorstep. Instead, it's a woman I've been trying to talk to. A woman who has been very elusive. But now she's just fallen right into my lap.

'Hayley?' I say, staring at the pale, pained person before me. 'Are you okay?'

Just like when I saw her through the window of her house, she looks exhausted and far from her best, but now there is no pane of glass separating her, I detect something else about her too. It's the strong scent of alcohol.

As I look into her bloodshot eyes, I figure she is drunk,

which makes me only want to help her even more. When she speaks, she proves me right.

'I need to tell you something,' Hayley says, slightly slurring her words while fidgeting with the long sleeves of her oversized sweater.

'What?' I ask, eager to hear it.

'It's about your house,' she goes on, looking past me into my home. 'It's about something that happened before you got here.'

I knew it. I was right all along. We're not the first people to live here. That note I found was real, not a prank. And my poor next-door neighbour is clearly battling her demons while being in on the big secret. Or maybe she's going to tell me something that's connected to her crying? Maybe Theo has something to do with all of this.

'What happened?' I ask, bracing myself for some terrible news.

'Hayley, what are you doing?' comes a cry from the street, and I look up to see Theo marching towards us. Suddenly, Hayley goes mute, but I can't let Theo's arrival stop her from telling me what's wrong.

'It's okay, you can tell me whatever it is,' I urge her before Theo fully reaches us. 'Please, just tell me.'

'Is she bothering you?' Theo calls out as he gets closer, talking to me this time. 'I'm sorry if she is.'

'No, she isn't,' I reply firmly before looking back to Hayley. 'Please, just tell me what you know.'

Theo has reached us now but I can tell from the look in her eyes that he's too late and Hayley is going to speak anyway. She is going to tell me whatever she knows.

That's until a very loud alarm sounds, a noise with such volume that it would easily drown out whatever she was about to say even if it hadn't just cut her off.

'What is that?' I shout, confused as to where it is coming from.

I'm also confused as to why it sounded at that very moment.
It's almost like it was set off to stop Hayley talking.
Was it?

TWELVE

'What's happening?' I cry, trying to make my voice heard over the deafening alarm that is already giving me a headache. Worse than that, it interrupted Hayley just as she was about to tell me something very important.

'We need to go,' Theo says then, grabbing Hayley's hand and pulling her towards him, but I get the feeling he is talking to the both of us.

'Go where?' I cry.

'We have to get off the estate,' Theo says before he and Hayley leave.

Now I'm left standing in my doorway, starting to panic that something terrible is either happening or is about to happen. If it is, I need to find my family immediately.

Christian and Kai are still at the gathering. Has something bad happened there? Are they hurt? In danger? Theo made it sound like we have to evacuate, but what are we evacuating from?

I notice more people coming down the street now. They are people I saw at the gathering. They have obviously left the barbecue behind and now seem to be heading for the exit just like Theo and Hayley are. But I can't see Christian or Kai among them.

I rush out of my house, leaving the door wide open but I don't care because I just want to know that my husband and son are okay. As I go in the direction that I last saw them, everyone else seems to be running the opposite way.

'You need to turn around,' somebody calls to me as they pass, but I ignore them and keep going because there's no way I am leaving here without my family.

I'm hampered by how quickly I can move thanks to my bump, but nobody else has such limits, so they are all moving much quicker than me.

What is everybody running from? My heart is beating wildly.

Then I see my husband rushing towards me, and, thankfully, our son is with him. But I don't stop moving until I reach them.

'Are you okay?' I cry, checking the pair of them for any visible signs of injury.

'It's so loud, Mummy,' Kai says, his little voice barely audible over the alarm.

'I know it is, darling,' I reply, relieved he appears to be okay, before looking at Christian. 'What's happening?'

'I'm not sure. Cesar just told everyone to leave,' Christian replies. 'Come on, let's go.'

I now change direction and join the crowd in heading for the exit, and the three of us pass our house, the door still wide open but it feels like there's no time to go back and close it. Very quickly, we make it to a patch of tarmac just off the estate where it seems everyone is gathered. Although I'm not sure if it is everyone, because as I look around, I can't see Theo or Hayley anywhere. Where has she gone? I really need to finish that conversation we were having before the alarm sounded. There's no sign of her in the crowd. I do spot Cesar, though. He is talking with a couple of men in construction clothing, and I suddenly wonder if all this panic and upheaval has something to do with the building work that is still going on over on the far side of the estate. At least the alarm is much quieter here, I think, and the reduced noise gives Cesar the opportunity to raise his voice and address the concerned crowd.

'My apologies for this. I'd like to thank you all for reacting to the alarm and leaving the estate as quickly and as safely as you could. The reason for the alarm you can hear in the distance is that there was a rather sudden, suspected gas leak during the construction of one of the new properties, so we decided it was safest to evacuate until we can be absolutely certain everything is okay. I'm sure it won't take too long. Thank you all for your patience.'

The calmness with which Cesar spoke about such a matter makes me think this might not have been the first time he has had to do this, and clearly, if there is an alarm in place, it might have been used before.

I decide to try and find out by asking the person nearest to me, a woman in her fifties who I notice held on to her glass of champagne from the barbecue despite all the rush.

'Has this happened before?' I ask her, wondering if she has lived her longer than me.

'Just once,' she confirms. 'The first week I moved in. I think it was a gas leak then too. I suppose it is a bit of an inconvenience, but I guess there are always a few growing pains with a new estate, especially one that is still being built. But it's better to be safe than sorry, right?'

'Of course,' I say. 'I'm at number fifteen. I was wondering, do you know if anyone lived there before me?'

I might as well try and get any information I can out of this person, but the woman frowns and shakes her head.

'We're all the first people in these houses,' she says while looking at me as if I've said something very stupid.

'It's just that—'

'Di,' Christian cuts in then and when I look at him, it's obvious he really doesn't want me to keep talking about it. The interruption is enough time for the woman to move on through the crowd and now she's already talking to somebody else. She wasn't much help anyway. Now I wonder if Arthur is around. But I can't see him, just like I can't see Hayley.

'Can we go back to the party yet?' Kai asks, but Christian tells him we'll have to wait.

'For how long?' Kai whines, and that is a good question. How long exactly does Cesar expect us all to just stand around out here, unable to return to our homes? And is it really necessary to evacuate the entire estate? Is that not overkill? Sure, a potential gas leak should be taken seriously, but it wouldn't cause a blast capable of wiping out every home here, would it? Shouldn't it just be the construction site that evacuates?

I guess these are all good questions for the man in charge, but Cesar is busy talking with the construction workers so I can't ask him yet. As I watch him, I think about how this could be another example of his controlling ways. If all it takes is an alarm to sound to get the residents to leave their homes and gather outside, what would stop him from using that alarm whenever he wanted to? Whenever it suited him to? Like whenever one of the residents might potentially be doing something he doesn't want them doing. Like having a conversation that was leading somewhere very interesting until that alarm interrupted it...

I try and tell myself that it was a coincidence that the alarm sounded just as Hayley was trying to tell me about what happened in my house before we moved in, but my paranoia about this estate won't allow me to put it down to that.

'I was talking to Hayley before the alarm went off,' I tell Christian.

'Who?'

'Our next-door neighbour, and she said she had to tell me something about our house.'

'What was it?'

'I don't know. The alarm interrupted us and now I can't see her anywhere. She knows something, and I think this alarm was used to shut her up.'

'It's a gas leak.'

'Do you believe that?'

'Why wouldn't I?'

'Because I don't think we should trust Cesar.'

'What are you talking about?' Christian asks with his eyebrows raised, an expression that instantly tells me he is struggling with my beliefs again.

It's infuriating not having the support of my husband in this. Why can't he see what I can? Something is going on and we seem to be the only ones here who don't know what it is.

'Look, all of this, from the alarm to the note to Cesar and his slightly strange ways, they're all just teething problems that come with us being in on the ground floor of this very exciting development,' Christian tells me, and it's clear he is doing his best to keep his patience, though it's rapidly running out. 'The last of the houses will be built, they'll all be filled and then everything will settle down. It's just a little messy at the minute.'

It's a waste of time trying to get Christian to share my concerns, so I decide I won't waste my breath. Instead, I'll save my energy for when Hayley is back. This alarm might be genuine, or it might be a decoy, but whatever it is, I'll see her again. Wherever she is now, she'll go back to her house and when she does, I will be ready to resume my conversation with her. When I do, I am not going to let anything interrupt it.

Not Theo. Not Cesar. And certainly not an alarm.

Hayley was on the verge of telling me something about my

house, something big, and I can't rest until I know what that was.

If Christian can't see the danger we might be in here, it's up to me to make sure our children are safe.

I'm getting to the bottom of this.

And nothing is going to stop me.

THIRTEEN

It was over sixty minutes before we were told we could safely return to our homes. Cesar tried getting the community get-together started again after that, but I think the barbecue had fizzled out by that point, much like the party atmosphere along with it. I didn't care because I wouldn't have gone back to the barbecue anyway. I only wanted to go home and look out for Hayley returning to her house. Despite standing by my window for what must have been hours, I never saw her return. I didn't see Theo either. My two next-door neighbours were conspicuous by their absence. They were the only people who seemingly weren't eager to get back to normality after the alarm had been turned off.

'What are you doing?' Christian had asked me several times as he had noticed how unsettled I had been as I stood by the window, but I didn't bother explaining to him what I was doing because he would have only told me to stop spying on the neighbours. Eventually, I gave up and went to bed.

It's the beginning of the week now and with my husband and son having left the house this morning, at least I have the time and space to do what I want without being judged.

I make a check on next door again via my bedroom window, but still fail to see Hayley or Theo. I do see a text from my mother come through on my phone, though, asking me how we are settling in and offering assistance if we need anything. Mum isn't always so eager to help and there have been times when I have gone weeks without a message from her checking to see if I'm okay. I got used to it, I knew Mum was busy, either with Dad or some rich friends, and it's not as if I couldn't call them if I needed something urgently. I guess Mum is having a slow morning if she's reaching out to me today.

I think about telling her about my recent concerns, but just text back to say everything is fine. That seems easier to fit into one message. I also don't really want my parents thinking the same as Christian, that the stress of the house move coupled with my pregnancy hormones is causing me to go a bit paranoid and loopy. Best to try and figure this out on my own. As I reply, I'm not even sure when my mum might have sent the message. The signal is so bad here that she may have sent it yesterday and my phone has only just received it now. That's another thing Cesar seems to have covered up during the sales process. Alarms may go off. Secrets may be kept. Oh, and your mobile phone is basically useless here.

Once the message is sent, or at least I think it's been sent, I decide to drag a few unpacked boxes to the window where I can work on them while still maintaining good visuals on Hayley's house for any signs of movement. Opening the first box, I quickly figure this is one that was packed by my husband. I can tell that by how everything in it was seemingly thrown in haphazardly. There isn't much organisation, and I consider just pushing the box away and leaving it for him to sort out. That would serve him right. It looks like a bunch of boring bills and documents anyway, most likely from the top drawer of his desk in our previous home office, so I'm sure I can find something more interesting to unpack. But knowing Christian as well as I do, if I leave this to him, this box will most likely sit in a corner for the next few weeks before I inevitably end up sorting it myself, so I might as well just do it now and get it over with.

Reaching in and taking out the pieces of paper that sit on top of the large pile, I see they are documents that relate to dull but necessary parts of adult life, like paper copies of insurance confirmations, banking identifications and even the duplicates of our wills are in here. This is all stuff that nobody really wants to look at, as it's a reminder that life doesn't always go to plan and bad things might happen; but it is important to have these stored in a safe place just in case they are needed one day, so I better get this all filed away correctly.

I work diligently, only pausing to glance through the window for any sign of Hayley or Theo, but there is still none. After a while, I'm practically at the point of working on auto-pilot, sifting through all these sheets of paper, when I suddenly pause. That's because I'm looking at a bank statement and while that wouldn't be unusual in itself, what is unusual is the number on the statement that is apparently in one of my husband's accounts. Like most married couples, we have a joint account, but like most couples, we had our separate, individual accounts that existed before we met, and neither of us ever closed those. It's always helpful to have a couple of spare places to move money around if need be. I don't have much in my personal account, though, as nearly everything goes through the joint one, and I always thought that was the case with my husband too. But not according to this bank statement I've just discovered.

According to this, my husband has over twenty thousand pounds secretly stashed away.

What is this money? Where has it come from? And why am I only just finding out about it now?

I check the date on the statement and see it is from a couple of months ago, so this definitely isn't some historical record. It's very recent, so recent in fact that I assume Christian still has this money now. It must have come from work as that's his only source of income. But why wouldn't he tell me about it? We could certainly use cash like this. Anybody could. Unless he doesn't have it anymore. But if not, I would really like to know what my husband has spent twenty thousand pounds on without discussing it with me at any point during that process.

For a moment, I blame myself because having always hated maths and anything else numerical, I have been more than happy to allow Christian to deal with the finances in our family. It always made sense too because he works in finance in his day job, so he would obviously be better suited to that than me. But perhaps doing so has allowed there to be a big blind spot in our relationship, though it is clearly no longer a blind spot.

I grab my mobile and try to call him but, as usual, the signal is terrible so if I want to speak to him now, I'll have to call him on the landline phone that we had fixed recently. I head downstairs and pick up the receiver before entering Christian's work phone number from my mobile. It is certainly more arduous making a call the 'old-fashioned way', but at least it works. Or it would if the person at the other end of the line answered their phone. Christian doesn't pick up, much to my frustration. It's not unusual when he's at work, so he could be in a meeting. He rarely communicates with me on weekdays during the hours of 8 a.m. and 4 p.m., and today is no different. Or it shouldn't be. But today is different because it's the first time I've discovered he has been hiding money from me.

I try one more time but am forced to give up and I'll have to wait until he gets home to have this discussion. But someone else is home. I hear a car door outside. I rush to the window, and I see Theo.

Leaving my house because I'm desperate not to ignore the first signs of life that have occurred at my neighbour's place since Saturday, I look around to see if Hayley is with him. I don't see her but at least I can ask her husband where she is.

'Is Hayley home?' I ask Theo before he can go inside his house, and while I know I am behaving like a very nosy neighbour, it's my only option if I want to find out what is going on. Theo spins around and when he does, I see that he looks tired. I also notice his T-shirt has some dirt on it, as do his jeans.

'No, she's not,' he says quickly before turning to carry on his way, but I keep talking to him.

'Where is she? It's just that we were having a conversation before that alarm went off and I really need to talk to her.'

'She's gone,' Theo says.

My blood instantly turns cold.

'What?'

'She won't be back, so you won't be seeing her again.'

Theo takes out his key to unlock his door, but I put a hand out to stop him.

'Where has she gone?'

'It's none of your business,' Theo snaps back, clearly irritated, and I get the sense he is extremely tired too. He looks like he hasn't slept and maybe he hasn't. But if he's been up all night, what was he doing?

The problem is, he has a point. His relationship isn't really any of my business. I'm just the woman next door, a woman he barely knows and who barely knew Hayley. Yet here I am asking all these questions when he just wants to go inside and be left in peace. I know how this must look. I don't want him to think I'm crazy.

'Please, I just want to make sure she's okay,' I say, making this less about myself in the hopes that he might be willing to talk. But it doesn't work. Theo pushes past me and enters his home before slamming the door and now I'm alone again.

No Theo. No Hayley. No answers.

I still don't know what happened in my house before I got

here and now, I don't know what happened to the woman who was about to tell me.

All I know is that Theo might have got rid of her before she could tell me.

Why would he do that?

Does he feel threatened by something?

Now I've expressed my concerns to him, does he see me as a threat too?

FOURTEEN

The only way I've prevented myself from being overwhelmed is by making a list. Hayley and the mystery of where she might be is on there, as is the mystery of this house and whatever potentially happened here with a couple before we moved in. At the top of the list, and the first thing I can hopefully tick off tonight, is ask my husband about the money in his account. Now Kai is finally in bed after another exhausting early evening bedtime routine, I can ask him without interruption.

'What's this?' I say as I thrust the bank statement I discovered earlier into Christian's chest while he lies on the sofa with a beer and a game of football on the TV. He thinks this is the part of the day where he gets to unwind after several hours of work and parenting duties, but I'm sorry to say, 'not tonight, hubs'.

'What?' Christian mutters as he puts his beer down and sits up before checking the statement.

'I found it in one of the boxes while I was unpacking,' I tell him, though it's not as if I need to because once he realises what it is, he will surely know that he was the one who put it in that box in the first place. Although I'm guessing it got bundled in with all the other paperwork, and if he had taken the time to properly sift through it all, he might have decided to get rid of it rather than bring it here and risk me seeing it.

'Erm,' Christian says and I wait for him to come up with a better answer than that. 'It's just our bank account.'

'No, it's *your* bank account, not the joint one. And while I knew you had a personal account, just like you know I have one too, I had no idea you had that much money in yours. I certainly don't have anywhere near that amount in mine. So where did all that money come from?'

Christian pauses before answering.

'It's from work,' he says. 'I got a bonus.'

'You got a bonus and didn't tell me about it?'

'It was going to be a surprise.'

'Well, it certainly is a surprise.'

'What's the problem? Most people aren't annoyed at having more money than they thought they had,' Christian says with a laugh, but he's totally missing the point.

'Most couples don't keep big amounts of money secret from one another,' I explain, though I shouldn't have to. 'Why didn't you just tell me? It's not as if we couldn't use the money, is it? And is it a bonus? Or is it from somewhere else?'

'Where else would it be from?' Christian asks, lowering the bank statement.

'I don't know. My parents, perhaps,' I reply with my hands on my hips.

'No, it's from work. I just told you.'

'Yes, but are you telling me the truth?'

'Of course I am. It was a bonus. You know how hard I've been working. I was saving it up and was going to surprise you with it once everything had settled down with the house move. Maybe suggest a holiday or something we could do as a family next summer. Or say that we save it for a trip to Disneyland with Kai when his little sister is a bit bigger.'

I analyse my husband's expression, as well as the tone of his voice. I can't tell for sure if it's the truth or a lie, but as the man I married, and as he has never done anything in the past to make me doubt him, I guess I have to give him the benefit of the doubt and trust him. We've always been a solid team, ranging from how we delegated tasks for our wedding organisation to how we handled the early sleepless nights of Kai as a newborn. He's on my side, not against me, so he could be telling the truth. Then again, he's not a total saint and he could be lying. He knows how much I am against taking cash gifts from my parents because I feel it would teach a bad example to our children if they think you can get through adult life just relying on hand-outs from other people. We don't need their money, barring an unforeseen disaster, and I certainly don't need to alleviate whatever guilt they might feel about not always being present parents by accepting money now over all the time they could have spent with me in the past instead.

'I just don't see why we have to have secrets,' I say, relaxing a little because at least this is one mystery that I seem to have solved. 'You should tell me about anything like this. We should celebrate your hard work and bonuses together. There's no need to keep things quiet.'

'I understand and it won't happen again,' Christian replies, offering to give me a hug and I accept his strong, wide embrace because I need his strength after today, not his weaknesses. As his toned arms wrap around me and I pick up a scent of his familiar aftershave, I feel slightly better about things.

'How about you take a break from all the unpacking and let me do it?' Christian says then. 'I'll go and do a few boxes now while you relax.'

I suddenly feel bad because he was relaxing before I interrupted him with the bank statement, but he doesn't take no for an answer, and very quickly, I'm the one reclining on the sofa while he goes upstairs to unpack some more. I'm grateful for this rare moment of normality and just wish there could be more moments like this, where I could enjoy my new home instead of worrying about that note.

I change the channel on the TV and find something more interesting than football to watch and for a few blissful seconds, I pretend like everything is okay. But it's not. How can I just watch TV while I still don't know what happened to Hayley?

I get up and go to the window to look next door but it's dark, so I can't see much. Then I go into the kitchen to make a drink, hoping that might distract my mind. It does to some extent, especially when I see that the bin is full and needs emptying. Rather than ask Christian to do it, I'll do it myself so I grab the full bag of waste and haul it outside to where the bin is stationed by the side of the house.

I'm expecting it to be extremely quiet outside, as it usually is around here at night, but I pause when I hear a voice. I quickly realise it is Theo and as I creep to the fence, I also realise that he is talking to somebody on the phone. I figure that out because I cannot hear anybody else speak in between his sentences.

I lean in closer to the fence to hear more but when I do, I quickly regret it as it only gives me more to worry about.

'I had no choice. She had to go. I had to get rid of her and I'm glad she's gone.'

If Theo knew I was eavesdropping, then he might not be talking so openly about who I presume is Hayley. But he doesn't, so I have just heard something I shouldn't have done.

I had to get rid of her.

What has he done to Hayley?

Is she dead?

FIFTEEN

I can see her.

Her face. Her long dark hair. That pale skin. Those desperate eyes. And her mouth, the one that was just about to tell me something important about my house.

I can see Hayley. Not right in front of me because she's not here. But I can see her when I close my eyes. When I try and sleep. That's why I'm still wide awake despite it being the middle of the night. Christian is snoozing. So is Kai. Even my daughter inside me is still. But I'm unable to rest.

I can't stop seeing Hayley. But it's no good seeing her in my imagination. I need to see her in real life. I might not know her well, barely at all, but as a human being, I'm still fearful for her safety and don't want any harm to come to her.

I need to find her.

I need to find out what Theo did to her.

I need to know where he has hidden her body.

I am convinced she is dead now, and the more I think about it, the more I am convinced her body is not far away. She vanished just after that alarm sounded and when everybody was heading for the exit. That was just after she was talking to me and when Theo had arrived back to interrupt us. It all happened so quickly, but I definitely didn't see either of them at the exit where everyone else was gathered. That makes me think Hayley never made it off the estate.

She's still here somewhere.

I get out of bed as quietly as I can, not wanting to disturb Christian, and I put on a few clothes in the dark before tiptoeing to the bedroom door. I creep past Kai's room and go downstairs, where I put on my coat and shoes and leave the house. There's a chill in the air but that's to be expected in the middle of the night. Hopefully, I'll warm up as I begin walking. I'm not going anywhere in particular, but I feel like I have to do something, more for Hayley than for me. I'm so worried about her.

There are a lot of places to hide a body around here.

I don't know where to start looking. I can't even believe this is something I'm having to think about. But if I don't try to find out what's happened to Hayley, who will? Where is she? Inside any one of the spacious, luxurious homes that surround me as I make my way down this street? Within the sprawling, luscious gardens at the rear of all these properties, gardens that could easily be home to a hastily dug grave? My imagination runs away with itself. What about all the stylish vehicles parked on the driveways? Could there be a body hidden away in one of them, just waiting to be transported elsewhere by a murderous driver with a terrible secret to hide? Or what about the fact that this aspirational estate is still only half finished and beyond the homes already built is a construction site where, eventually, more houses will spring up and be sold to wealthy families looking for their forever home? A place with lots of holes just waiting to be filled with concrete would make an excellent place to bury a body, right? I wonder if Hayley is already destined to end up buried beneath a house that will one day be occupied by a loving family who have no idea what is hiding under their feet.

That would make it another home that harbours a secret.

Another home like mine.

It feels like a hopeless task. But it's always the moment when everything feels lost that things begin to turn – and that's exactly what happens next. I see something straight ahead on this otherwise deserted and silent street. I snuck out of my home ten minutes ago and I thought I was the only one out here at this time of night, but I'm not because I see movement in the darkness.

I rub my eyes as if trying to check that I'm awake and not still dreaming, but I can't be sure as I keep watch.

I see two figures coming out of a house and as I stare at them, I see they are heading to their car. I also see that they are carrying something between them. It's long and thin and wrapped inside plastic sheeting, so I can't make out exactly what is inside. They are holding an end each, moving the heavy item as quickly as they can, but it's not easy. They pause, taking a quick break before carrying on, and it's enough time for me to freeze and hold my breath: I think I might know what it is.

Is it what I'm looking for?

Is it the person I have been anxiously trying to find?

Is it poor Hayley?

If so, are these two people moving it the killers?

I dare not move a muscle for fear of being seen. If I am, I will end up wrapped inside that plastic too, being carried to the back of a car before being driven away and buried in the woods. I have to stay still. I have to stay silent. I cannot let the killers know I have just caught them in the act.

That's when they both turn and look at me, and my heart beats faster as I realise I have been seen. I instinctively hold my breath, as if that will somehow make me invisible, and I wish it would because now I could be in danger.

They don't drop the body they are carrying as our eyes meet. But I know what they are thinking.

Is there space inside their car for two bodies now?

I imagine they could figure out what I am thinking at this exact moment too. It's a simple thought, but a strong one.

I'm thinking that I should never, ever have moved here.

Before the men can do anything to me, I grab my phone from my pocket and even though I always have a poor signal here, modern phones allow the user to still make an emergency call. As the men continue to stare at me from a dozen or so yards away, I stay on my guard while I am connected. When I am, I waste no time explaining what I see.

'Yes, I need the police. I think somebody has been murdered and I think I'm looking at the body!'

SIXTEEN

I feel like I should run to save myself. To save the child inside me. The men carrying the body certainly heard what I just said on the phone, so it's surely only a matter of time until they try and shut me up. But it doesn't matter if they try because the police are on their way now, and I'm hoping that means that they are not going to get away with what they have done.

Or what they might be about to do.

I also hope it means Theo won't get away with his part in this too. If he killed Hayley and arranged for these two men to help him hide the body then he is going to end up behind bars. I will make sure of it, even if it's the last thing I ever do.

But as my heart races impossibly fast, I fear that I have just been incredibly selfish. I wanted to resolve the mystery of the note, and to get justice for Hayley, but what about the people who depend on me? My son. My unborn daughter. And my husband. What if I have placed myself in danger and they lose me?

That's why I'm still ready to run. But strangely, despite what I just said on the phone and despite being caught in the act, the two men are not coming towards me to try and shut me up. They are simply looking at each other with a bemused look on their faces. Then one of them speaks.

'Can we help you?' he asks me, which seems a strange thing to say if they have something to hide.

I don't reply, and the two men share a quizzical look before they address me again.

'It's very late to be out,' I'm told. This immediately makes me worry. Is it a warning? Are they hinting that I should have stayed home, in bed, where it was safe? But because I haven't, is it now too late?

My thoughts are so scrambled from a recent lack of sleep that it's hard to think straight. That's why again I choose to say nothing, though it's less out of choice and more out of the deep-seated fear that has consumed me ever since I saw these men sneaking around out here in the dark.

The awkward silence that lingers is eventually broken by the sound of sirens in the distance. The police response has been a quick one, quicker than I expected, but the closer they get, the more I start to fear something is wrong. If those men do have a body in the carpet, why aren't they trying to get away with it now? Why are they still here despite the sirens approaching? And why has one of them just asked me if I am okay?

'Can you hear me?' one of the men says before repeating his question. 'Are you okay?'

I don't know what to say and as the police reach the estate and this serene suburban space is transformed into a chaotic mess of blue flashing lights and screeching tyres, I fear that I am the one in the wrong rather than the two men carrying the rolled-up body. A thought occurs to me, what if it isn't a body? What if the dark street, coupled with my paranoia, has led me to jump to a very large and very incorrect conclusion?

It's too late now. The police are here. I guess they will be the ones who find out the truth.

Either those men are in the wrong.

Or I am.

As the police cars park on the street, I see the residents in the houses opening their doors and stepping outside to see what all the noise is about. Unlike many of the other streets here, the homes on this one are mostly occupied so there is a large crowd gathering very quickly. Why wouldn't there be? It's not every night that the police come to visit. But while all these residents are standing around and watching on with interest, they are not the only ones. The two men with the rolled-up item are watching too. They have lowered it to the ground now, but they are still standing with it in plain sight, and as the first police officers approach both them and me, I have realised these men seemingly have nothing to hide.

That must mean I am wrong.

'Who made the call?' I hear an officer cry out, and I have to raise my hand to own up to that one. The officer approaches me while he directs a few of his colleagues over to the two men – and the fact they still don't run is another strong indicator that they are innocent.

'We were told there was a body here,' the officer says to me as he looks around. 'Where is it?'

'I thought that was a body,' I say as I point towards the two men. Very quickly the officers with them make a check on what they were carrying and, when they do, I see what I should have done ten minutes ago.

It's not a body.

It's a carpet.

I'm so embarrassed and it's only the dark sky overhead that is surely preventing everybody from seeing my blushing face.

I want to explain to this officer. Make him understand that I've been worried for my neighbour and that I couldn't sleep so I came out here for a walk, and because it's dark, and because I'm so worried, I mistook one thing for something else. I don't want to do all that, but I guess I need to because there are a lot of officers here who will want an explanation, just like all these residents will too. Before I can make a start on that, though, somebody else who wants an explanation arrives on the scene and as he does, I can see how exasperated he looks.

'What is going on?' Cesar cries as he comes towards us. 'Who called the police? What's happened?'

I'd love to say that this is none of his business, just like I'd love to say the same to all these residents still gawking from their doorsteps, but as they all live here, they have a right to know why there is a large police presence near their homes in the early hours of the morning. They presumably all want to know if they are safe. In Cesar's case, he also wants to know who has made a mockery of his supposedly 'crime-free' estate.

'It appears there has been a mix up,' the police officer I just spoke to says as Cesar reaches us.

'A mix up? What about?'

The officer looks to me then as if I should be the fool to explain it rather than him.

'I was looking for Hayley. She's gone missing and I thought that she had been hurt, so when I saw those two men moving what looked like a body, I panicked and called the police.'

'A body,' Cesar spits back. 'That's a carpet!'

'Yes, I know now. It's dark and it has the same shape and it's the middle of the night. Why were they moving it at this time? I thought it was suspicious.'

Do I sound like a crazy person? I was so sure of what I saw, but the terrible combination of tiredness and worry seems to have conspired against me.

'They're probably doing it at this time of night because they work for me and they have a lot to do to get this house finished,' Cesar says. 'As long as they work quietly, they can do so through the night. I told them not to disturb the residents, which they haven't done. You have.'

I try to explain myself further then, but Cesar storms off and I see why a moment later. He's addressing the other residents.

'My apologies about this very inconvenient wake-up call. I want to assure you that everything is fine, and you can go back into your homes now. My apologies again. This shouldn't have happened.'

Even though Cesar is talking to everyone else, it feels like that last line was directed at me. *This shouldn't have happened.* But it has, and there are strong reasons for that, and they go beyond me mistaking a shape in the dark for something else. That's why I intend to explain to not only Cesar, but the police officer who is still with us.

'My next-door neighbour has gone missing, and I think something terrible has happened to her,' I begin, trying to keep my voice low so the residents who are trickling back inside their homes don't hear and stay outside. I also make sure to keep the urgency in my words because that is crucial in getting the police to take me seriously. 'You need to go to her house and look around. You also need to talk to her boyfriend, Theo. I think he has something to do with her going missing. I overheard him on the phone telling somebody that she had to go, and he was glad she was gone and—'

'That's quite enough,' Cesar says, snapping my sentence in half. 'You have disturbed all these people for no good reason, not to mention wasting police time. And all for what? Some figments of your imagination?'

'It's not a figment of my imagination! Okay, I was wrong about this and I apologise for that but Hayley has gone missing,' I maintain as I keep my pleading eyes on the police officer. 'Go to her house now and ask her boyfriend where she is. They're at number thirteen. I'm at fifteen, so that's why I know something is wrong next door. Please, go and speak to the man who lives there and ask him where his girlfriend is.'

'There is no need to do that,' Cesar tries, but to my relief, the officer does say that he will get somebody to make a visit to Theo's home.

'Thank you,' I say, but Cesar is still far from happy, and while the officer leaves us to go and speak with his colleagues, Cesar steps in closer to me with a menacing look in his eyes.

'What do you think you are doing? Are you deliberately trying to ruin me and this estate? Making false accusations about dead bodies and missing women? Are you trying to ruin sales and kill this estate's reputation for no good reason? Have you any idea how much an incident like this could cost me?'

'What? I don't care about sales or reputation, and I certainly don't care about your money. I just care about a woman going missing, a woman who was about to tell me something very important but was conveniently cut off by that alarm before she could, and I haven't seen her since. But Theo knows where she is. Maybe even you do too.'

'Me? What are you talking about?'

'I know something happened in my house before we moved in and you're deliberately concealing it. I think Hayley knows it too, which is why she has vanished. What have you done to her? Where is she? Is she alive? And what happened in my house?'

I'm getting frantic and losing what morsel of control I have, like a woman possessed and that's probably not a good thing to do when the police are around to witness it. But unlike me, Cesar is not losing his cool. All he does is step even closer to me and with his face inches from mine, he only has to whisper for me to be able to hear him.

'If you think this place is so bad, just leave. I'm not stopping you. Am I?'

That last part feels ominous. Is he trying to show who is really in control here? Is he implying that he could stop me if he wanted to?

It feels like he's goading me into going. Maybe he is bullying me. But whatever he is trying to manipulate me into doing, I won't back down.

I think I know what he's up to. He's only trying to help himself.

That's why I say what I do.

'I'm not going anywhere. Not until I have found out the truth about whatever is going on here.'

SEVENTEEN

Despite having crept out of my house so my family were undisturbed, it's a very different story when I return. I already know they are awake because I can see lights on inside as I reach the front door, and when I walk in, I find Christian in the kitchen with Kai. My son is eating a bowl of cereal, even though it's a few hours away from normal breakfast time yet. As for my husband, he has a cup of coffee in front of him, so I guess he's given up on getting any more sleep too.

The only question is, how long have they been awake?

'Mum!' Kai calls when he sees me, and he abandons his bowl and spoon to rush towards me instead. 'The police are outside! Did you see them?'

'Yes, I did,' I say, which is about the simplest answer I can give him without letting on that I was actually the one who summoned them here. Then I have a question for him. 'Why are you not in bed?'

'I heard all the sirens, so I got up!' he excitedly proclaims. 'I saw the cars go past, but then I couldn't see them, so I came downstairs for food.'

I can't help but smile at his innocence. If only everyone in this world was as pure as my little boy. But they're not, which is why I made that emergency call, and the ominous conversation that occurred after it with Cesar is still replaying in my mind even now I'm home.

Judging by how excitable my son is, I think it's pointless trying to get him back upstairs and into bed. He's going to be exhausted all day for sure, but he won't be the only one and I notice Christian take a sip of his coffee as he watches us.

'Are you okay?' I ask my husband as Kai returns to his cereal.

'I could ask you the same thing,' he replies quietly. 'I woke up and saw you weren't here, and I was worried, especially when I heard the sirens. I tried calling you but—'

'No signal.' I finish his sentence for him. He nods, and I feel incredibly guilty for making him worry. I can also tell he has done his best to not let Kai worry, which is probably why he has distracted our son with food and also why he isn't getting more annoyed with me in front of him now.

'This was you, wasn't it?' he asks me, though it might not even be a question, more a realisation.

'I can explain,' I say, but Christian holds up a hand.

'Later,' he replies, looking fatigued and I feel bad because I know he has a long day of work ahead of him, so this is the last thing he needed. He's also smart enough to know that whatever story I have involving myself and the police is probably best not recounted in front of Kai. We'll have this conversation later. I can't say I'm looking forward to it.

'I'm going to take a shower,' Christian says. 'Then maybe I can answer a few work emails before going into the office. I have got a couple of hours to kill now.'

I watch him as he leaves the kitchen, hating that he is annoyed at me, and aware that he must know all this disruption has been caused by me and my wild theories.

'Mummy, can we watch TV?' Kai asks then and I don't have

a better idea, so I agree, and my son quickly carries his bowl into the lounge before finding his favourite show to watch. It's one he made me download all the episodes of so he can access it anytime, some show about a cartoon hedgehog character who goes around the woods saving all the other animals there from various dangers. It's very kid-friendly, and there are a few lessons in there, so at least it's not at risk of turning my son's brain to mush. There are even a few lessons in there for the adults who are forced to watch too, and maybe I need them as much as my son does.

I sit with Kai in mostly darkness, only the light from the screen illuminating the room in intermittent flashes, but the flashes from all the police cars are a thing of the past. It's quiet out there, so I guess they've either gone or at least most of them have. But did they do as I requested? Did they go and speak to Theo? I doubt they have. I would have seen them when I got back here.

I can't be the first person in the world to be frustrated by apparent inactivity on the part of the police, and I can't also be the first person who feels like they have to take matters into their own hands if something needs to be done. But there's little I can do while I'm sitting here beside my son waiting for the sun to rise.

There is one thing I can do, though.

I can feel my sense of injustice growing by the second.

Cesar, and indeed Theo, are being allowed to get away with whatever is happening. Poor Hayley seems to have already paid the price for knowing about a secret connected to this house, and I have to fear that whoever was in our house before us paid the price too. All signs are pointing to the fact that if I don't drop this, I may end up in danger as well.

As a mother, it seems like the obvious decision to just stay out of it, mind my own business and keep my family safe in our little bubble of peace. But as I look at my son's face lit up by the

TV screen, and as I feel my daughter wriggling around inside me, I can't see how I can ever let them live in a world where people who do bad things are allowed to get away with it. As their guardian, and just like this TV show, I am here to teach them right and wrong. To stand up for yourself. To not back down in the face of a warning like the one Cesar just gave me. That's why I already know what I am going to do, just as soon as my husband and son have left the house today and I get my first window of opportunity.

I am going to do what the police have not.

I am going to go to Theo's home and do some investigating.

The only difference is, I won't knock first and ask to come in.

I will find a way in.

I know that will mean I am committing a crime to try and solve a crime. I also know it means the police could be after me and not somebody else if they do come back here.

But what choice do I have? I can't ignore the fact my neighbour has gone missing. And I need to protect my family.

My son loves his brave characters on TV.

It's time for his mum to be brave in real life.

EIGHTEEN

'Try and get some sleep. You'll feel better if you do.'

Christian's words to me as he leaves the house are not just meant to be helpful, but also a subtle reinforcement of how tired he is after my actions woke him in the night. He knows that sleep is not possible for him now that he has to take Kai to school and then go to work, so essentially, he is saying it's not possible for him to feel better anytime soon. If I was to take his words deeper, I could take them as him being unselfish, looking out for me to get some sleep despite it being my own actions that caused him to lose his. If so, that only makes me feel worse about how tired both he and Kai look as they head to the car. I feel guilty but I don't have time for overanalysing things this morning. I just wave my loved ones off before closing the door to keep up appearances. Christian will presume I'm going to go back to bed as he sees the door close. Although he is wrong and no sooner have I heard his car leave than I re-open the door and look at the house next door.

There is no car there either. I saw Theo go out about half an hour ago, and as he is yet to return, this is the window of opportunity I have been hoping for ever since I made the decision to try and gain entry to his home to look for clues as to what happened to Hayley.

This is it.

Potentially now or never.

So I go.

I don't head for the front door of Theo's place because one, I know it will be locked and two, I don't want anybody to potentially see me creeping around here. Cesar caught me the last time I was at this house. That's why I head straight around to the rear of the property as quickly as I can and, within seconds, I am in my neighbour's back garden.

Away from prying eyes back here, I instantly try the handle on the back door, but alas, it's locked. I had to expect this would be too, especially if Theo really does have something to hide like I think he does. There's no way he would risk his secrets being uncovered easily. But I'm trying to uncover something easily now. That's because I'm searching around his back garden for a hidden key. I'm hoping there is one here somewhere, a spare key that he has stashed away in case he ever forgets his usual key and finds himself locked out. It's a common thing for home-owners to do, leave a key under a plant pot or some other such place, out of sight of any potential burglars but there just in case the people who live there actually need it to get inside. Despite looking under numerous plant pots and turning over various large rocks in his garden, I cannot find a hidden key anywhere. Maybe he's too smart to have one. But I'm still not giving up.

With the door locked and no windows open either, it's become clear to me that my only way in is by using force. I'm going to have to break in rather than simply trespass, so that's what I prepare to do as I pick up a rock and feel its weight. But what's the best way of doing this? Throw it straight through a window? That will make an awful lot of noise. Maybe there's a subtler way. What if I was to try and break the back door handle and along with it the lock? Could that work?

It's insane to me that I am even contemplating these choices, but the fact that I am is just a sign of how far I am being pushed in pursuit of the truth and how far my worries over Hayley are taking me.

I raise the rock above the handle before bringing it down with as much force as I can muster, and I hear a loud crack. The handle is still intact but that definitely did some damage. Let's try again. I repeat the action and, this time, the handle breaks and I hope the lock has been damaged along with it. There's only one way to find out, so I take hold of what is left of the handle and try and turn it. When I do, the door opens.

I'm in. The first thing I do is throw the rock over the fence into my garden, and I hear it land with a loud thump on my lawn. If Theo calls the police, I don't want them finding the evidence of the item that the intruder used, so it's safer over there than it is left lying around here near the damaged back door.

Only now do I go inside and, as soon as I do, I see that I am in the kitchen. I expected that because I assumed all the houses in this part of the estate were designed with exactly the same layout, and it appears that I am right. While I was initially against this cookie-cutter style design when I first looked around the estate, the predictability of it is now my friend because it will mean I can move around this home without wondering which room I am going to walk into next. Instead, it means I can wonder what it is that I might find in these rooms.

Everything looks as I would expect it to in this kitchen. Not only does it have the same layout as mine, but I see that Theo uses the same shelves to store the same kind of cooking utensils, and while the fridge magnets and the things pinned on the noticeboard are different, everything else in here is very similar to my kitchen next door.

So I move on.

I pass through the hallway before checking in on the dining

room and lounge, but again, everything seems normal, or at least in terms of the furniture. I'm not just looking at the tables and chairs; I'm looking for signs of Hayley and, very quickly, I realise that it's obvious there is nothing of hers here. I can't see any female clothing lying around, not a woman's coat on a hook in the hallway or a lady's sweater drying on a radiator or strewn over the arm of a sofa. Nor can I see any make-up or hair products like a stick of lipstick left out on the coffee table or a hair bobble or clip casually lying on the carpet. The more I look around downstairs, the more I only see evidence of a male presence, and while I knew Hayley had gone, it does seem rather quick for every single trace of her having lived here to have gone too.

It's time to look upstairs.

My heart rate quickens as I climb the staircase, well aware that when I was on the ground level, it would have been easier for me to make a quick escape out the back door if I needed to. Now I'm upstairs, getting out of here fast won't be as simple. It might even be impossible. But I'm still going up because if I'm here to look for clues, I have to look in every room – especially the bedrooms – the most private part of any home.

I expect to see the same four doors up here as I see when I'm upstairs in my own home and sure enough, I do. I also expect to find the bathroom behind the first door and I'm right again. Once more, there are plenty of male toiletry items but nothing that might belong to a female, so I move on to the next door.

In my house, this next room is already earmarked as the nursery for my daughter, but as Theo and Hayley don't have children, I'm not sure what they might have used this room for instead, so there is some suspense as I open it. It quickly evaporates when I see that the space is used for a home gym, and barring a few dumbbells, a resistance band and a foam mat, there isn't much else to see.

The next room is Kai's bedroom in my house, so what is it here? It's a home office and as I regard the desk drawers, I am eager to snoop around inside them. Unfortunately for me, these drawers are locked. Is that because they contain confidential work documents that are supposed to be protected when out of the office environment? Or is it because they contain something else, something that relates to Hayley and her disappearance, and potentially, the past of the house next door?

Trying to break into these drawers will take time, and might not even be possible, and there are still a few rooms to have a look in first, so I decide I'll only come back to this if I fail to find anything elsewhere. But as I move on to the master bedroom, my hopes are high that I will find something relating to what Theo has done to Hayley. He can't have removed all trace of her, surely.

It frustrates me that I am the one having to conduct this search rather than the police, but I can't let that frustration at being the only one who thinks something bad happened here distract me from the task at hand.

Keep looking.

Keep hoping to get lucky.

As I enter the master bedroom, the first thing I notice is that it is incredibly tidy. I see the bed, a couple of bedside tables and a large wardrobe, as well as the door to the ensuite. There is no mess in here, no clothes on the floor or even a crumpled duvet. Everything is in place and the bed is made, and while it might just seem like the homeowner is a neat person, to me, this sets off further alarm bells. If Theo was upset about Hayley leaving, or devastated at the breakdown of their relationship, would he be living like this? Or would there be signs of his mental struggle, like half-consumed food and drink next to the bed, the curtains drawn in the daytime, or other mess from where he didn't have the energy or the will to hang his clothes in the wardrobe? What upset, broken-hearted person makes their bed neatly every morning, as well as keeping everything else in the room pristine? To me, this looks like the bedroom of a man who is acting as if nothing momentous has happened recently.

Is Theo a psychopath? Is he capable of feeling little or no emotion? Could he really have got rid of Hayley and carried on as if everything was normal?

I look in the wardrobe but find nothing of interest there, just Theo's clothes, so I move on to the bedside table. I guess the first one I look inside belongs to him because it's full of men's socks and underwear, so I move onto the other table. This must have been Hayley's, so what might I find inside? As I open the drawer, I'm expecting it to be devoid of her things like everywhere else. But it's not. There's a small notebook inside, so I take it out and open the pages. Very quickly, I realise what it is that is written in here. That's because I see my name mentioned.

I have a new neighbour. She is called Dionne.

As I look down the page, I see all the things that are written are *about me*.

I hold my breath as I read.

I'm worried about her. I need to help her. She's in danger...

I look to the next page as my heart pounds in this silent home.

This can't carry on. I need to tell her. I need to warn her...

Oh my god, I wish Hayley would just write what it is so I can read it and find out now. Whatever it is, she was clearly grappling with it for some time.

I turn the page, desperate to see if there is more, but before I can, I hear a loud sound that is more than just the blood rushing in my ears from my erratic heart rate.

I hear something that causes me to almost drop the notebook and run for my life.

I hear the front door unlocking downstairs and the sound of a man whistling as he enters the house.

Theo is home.

NINETEEN

Why did I go upstairs? Why did I trap myself up here?

Theo, a dangerous, unpredictable man, a potential murderer, is home and where am I?

I'm stuck in his bedroom with no chance of escape.

I want to run, but I know I can't hope to simply get down the stairs and sneak past him without him seeing me, so I have to look to Plan B.

Hide.

With the notebook still in my hand, I look around the room for a potential hiding spot and very quickly my options dwindle down to either inside the wardrobe or underneath the bed. In a split second, I make the decision that if Theo comes in here, he is more likely to open the wardrobe doors than he is to get on his hands and knees and look under the bed, so I lower myself down onto the soft carpet before attempting to crawl into what I hope will be a safe space. But while the bed is raised higher than my own, giving me a little more room than if I was attempting this in my own house, it's not easy in my condition. My bump gets in the way of flexible movement, and for a second, I fear that I have made the wrong choice. I should have gone for the wardrobe instead, but it's too late now. I just about manage to get myself under the bed, and while it's uncomfortable, I am now hidden as best I can be.

As I get into position, lying underneath the bed with only a small backpack for company under here, I am praying that Theo has just come home because he forgot something and that once he has it, he will go out again. Then, as soon as he leaves, I can make my exit too, but I can't go anywhere while he is down there. If he doesn't leave the house, my best hope is that he comes up here and goes into the bathroom, because I could potentially get out then while he is preoccupied in there. But it's all hopes and wishes, and the frightening truth is, I can't make my next move until Theo makes his.

So what is he going to do?

I listen out for him and hear his footsteps in the hallway as he moves around. He's still whistling, another sign that he is content rather than heartbroken about Hayley not being here, and I'm further convinced he is a psycho. Hayley might not even be the first woman he has made disappear. There might be others. If there are, there's no doubt he will make me disappear if he finds me hiding under his bed.

My mind spirals in a panic. I think about Christian, Kai and how they would be left with so many unanswered questions if I just vanished. They might never know what happened to me. Kai would wonder why his mummy just left and most likely take that trauma with him into adulthood. As for my husband, he'd probably either throw himself into work to cope with the grief or throw himself into his wine collection, neither one being good solutions. Then there's my unborn child. If I go, she goes with me.

I have no choice.

I have to get out of here.

I have to live.

Suddenly, the whistling stops. So do the footsteps. The only thing that carries on is my pounding heart.

What is Theo doing? Has he heard me? Has he noticed something is wrong? Has he seen the damaged back door handle? If the answer to any of those questions is yes, my chances of getting out of here alive have diminished.

I still can't hear him. Where is he? As creepy as a man like Theo is, I doubt he possesses the ability to float up the stairs and into this bedroom, so I'm confident he is still down there on the ground floor. At least I am until I hear a very awful sound.

It's the sound of footsteps on the staircase as he ascends it.

He's coming up here. He's getting closer to me by the second. If he enters this bedroom, how am I ever going to be able to hold my breath long enough that he won't hear me?

I let go of the notebook, leaving it to lie on the carpet beside me and instead, clamp one of my hands over my mouth in a desperate bid to stop myself crying out in fear or making any other noise that gives away my position. If I was watching a film now and saw some poor character in this situation, I'd simply sit there and think they only need to be quiet, and they'll be fine. But it's easy to think that from a comfortable seat on the sofa while watching television. It's a different reality when you're actually the person hiding and trying everything possible not to make a single sound.

The faster my heart goes, the faster my breathing is, and that means it's impossible to stay perfectly silent. What if I start hyperventilating? I can't do that quietly, can I? I start panicking as Theo continues to climb the stairs, and I'm already about to give up and start begging for my life to try and save some time.

But then something unexpected happens.

There is a knock at the front door.

And it's enough to get Theo to stop.

Who is it? Who has potentially just saved me? Who might I owe my life to?

I listen out as I hear Theo walk back down the stairs before he opens the door. When he does, I get my answer.

I know who is here.

It might just be the best possible outcome.

It's the police.

TWENTY

'Can we come in?' I hear a strong male voice say, and I recognise it. It's the police officer who spoke to me last night on the street when I thought I had witnessed two men trying to dispose of a body. I urged that officer to come here and investigate Theo over Hayley's disappearance, and while it seemed like my pleas had been ignored, I must have been wrong.

The police are here to talk to Theo about a potential crime.

The problem is, they're here while I'm hiding in his house, currently committing a crime of my own.

If it was extremely important that I remained undiscovered when it was just Theo and me, it's still more important that I'm not found now. Should the police learn about my break-in, they will surely arrest me on the homeowner's request. While police custody might be preferable to the fate that I feared was awaiting me just a few moments ago when Theo was coming up the stairs, I'd rather not be arrested if I can help it. Not only is a criminal record the last thing I need and a terrible example to set for my children, but it would surely reduce my credibility in the police's eyes when I tell them to keep investigating other things that have happened here. I need to stay hidden, but it might not be for long. If Theo is arrested, he'll be taken away and I can get out of here then.

But will he be?

'What's this about?' I hear Theo ask, which I suppose he has the right to, though he must secretly be aware of why he is suddenly under the spotlight of local law enforcement.

'We just have a few questions for you. It won't take long, so if we could come in that would be great,' the officer replies, and I get from that dialogue that he must have at least one colleague with him. Sensible to have backup, especially where a man like Theo is concerned. At least if things do go wrong for me here, Theo is the outnumbered one, not me. But what will happen?

The talking seems to stop downstairs, but I can hear movement, and I assume Theo has allowed the officers inside. That is brave of him, but perhaps he is confident of talking himself through this situation.

He's a good liar.

He'll certainly need to be now.

I hear murmurings then but can't make out the words, and I realise they must be continuing the conversation in another room. Now they're no longer in the hallway, I can't hear them, which is not ideal because I want to know exactly what they are asking Theo and what answers he is giving them.

Should I risk leaving my hiding place to try and eavesdrop?

It's surely too risky. What if I trod on a creaky floorboard and everybody downstairs realised there was someone above them? I should stay here where I have been safe so far. But then I think about how this is a new house and, just like mine, there are no creaky floorboards, so maybe I could crawl out from under here and creep to the top of the stairs without giving myself away.

I decide to take the chance because I'm so desperate to hear Theo's conversation with the police, so I make my move.

Crawling as quietly as I can, I get out from under the bed,

but being sure to take the notebook with me. Then I tiptoe to the top of the stairs and brave a look down, though I can't see anyone down there by the door. I can hear the voices much better out here, though, so I listen in.

'You understand we have a duty to follow up on any accusations,' I hear the officer say.

'Of course. I understand,' Theo replies. 'But if she is going to accuse me of doing something like harming my girlfriend, I am going to have to accuse her of harassment.'

What?

'I've done nothing but try and welcome her since she moved in here, but maybe that was the problem,' I hear Theo go on. 'Dionne is obviously obsessed with our lives and has come to this wild conclusion that I have hurt Hayley. My best guess? She's a bored housewife with a big imagination, and while I appreciate you have to look into these things, I wish she wasn't wasting your time and mine with this nonsense.'

I'm furious at Theo and how he is making me out to be the problem. How dare he talk about me like that to anyone, let alone the police. I feel like marching down there and defending myself. I'd love to shut him up by handing this notebook to the police to let them read Hayley's entries. Then they would see that I'm not the crazy one. How would he talk his way out of that?

But I can't do that. If I did, Theo would have me arrested for breaking in and I'd have legal problems of my own. I just need to get out of here without anyone seeing me, finish reading everything there is in this notebook and then find a way of getting it into the hands of the police without incriminating myself. I could give it to them anonymously, that might work. I just need them to read this. When they do, they'll see what I see.

Hayley was afraid.

And Theo has silenced her.

But he can't silence her written words.

I can't quite hear what is being said now as the voices are too low, but I dare not get any closer either, so I stay where I am. While I do, I wonder why Theo didn't get rid of this notebook. He must have read the entries in here. If I found it easily enough, he must have found it too. He's obviously done a good job of getting rid of the rest of Hayley's things, so there's no way he would have missed this notebook. Is he so confident that he didn't deem it a threat? It's impossible to know what Theo is thinking. That's what makes him so dangerous.

I hear more conversation but can't make out what is said, until I am forced to freeze and hold my breath when Theo and the officers suddenly return to the downstairs hallway. They're right underneath me, just at the bottom of this staircase that I am lingering near, and if any of them were to come up now then I'd definitely be caught because I can't run without making too much noise.

But none of them do come up. All that happens is Theo opens his door to apparently wave the officers goodbye.

Why are they leaving? Why aren't they arresting him? What explanation did he give them as to where Hayley is? I don't know but it must have been a sufficient one if they are leaving without putting him in handcuffs.

Against my better judgement, I brave another look over the top of the staircase, and when I do, I see the officers departing while Theo stands watching them go, entirely unencumbered, no handcuffs in sight.

Then he closes the door and it's just me and him again.

If he can handle the police so easily, I wonder how easily he could handle me if he discovers me up here. I don't want to find out, though. If I have to, I am determined to do a lot more than they did.

Then it seems I might just get my chance to prove it.

Theo is coming up.

I instinctively step back away from the staircase before looking around for somewhere I can hide. It has to be no more than a couple of steps away or there will be no way I can get there in time.

I see a doorway and step through it before hiding behind the door, and I'm out of view just in time as Theo reaches the top of the stairs. I can hear his movements only a few feet away from me and I hold my breath as I wait to see where he will go next.

The answer is the bathroom and when I hear the door close behind him, I realise this is my chance.

I have to go.

Now.

Leaving my spot, even though every muscle in my body is telling me to stay hidden, I move as quickly and as quietly as I can, passing the closed bathroom door before reaching the stairs. Then I descend in the same fashion, feeling like my heart is skipping beats, though I'm careful not to skip any steps in case I fall and make too much noise.

I glance nervously over my shoulder to check the bathroom door hasn't opened, but it's still closed and as I make it to the bottom of the stairs, I feel like I have a strong chance of getting out of here safely.

I head for the back door, the same way I came in, as I figure it's the quickest way out. The front door might have been locked, but at least I know the back door can't be because it is broken. I'm also unsure if the police might still be outside, so best to leave via the rear and be as discreet as I can.

I head into the kitchen and the back door is in sight. From this side, everything looks normal, which must be why Theo hasn't noticed anything awry. But as I open the door and see the other side of it, I see the damaged handle that gives away the fact that someone gained access into here illegally.

I feel the fresh air on my face and now I'm just about to step into the garden, safe in the knowledge that I'll be home in less than a minute.

I've done it. I've got away and best of all, Hayley's notebook is still in my possession.

'What do you think you're doing?' the voice suddenly says behind me, and I don't have to turn around to know who it is and what has happened.

It's Theo.

He's caught me.

I guess I'm not making it home safely after all.

TWENTY-ONE

'I'll ask you again,' Theo says as he takes a step towards me. 'What do you think you are doing?'

Considering he has just caught me intruding in his home, Theo seems very calm. Disturbingly so. If he was angry or rushing towards me then I'd at least react instinctively, turning and running away in a desperate bid to escape his wrath. But he isn't doing those things. He is getting closer to me but ever so slowly and he isn't raising his voice, suggesting to me that he doesn't want to frighten me any more than I already am. He might not want to startle me because he knows I'll run. Better to keep me here than have to chase me out into the street. But because I haven't moved a muscle yet, he is close enough now to reach out and grab me, so even if I do try and run, I fear I've left it too late.

I don't know how he got down those stairs so fast but now he's here, he doesn't need to be quick.

'Don't come any closer,' I snap at him, standing my ground and showing my strength. 'Stay where you are, or I swear I'll scream so loud that all the neighbours will hear me.'

That does enough to prevent Theo from taking another step, but though he stands still, he is now smirking, suggesting my show of strength didn't have quite as much impact as I might have hoped.

'I'm not going to hurt you or do anything to make you scream so all the neighbours hear,' Theo says, putting his hands out to show me he means me no harm. 'But I would like to know why you are in my house. You understand I have the right to know, don't you?'

'You know why I'm here,' I reply, not quite as calmly as Theo just spoke. 'You've hurt Hayley. You've shut her up before she could tell me whatever she was going to say. You're dangerous. You might have fooled the police, but you're not fooling me.'

'Ahh, the police. I guess if you were hiding upstairs then you know they were just here,' Theo replies. 'I have you to thank for that little visit.'

'Okay, so they're gone. You're a good liar, but they won't believe you when I show them this,' I say as I raise the notebook, allowing Theo to see that it is in my possession now.

'Why have you got that with you?' Theo asks, still calm on the outside, but his nerves must be jangling beneath the surface.

'Because it's evidence!'

'Evidence of what?'

'Evidence that Hayley knew something bad had happened at my house, and it proves my story right. She was silenced before she could tell me, which makes me think that whatever she knew, you were at the heart of it.'

I am so confident that I don't even pause for breath.

'This is why she stayed in the house all the time. This is why she was drunk when she turned up on my doorstep. Why she looked so afraid. Because she was afraid of you. She felt trapped and scared and alone, but she still tried to help me. But it's cost her everything. She's gone, but I won't let her death be in vain. I won't let you get away with whatever you have done. It's over, you understand? Whatever secret you are hiding, it's all going to come out and this notebook is going to help me prove it!'

Only then do I pause and allow Theo to speak, and the reason I am doing so is because he is still not doing anything to threaten me. But it could just be a ploy to lure me into a false sense of security, so I am remaining on my guard, my fingernails gripping the notebook tightly.

'Yes, you're right. Hayley is gone,' Theo says. 'And yes, you are right about her staying in the house all the time and being drunk when she visited you. But that's it. You're mistaken about everything else. You're certainly mistaken if you think I have hurt her to try and cover up some big secret about your house.'

'No, I'm not. I heard you on the phone. I heard you telling somebody that Hayley had to go.'

'You were eavesdropping on my private conversations?'

'I heard you over the fence. So explain that!'

Theo takes a deep breath as my own breathing continues to be shorter than it usually is.

'I was talking to one of my friends. He was worried about me, so I was explaining what had happened.'

'He was worried about *you*? Why would he be worried about you?'

'Because he knows what I've had to put up with recently?'

What is he talking about?

Theo surprises me again then by taking a seat at one of the stools beside his kitchen counter.

'I told Hayley to leave and the reason I did that is because she had become very difficult. She was not the woman I had originally started dating. She had become paranoid and aloof. She had developed a serious drinking problem. And despite me trying all sorts of things, she refused to open up to me and tell me what was wrong, so in the end, I had no choice. I told her I couldn't carry on like this. The incident at your house was the final straw. We are now separated, but I can assure you she is safe and well.'

Theo talks with such conviction, but can I believe him?

'The things she has written in here,' I say as I raise the notebook and recount some of them. '"She's in danger. I have to help her. I have to warn her." Hayley is talking about me, right? So that proves she knew something and was trying to help me. So isn't it a big coincidence that she has gone just before she told me? And that alarm sounded at just the right time? I know you and Cesar are hiding the truth.'

Theo frowns.

'You think that is Hayley's notebook?' he asks me as he looks at it.

'What? Yes, it's hers,' I say, but Theo is frowning.

'Nope. It's mine,' he says. 'Anything written in there was written by me.'

I was not expecting that.

'What? You wrote these things?' I ask him as I open the notebook and flick through the pages again.

'That's right. I was trying to make sense of what was happening with Hayley, so when I refer to somebody as *she*, it's Hayley, not you. I was saying I was worried about her. About her paranoia and her drinking. And when I said I had to warn her, it was because I was going to tell her that I couldn't carry on like this and we were over unless she changed her ways.'

I re-read the sentences I just spoke out loud, only this time from the new perspective. Suddenly, what Theo has said might make sense. Instead of these being the frightened ramblings of Hayley, they could just as easily be the frightened ramblings of Theo, a man who was worried about his girlfriend's apparent unravelling.

'Why do you think it was just lying in the bedside drawer

upstairs?' Theo goes on. 'If I was trying to cover up something and hide any evidence, wouldn't it be gone if it belonged to Hayley? But it doesn't, so it was here. It's here because it's mine.'

I'm trying to process all of this. I'm trying to see if I could have got this so wrong.

'I'm not hiding anything,' Theo goes on. 'And I don't think Cesar is either. The truth is not as interesting as that, unfortunately. The truth is Hayley and I have separated, and while I still care about her and wish her the best, we couldn't continue as we were. The writing had been on the wall between us for a while. We were drifting apart, so I made the difficult but necessary decision and told her that we had to be over. So she has left. Now I'm here trying to get on with my life, but I hope you appreciate that having you and the police poking into my personal affairs is not making any of that easier.'

I look up from the words in the notebook and stare at Theo, and now I see him in a different light. I don't see a devious, cold and calculating man. I see a man whose heart is aching over the end of his relationship. He doesn't look strong or dangerous anymore; he looks weak, tired, and fed up with all the recent drama in his life. The toll of Hayley's drinking and mood swings has clearly weighed heavily on him, and I realise I feel exactly the same way about the toll all my recent worry and anxiety has taken on me. But while Theo might be feeling a little better now he has taken decisive action on his problems, I know that I'll only feel truly better if I know where Hayley is.

'Where has she gone?' I ask him. 'If you can prove to me that she is safe and well then I will leave you alone.'

I hate how I might be coming across to Theo, but I am a natural worrier and if he didn't realise that already, he will now. As he contemplates answering me, I think about giving an example of how much I do worry. I could tell him about how I always used to insist that my friends messaged me when they got home from a night out we had enjoyed, just so that I knew we were all safe in our beds and none of us had fallen foul of any trouble on our separate ways home. Before I have a chance to explain, he finally answers me.

'She's with her sister in the Midlands,' Theo replies.

I think about that, and it calms me slightly to have a location for her that sounds safe. But there's still the matter of what she was trying to tell me.

'I don't know if this is asking too much, but could I have her number?' I ask next. 'It's just that I'd like to speak to her about whatever it was she was going to tell me before the alarm interrupted us.'

'I'm not sure that's a good idea. She needs to get herself better and focus on her recovery.'

'But she had something to tell me.'

'She was drunk,' Theo says with a sad sigh. 'I saw it first hand and a lot more than you did. Most of what she said in these past few weeks has been nonsense. It was all the alcohol talking. I don't think you should take much notice of any of it, I'm afraid.'

'Something must have caused her breakdown! You said she wasn't always like this.'

'I guess something did. I don't know. She never told me. I do know that her father had a troubled past with alcohol, so I fear she may have inherited that gene. If so, maybe this was always destined to happen and we're just two people who were caught in the crosshairs when it did.'

Theo really is talking like a man who feels sorry for himself rather than a man who is trying to talk his way out of something bad he did. He must have come across this way to the police as well, and I presume he provided them with an address for Hayley so they could look into her wellbeing and definitely rule him out of any potential wrongdoing. Has all my paranoia and stress caused me to accuse an innocent man of something terrible?

Maybe Theo is okay.

Maybe Hayley is okay too.

If so, I really should leave him, his notebook and his house alone.

Assuming Theo lets me.

TWENTY-TWO

I rush home, grateful it's not far to go because I feel exhausted and weak. What was I thinking, breaking into my next-door neighbour's house? It was insane of me to commit a crime as serious as that at any time, but doing it while pregnant? I could have been arrested and sentenced and then my baby would have been born in custody. My daughter's first experience of life would have been seeing her mother surrounded by police officers waiting to take her back to her prison cell as soon as the birth was complete. Maybe my paranoia is causing me to imagine the worst-case scenario and the reality is that I might only get a community service order or a fine for my crime. But how can I not worry when I've always been a law-abiding citizen?

Maybe everyone else is right and I'm wrong.

Maybe I am losing my grip on reality.

After the nerve-wracking ordeal of hiding in Theo's home only to end up getting caught, and the embarrassment when he explained how the notebook was his, not Hayley's, all I want to do is get inside my house and hide away. But no sooner have I walked in than I find that I am not alone.

'Dad?' I say as I spot my father coming out of my kitchen with a piece of toast in his hand.

'Ahh, there you are. I've been looking everywhere for you. I did knock but there was no answer, and when I tried the door, it was open. I was wondering where you had got to.'

My dad takes a bite out of his toast, although his slim appearance makes me think it's his first carb in a while, and he looks like he has made himself very much at home in my absence.

'Where were you?' he asks me with his mouth full, but that's tended to be one of my father's bad habits throughout life, as if so much of what he has to say simply cannot wait until he has finished chewing.

'Erm…' I stall, really not wishing to tell him what I've been doing, so instead, I decide to use another one of his bad habits against him. *Answering a question with another question.*

'What are you doing here?' I ask, wondering how I could have missed seeing his car parked out front, but then I was in a bit of a panic. I suppose I still am.

'I've come to see how you are settling in,' Dad replies, finally finishing his toast, although I hear more pop out of the toaster behind him, so I guess he is peckish this morning. 'We've barely heard from you. It'd be nice to know how our daughter is doing.'

I almost feel like saying 'you've never been that bothered before' but hold my tongue because I don't have the energy to get into a heated parent-child debate at this time.

'I'm fine,' I say. 'I've just been busy. You know how it is with a house move, there's so much to do.'

He certainly does know because he and Mum move all the time. London. Scotland. The south of France. They go wherever their money and their mood takes them before coming back and starting all over again, and they don't always sell the properties they bought along the way. I have no idea how many houses they currently own, and I'm hardly going to ask them explicitly, but if people wonder why there is a housing crisis, my parents might have the answer for them.

'Well, it's nice to see you in person,' Dad says casually. 'Have you had breakfast? There's more toast in here. Why don't we sit down and have something to eat and a cup of tea and let's catch up while the house is quiet.'

The house is quiet with Christian and Kai out, but this is still really not a good time.

'I didn't sleep well,' I confess, though I quickly regret doing so because I know Dad will ask why and I don't want to mention the police, so I put my hand on my bump. 'She was wriggling all night.'

'Oh, I see,' Dad replies, looking a little useless like any man does when they can't relate to the stresses and strains of carrying a child.

'I'm sorry but I might just go upstairs and take a shower and then try and have a nap,' I tell my father, hoping he will understand and leave. 'Is that okay?'

It feels weird having to ask for permission to do something in my own home, but I guess the habit of a child asking a parent for permission dies hard.

'Of course. Whatever you need to make yourself feel better,' Dad says to my relief.

'Thanks,' I say as I turn for the stairs. 'Are you okay to let yourself out?'

I figure he is because he had no problem letting himself in, and Dad confirms that he'll manage but not without asking if he can just grab the toast he made before he goes.

'Enjoy your breakfast,' I say with a weary smile as I climb the stairs, and as Dad finishes up using my food in the kitchen, I go in search of something that will make me feel better.

My first port of call is the shower, and I undress before turning on the hot water and stepping under its soothing spray. As I wash my body, I try to cleanse myself of all my worries too, but it's impossible. While the soapy suds disappear down the drain without much effort, the thoughts of Hayley, Theo, Cesar and this house do not, and by the time I get out of the shower, I'm still to achieve peace of mind. The next thing I try is getting into bed and as I dry myself off and slip into my pyjamas, I am ready to hide under my duvet for the rest of the day. Before I can do that, I hear a noise. It startles me at first because I haven't actually heard it before.

It's the landline phone ringing.

Christian initially moaned about us not needing it to be fixed because he said a signal booster kit would do the job, as everybody rings mobile phones these days rather than landlines, but he's obviously wrong because somebody is calling us now on that very landline.

As I head to the upstairs phone, I wonder who it might be who is calling. I sent out our phone number to all our friends, so maybe it's one of them checking in to see how the house move has gone and arranging a time when they might get to come see our new place. Maybe getting a date on my social calendar is exactly what I need, so I pick up the phone and answer eagerly.

'Hi!' I say, waiting to hear a familiar voice at the other end of the line.

'Oh hello, I was just trying to reach Rosie,' the unfamiliar female voice replies.

'Sorry, who?'

'Rosie. Or Jordan. Are they there?'

'Sorry, I think you must have the wrong number,' I reply. That seems to be the only explanation as to why this person is asking for two people who don't live here.

'Oh, this was the number they gave me,' the woman replies. 'It was a few months ago now. I've been meaning to call sooner but you know how life is, things get in the way. Although I haven't heard from either of them in that time so I was worried. Are they okay?'

What part of 'you must have the wrong number' does this woman not understand?

'I'm sorry, but like I said, there is nobody here by either of those names,' I repeat and now I'm preparing to end the call.

'There must be. This is the number they gave me to their new address. They can't have left already, can they?' the woman goes on, continuing the conversation.

'Their new address,' I repeat, more to myself than for this woman's benefit. 'Wait. Are you saying Rosie and Jordan lived in this house?'

'Yes. This is number fifteen, Evergreen Drive, is it not?' the woman says, and my hand grips the telephone tighter. This is it. This is the proof I needed. Somebody did live here before us. A couple by the names of Rosie and Jordan. Getting this landline connection fixed means I am now using the same number they must have used, which is how the person has been able to reach me. So this means Cesar was lying. But where are Rosie and Jordan now? This woman on the phone obviously doesn't know. *But Hayley did...*

'What's your name? Where are you?' I ask the woman urgently. 'Are you nearby? Can you come to this address because I really need to talk to you. I was told that we were the first people to live in this house, but I've obviously been lied to, so I need you to come here and help me prove that—'

I hear a loud clicking sound at the other end of the line.

What has just happened?

Did the woman hang up on me?

It takes me a few seconds before I realise what has actually happened.

She didn't hang up on me at all.

The call was disconnected from my end.

TWENTY-THREE

There could be all sorts of reasons why a call might get disconnected. A bad line. Bad weather. Sheer bad luck. I don't believe it's a coincidence.

Just like when Hayley was about to tell me something important only to be interrupted by the alarm, this call was ended on purpose at the most inconvenient time. Being denied the truth once could be deemed unlucky, but twice, no way. Somehow, someone on this estate must have heard my phone conversation and ended it abruptly before it could go any further. That's because I was only seconds away from arranging to meet the mystery caller so we could confront Cesar together and demand to know what's happened to Rosie and Jordan. She was my proof that I am not just imagining all of this.

I thought I was going mad. I feared I was losing my mind. But the note was real. Someone was here before us and somebody was trying to warn me, just like Hayley was.

Now somebody else ended this call.

Somebody who is doing everything they can to keep their secret buried.

I give up trying to get the upstairs phone working because

it's clearly dead, so I run downstairs to try the one down there. This one is fixed into the wall in the hallway on a table by the door, so I pick up the receiver to see if there is a dial tone. But there's not. It's the same as the one upstairs. Totally useless.

'What is going on?' I say out loud to myself as I check the phone cable that goes into the wall, but I can't see anything wrong with that either. But there must be something wrong, otherwise my call wouldn't have cut off and I'd still be talking to that woman now. I'd know her name already, as well as knowing exactly when Rosie and Jordan told her they had moved in here. Best of all, I'd know exactly when we could meet up to discuss this further and, if need be, alert the police. No longer would I just be a lone woman with a paranoid imagination. I'd be part of a pair, two women with a story to tell that the police would have to believe. My husband would have to believe it too, and that would mean a great deal to me. I crave his support just as much as I dread his doubts. It would also mean a huge amount to me to catch Cesar out because I know he is behind all of this. I bet he sounded that alarm and I bet he cut this call. I just need to prove it, and that woman was my best bet. Except she can't phone me back if the damn phone isn't working.

I do not have the technical expertise to figure out how to diagnose or fix the problem with my phone, so I have no choice but to contact an expert. I use my mobile phone to go online to the website of the company that connected the existing landline and through a customer service chat, I request that they send out an engineer urgently to my address. As I wait for them to arrive, I pace around my house like a caged animal, feeling as frustrated and restrained as they might do at a zoo.

I seem to be thwarted at every step, like somebody else is controlling my life and I can't get out from under their power. It's felt this way ever since I moved into this house.

. . .

It takes two hours for the phone engineer to arrive, and no sooner has he parked his van and climbed out from behind the steering wheel, than I am rushing towards him. I'm keen to get the phone fixed as soon as possible, but I also want to know exactly why it stopped working at the precise moment it did. Most of all, I want to know if he can trace the fault to the point where we can find out who actually caused it.

The poor engineer listens to everything I have to say before he's even made it into my house. He responds by very politely asking me for a cup of tea while he works. I realise I'm better off leaving him to get on with the job than bothering him anymore, so I plan to go into my kitchen while he gets started inspecting the phone in the hallway. But just before I do, I feel like I need a proper answer on my most pertinent question.

'What could cause a phone line to suddenly cut out?'

The engineer sets down his box of tools before scratching his head.

'This is a new-build house, right? Well, it's very common for there to be issues with things like phone lines and signals, etc. in these new properties. Believe it or not, things are often much better in the older houses.'

'I get that, but this phone line was only recently installed. So it can't have broken already, can it? What if it's been tampered with?'

'Why would anyone want to tamper with your phone line?' the engineer asks, eyeing me suspiciously.

Where do I start? I feel like saying to him, but I better not, so I shrug my shoulders before going into the kitchen to make his tea.

As the kettle boils and I make the engineer his drink, I think about the woman who phoned. She sounded so sure that there were a couple called Rosie and Jordan who lived here. She mentioned they had been here a few months ago and it had taken her a while to get around to calling. As I think about that timeline, I see that it fits. A couple could have been here a few months ago because that leaves enough time for them to have gone and then for us to have viewed this house, had the offer accepted and moved in. The only questions are: why did that couple leave and why did Cesar pretend we were the first ones here?

'Any progress?' I ask the engineer as I take him his tea, but considering I've only given him five minutes, he's well within his rights to let out a deep breath and look at me with a hint of exasperation on his face.

'Give me a chance,' he says before smiling and accepting the tea.

I need to follow his advice, so I go and take a seat on my sofa and drum my fingers nervously on the arm of it as I wait for an update.

It takes a lot longer than I would have hoped, and the amount of huffing and puffing coming from the engineer as the time ticks by is further evidence that finding the root cause of this problem is not an easy task. It takes so long that Christian arrives home with Kai, which means I'm going to have to explain to them why there is a stranger in our house.

'There's a problem with the phone,' I tell Christian as Kai very sweetly says hello to the engineer.

'What? We've only just had it fixed,' he says.

'I know,' I reply with my eyebrows raised. 'But guess when it broke? It broke during a phone call I received from a woman who was asking for the couple who lived here before us.'

'What?' Christian asks as Kai continues to stand by the engineer, watching him work.

'A woman called here asking for Rosie and Jordan. She said she was given this number for them when they moved in.'

'It must have been a wrong number,' Christian says simply, not sounding surprised in the slightest, which I would have presumed he might have.

'No, because she gave me our address. She knew it exactly, so she wasn't mistaken. Somebody was here before us. This is the proof. This is what I've been telling you and this is why we need to go and speak to Cesar because he's been lying.'

'Maybe it was a prank,' Christian tries then.

'Like the note was a prank?' I ask him. 'Isn't that a big coincidence? Two pranks on the same house?'

'I don't understand what you think this means,' Christian says, keeping his voice down in front of the engineer, who admittedly does look a little uncomfortable to be witnessing an increasingly heated discussion between a husband and wife.

'It means that we were led to buying this house under a false pretence,' I say. 'We were sold a house that had never been lived in. But it has been, so we could get our money back. Maybe we could even sue.'

'Sue? Why would you want to sue anybody?'

'Because I don't like being lied to.'

'Lying isn't a crime by itself,' Christian says, as if there is no issue here. 'And there surely isn't an estate agent in the world who doesn't embellish the facts in order to get a sale.'

I don't get it. Why isn't my husband being supportive? Why isn't he on my side? The longer he behaves like this, the less I recognise him as the man I chose to marry.

'Cesar is hiding something,' I maintain defiantly. 'This woman who called knows a lot about this house and the people who lived here, which means you should be just as interested in her as I am. I was in the middle of getting her to come here so we could confront Cesar together. Then the line cut off.'

'Why are you saying it like somebody deliberately did it?' Christian asks me, but before I can answer, the engineer does so for me.

'Because they did,' he says, holding up a broken wire from behind the wall socket. 'This line has been cut.'

'On purpose?' I ask for clarification, and the engineer nods, so I look at Christian again.

'See! Now do you believe me?' I say to him, expecting there to be no other possible thing for him to say except yes.

'Do you think this is doing you or the baby any good?' Christian asks me then, making me feel bad, as if I am deliberately choosing a stressful life over a peaceful one at the expense of our unborn child's health.

I hesitate to answer, mainly because there's no way I can say all this extra pressure is good for us, and Christian speaks again.

'I've got work to do,' he says as he takes his laptop bag and heads upstairs, leaving me to deal with both the engineer and the mystery as to who cut the phone line. But as I watch him go, I feel uncomfortable about his reaction.

Somebody has tampered with our phone line, and he isn't bothered? He carries on as if everything is normal?

Why would he do that?

I really don't want to think it, but the more I try to ignore the thought, the more it presses to the forefront of my brain.

The only reason that makes sense as to why he would try and dismiss or ignore all of this is because it's not just Cesar who is hiding something.

My husband is too.

TWENTY-FOUR

Another sleepless night, although this time, I forced myself to remain in bed. But even though I stayed home through the night, I plan to get out in the day, and once Christian and Kai have left, I depart too. The engineer said he needed to come back later to fix the phone, as he didn't have the parts he needed with him, so there's no point staying in hoping that the phone might ring again. I have asked him how I can get my phone records so I can try and get the number who called and ring them back myself, and he told me it can be requested. In the meantime, I am going for a walk, hopeful that the fresh air will help me arrange the cluttered thoughts in my mind.

It's a sunny day, but my mood is not lifted by my exposure to the rays, mainly because I'm feeling so down about the fact that Christian and I seem to be at odds with each other. He should be on my side in this, but he isn't. Every time I look at him, I see someone who looks tired, but not from work or parenting.

He's tired from me.

I appreciate that I am bringing a lot of stress to our lives with my obsession with finding out what happened with our new home, but what am I supposed to do? Pretend everything is normal? I know he's worried about the effect all this stress might be having on our unborn daughter, and I am too, but it's not as if I can just leave things alone. I didn't phone the house and ask for two people who no longer live there, nor did I cut the phone line. Somebody else is interfering in our lives, and therefore making it impossible for me to think about anything else but finding out who it is and why they are doing it. We might not be safe in our house.

I am considering going to Cesar's, if only to tell him that I am onto him. Despite his antics with the phone, I *will* speak to that woman again and I *will* find out what happened to Jordan and Rosie. I know it is a terrible idea, plus it could potentially be putting myself and my baby in harm's way. Perhaps being alone with Cesar in his house is too dangerous a risk to take, especially if I confront him with my growing knowledge. And what would Christian think if he knew what I was up to while he was busy earning money for our family? He thinks I'm resting, not investigating, so maybe going to Cesar's is not the best idea.

But while I'm busy deliberating my next move, I find myself walking in the direction of Cesar's and, as I see his house, I tell myself I will just give a cursory glance at his property as I pass. That's not illegal. I have the right to walk down this street and look at the houses here. Nobody can stop me doing that.

His house is just ahead of me, and I slow down a little, not wanting to rush past because who knows what I might catch a glimpse of in his windows when I walk by? Just before I can get there, though, I see the door open, so I hang back behind a hedge, expecting to see the owner of the house coming out.

But it's not Cesar who leaves.

It's not even Theo.

It's my husband.

I watch as Christian leaves Cesar's place, and as I see him approaching his parked car, I wonder if Kai is in there. I can't see my son, though, and checking the time on my watch, I note that school has already started, so Christian must have dropped him off there and then come back here. He's going to be very late for work, but there was obviously something that he had to discuss with Cesar that was more important than pleasing his boss.

I need to find out what it is and why he didn't tell me where he was going.

'Christian?' I call out, and my husband stops and looks down the street right at me. I step out from behind the hedge. He looks flustered at my sudden appearance.

'What are you doing?' I ask him as I get nearer to him and his car, and as I do, Christian glances back at Cesar's house, though there is no sign of the owner coming out to join us. I might request that he does unless my husband tells me exactly what this has been all about.

'Di? What are you doing here?' he asks me as if I'm the one sneaking around rather than him.

'I'm going for a walk. Why are you here? Shouldn't you be at work?'

I reach Christian and he looks even more nervous up close than he did from afar.

'I'm on my way there now,' he says, and as I glance in the car, I see that Kai is definitely not in there, so at least he isn't late for school today. It's just my husband who has gone off his usual routine.

'What were you doing in Cesar's house?' I demand to know.

'I'll tell you later. I really need to get to work,' Christian says and, to my surprise, he gets in behind the wheel and closes the driver's side door. Is he really going to just leave without explaining this to me?

'Christian, wait!' I cry and I try to open the door, but it's already automatically locked. He starts the engine then, and I fear he is going to drive away, but he does at least do me the courtesy of lowering his window so he can say one more thing.

'I have to get to a meeting. I'm sorry. I'll tell you all about it tonight, but everything is fine, so don't worry. Have a good day.'

With that, he takes off, speeding away down the street and leaving me standing by the roadside with even more questions in my head than I had when I left my house earlier. If he won't tell me what all that was about, someone else will have to.

I storm towards Cesar's front door and start banging on it, knowing he must be in there because Christian was in there too, and he wouldn't have been in there alone. But despite all the noise I am making, Cesar does not open his front door.

'Dionne?'

I spin around at the sound of my name to see Theo standing in the street behind me.

'Are you okay?' he asks, though he must know the answer to that question considering how worked up I am.

'No, I'm not,' I reply, just in case he was in any doubt, and I turn back to the door before banging on it again.

'He might not be home,' Theo says as he gets closer.

'He is home! I know he is, and I want to speak to him!'

'Then he obviously doesn't want to speak to you,' he says as he reaches me and tries to calm me down. I push him away initially before he says the one thing that does make me reconsider.

'You need to stop this. It's not good for your baby.'

I instantly realise he is right and stop banging on the door, and then my eyes fill with tears.

'I just want to know what is happening,' I sob, a simple truth, but one I can't seem to find.

I stop short of crying into Theo's shoulder, but he does

provide support to me as I stand beside him and try and dry my eyes.

'Come with me. I've got something that will cheer you up,' he says then, and he walks away before pausing to wait for me to follow him.

But should I?

TWENTY-FIVE

'Just this way,' Theo calls out to me as I continue to walk behind him, following him to wherever he is taking me, though I'm still not sure if it's a good idea. We've left the streets and the houses behind and we're walking uphill along a dirt track in the wilderness that surrounds the estate. There is grass on either side of us and tall trees ahead but no sign of anybody else and I'm on the verge of turning back because this is making me feel uneasy.

Why would he want to lead me out here?

Unless this is where he led Hayley before me?

'That's far enough,' I say, stopping. 'If you won't tell me where we're going then I'm going back.'

I turn around to show I'm serious, but Theo doesn't come after me.

'Look at this,' he tells me then and when I turn back, I see him at the top of the track, gesturing out to something I can't quite see from down here.

Half of me still wants to leave but the other half is curious enough for me to keep walking uphill rather than down and as I reach Theo, I see what he was trying to show me.

Between the tree, and below the dip of this hill, is a fantastic view of the estate we have just left behind as well as miles of unspoilt countryside beyond it.

'Pretty nice, huh?' Theo says with a grin on his face. 'I came up here for a run one day and noticed this view. Now I try and come up here every day if I can. It always makes me feel better, so maybe it'll work for you.'

While the view is beautiful, I look away from it to see Theo's expression, as I'm trying to figure out if he really has just done something incredibly nice for me without any agenda. It seems like he has, but the question is: why?

'I broke into your house,' I remind him, though I'm sure I don't need to. 'I've accused you of hurting your girlfriend. I got the police to question you.'

'Yes, I haven't forgotten about any of that,' Theo says with a chuckle.

'So why are you being nice to me?'

'Because I think you need it,' he replies. 'I think you need a friend around here and, while we might never be close friends, I want you to see that I'm not a bad guy. I'm just your next-door neighbour who broke up with his girlfriend and is trying to get on with his life. But my crazy neighbour won't let me.'

He smiles to show me that the last part of what he said is meant to be a joke, and it succeeds, because it does make me laugh.

Despite what has happened between us, he is right. I do need a friend here. I'm constantly second guessing everyone, thinking they are all against me. I'm assuming they're all hiding something from me, and now I'm even thinking that about my husband. It's exhausting, but right now, what Theo is doing is the nicest thing anyone here has done for me since I moved in. The only thing stopping me from truly enjoying and appreciating it is my paranoia.

I look back at the view and take several deep breaths. As I do that, Theo sits down on the grass beside a tree and enjoys the same view from that vantage point. After a few seconds, I decide to join him.

'I'm sorry,' I say to him. 'I'm sorry about all the things I did. I hope you can understand that some weird things have been happening and I'm just trying to figure out if any of it affects me or my family.'

'It's okay, no need to apologise,' Theo replies. 'You have a lot of people to look after. You're only doing what you should be doing as a protector.'

It's nice of Theo to give me that reassurance, but it also makes me wonder why my own husband wasn't giving it to me first.

'Maybe I could handle other people having secrets,' I say to Theo as he tugs out a few strands of grass and then opens his palm to watch them flutter away in the breeze. 'But not my husband. I feel like he is hiding something too. The way he doesn't seem worried about what might have happened in our house. It makes me think he already knows what it was. Maybe he knew before we even moved in, and maybe he didn't tell me because he knew I wouldn't want to move here if he did.'

Suddenly, I worry that I have revealed too much about the concerns I have over Christian. The intimate inner workings of my marriage should not be discussed so openly with a person who is still practically a stranger to me, so have I told Theo too much? If I have, he doesn't look embarrassed or unsure. He's just looking at the view, so I do the same.

I stare out at the estate below us, at all the houses, some of them occupied, some of them still waiting to be bought and, beyond them, some still being built. As much as I want it to, this place does not feel like home and I'm afraid it never will.

'Please will you be honest with me,' I say to Theo, feeling like my mistrust of him has always clouded my behaviour towards him, but needing to give him, and myself, another chance. 'You were here before we were so you would know more than I do. Was anybody in our house before us? Was there a couple called Rosie and Jordan?'

Theo stops pulling out small clumps of grass and looks at me while I hold my breath. Having been so nice to me, I feel like whatever he says next will be the truth.

'I have never seen anybody else living in that house other than you,' he tells me, so I guess I'm going to have to accept that. 'But...'

'But what?'

'When we bought the house, I was working away, so it was only Hayley who moved in at first. We were among the first residents here, and Hayley confirmed as much when she told me how few people she had seen around. She only mentioned one guy; Arthur, I think his name was. That made me feel guilty about being away. She was here for just over a month while I was away on business abroad. But I've been here ever since I arrived back from that trip, and in all that time, I have not seen anyone else in your house but you. I say all this because I am letting you know that there was a small period of time when I wasn't here.'

'So there might have been another couple before us!' I cry, realising there is a suitable gap in the timeline that could fit my theory. 'When Hayley was here alone, she would have seen them, right?'

'I suppose so, but she never mentioned anybody,' Theo replies. 'We spoke on the phone almost every night while I was away, and she never told me about anybody moving in next door.'

'Are you sure?'

'Yes. Well, I mean, I can't remember every single thing we said in those phone calls. I was working a lot and I was tired and I wasn't sleeping too well in the hotel. I never sleep well in those places. And I admit to being a typical guy, which means my mind does wander occasionally and I miss half of conversations if they're not about sport. I'm pretty sure she never mentioned we had new neighbours.'

'But there was time for two people to be there. You just admitted it yourself. Maybe that's what she was trying to tell me. Maybe something terrible happened to them and that could be why her behaviour suddenly changed. You admitted she wasn't always like this. She didn't always drink too much and act weirdly. When did all that behaviour start, exactly?'

I wait with bated breath for his answer.

'When I got back from that trip,' Theo quietly admits.

'Oh my god, this is it!' I cry, leaping to my feet.

'This is what?' Theo asks, not catching on.

'This is how you get Hayley back,' I tell him. 'If we find out what she knows, what upset her so much and caused her drinking, you two can be together again. She's obviously afraid; that's why she acted the way she did and it's probably why she hasn't come back here since you told her to leave. We have to find her and talk to her. Can we do that? You said she was at her sister's. We can go there now, can't we?'

I'm expecting Theo to say yes and then all we have to do is drive there. Except Theo doesn't stand up as if he is willing to do just that. He remains static, meaning my progress in finding the truth stays the same too.

'Come on, let's do it,' I urge him. 'You said her sister's place was in the Midlands. We could be there by lunchtime. Let's go.'

'No.'

'Why not?'

'Because she's not at her sister's,' he admits.

'What? You said she was there.'

'I lied.'

'Why would you do that?'

Theo doesn't answer.

'Where is she?' I demand to know.

'I can't say,' Theo replies quietly.

'Why not?'

Again, no answer.

'Theo, why not?' I cry and my voice is so loud that it might just carry down the hill to the homes below us, but I don't care.

Finally, Theo responds.

'Because Cesar told me not to.'

TWENTY-SIX

The serenity at this scenic viewpoint is spoilt by the fact that the person who brought me here, a person who I thought was looking out for me, has just admitted to lying. Not only that, but he has also admitted to something else. Cesar has played a part in Hayley leaving.

'Why would Cesar prevent you from telling me where Hayley is?' I ask Theo as he finally gets to his feet and joins me, no doubt because this conversation has taken a very serious turn.

'Dionne, please calm down. Honestly, I don't want you to get too worked up because of the baby.'

'I'll be a lot less worked up if you tell me what is going on! So if my baby is your concern, start explaining.'

Theo is startled, but wisely no longer tries to get out of anything by using the excuse of my unborn child.

'You lied to me, and I deserve to know why,' I go on. 'Or I will call the police right now and have them come back here and question you and Cesar, and I will keep getting them to do that until one of you cracks under the pressure and tells the truth.'

'I only lied because I was trying to protect you,' Theo claims.

'Protect me from what?'

'From him.'

'Who?'

'Cesar. He's obviously got something to hide, but I swear I don't know what it is.'

'But Hayley did?'

'Yes, I think so,' Theo confesses. 'I mean, she never told me what it was, but you are right. Something triggered her drinking and her mood swings. It was a relapse because she'd struggled with substance abuse before, earlier in our relationship, albeit on a lesser scale. I thought those days were over and she was doing much better, but I was wrong. I'm guessing you were doing much better before you got here too, right?'

That couldn't be more correct, so I nod.

'Cesar knew that Hayley and I had been having some diffi-culties,' Theo goes on. 'He'd heard us arguing before. He'd seen her drunk and crying in public. He came to visit me one night, while Hayley was in bed upstairs, and he told me he didn't like it. He told me it was not a good image for the estate, and he wanted Hayley to sort herself out before more people moved in here or he would have to ask us to leave.'

'What? He can't do that! You bought the house. You decide when you leave, not him.'

'That's what I thought, but Cesar was adamant that he only wanted what was best for this estate and if we didn't fit in here then we would have to find somewhere else to live. I told him that he didn't need to involve himself in our domestic issues, but he didn't care about our privacy. I know now that he doesn't care about anybody's privacy here. He only cares that he sells all these houses and makes a lot of money.'

'So what happened?'

'You remember the day the alarm went off? The day Hayley had come to talk to you?'

I nod again because I wouldn't forget that.

'He had one of his assistants take me and Hayley to one side during that evacuation. He said he wanted to make sure we were okay.'

'That's why I couldn't find either of you during the evacuation?' I ask, and he nods.

'We were taken to one of the unoccupied houses and then Cesar joined us. He said that he was willing to buy our home back from us so we would leave here. I laughed as I thought it was a joke, but he was serious, so then I asked him why he was so desperate to get rid of us.'

'What did he say?'

'He just repeated what he had already told me about wanting this estate to have a good reputation and our domestic disruptions were not helping him.'

'So what happened?'

'I refused and said we weren't going anywhere. I presumed that's what Hayley would do too. But she didn't. She said she wanted to leave.'

I can see that Theo is cut up about that fact because by leaving here, she has obviously left him too.

'What did Cesar say to that?' I ask him.

'He said if Hayley wanted to leave then it was okay if I stayed. He clearly saw her as the problem, rather than me. I told him I wouldn't be able to afford to stay in the house on my own. We had a joint mortgage. Hayley obviously wouldn't leave without her money either, so it seemed like a dead end. That was when Cesar offered to buy out her half of the house. He would give her cash, that day, if she left. As for me, I could stay and only owe my remaining half, meaning it wouldn't cost me any more to be on my own.'

'What did you say to that?'

Theo laughs.

'I said it was ridiculous. It would cost him a fortune, but more than that, it would mean me and Hayley splitting up and I didn't want that. At least I didn't until…'

'Until what?'

'Until Cesar urged Hayley to think about what was best for her, and she then admitted that she wanted to leave me.'

I frown because this is not sounding like a very typical way for a couple to break up.

'Cesar manipulated her into leaving you?' I ask, and Theo shrugs.

'I don't know. Maybe. Or maybe the damage was already done between us and Hayley would have left soon anyway. He was just giving her an easy way out and she accepted it. In the end, I accepted it too. It was too heartbreaking to try and fight for Hayley when she clearly no longer wanted to be with me.'

It's a sorry story and I can understand why Theo has done his best to keep the finer details of it a secret from me, a woman he barely knows. He probably wouldn't even want to tell this tale to his closest friends. It simply invites too many questions, let alone probably causes him great embarrassment. The end of his relationship with Hayley was more like a business transaction than a parting of two considerate souls.

'So that's it? He gave Hayley the money and she left?' I ask as Theo nods. 'I don't understand, though. Why the big secret about where she has gone? Why can't you tell me?'

'It was one of the stipulations of the deal Cesar was offering us. He told me that if I stayed here, I was not to talk about this with anyone and I was certainly not allowed to tell anyone where Hayley had moved to.'

'Doesn't that sound very strange to you?'

'Of course it does. But what was I supposed to do? Hayley wanted to leave me, and I didn't want to have to go through a house move on my own, so I accepted. She left, I got to stay in the house, and I thought I would try and move on with my life. But it's been impossible.'

'Because of me?' I ask.

'Well, yes, partly. But I'm not stupid. I know something is wrong. I know Cesar is trying to cover something up and I think it's safe to assume that Hayley knows what it is. She won't answer my calls or texts and while I have tried her sister's, she's not there, so I have no idea where she is, which the police believed because there is no evidence to suggest otherwise. I'm worried for her, of course, but a big part of me is also worried that she really doesn't want to ever hear from me again and this is just her way of rejecting me. I don't know for sure. All I do know is, I've left Cesar alone and he has done the same to me and maybe that's the safest thing to do.'

I hold a hand to my aching head and try to make some sense of it all. There's only one possible solution.

'We need to get the police to investigate Cesar. Find out what he is hiding. If we can't find Hayley, we need to expose him. Let's do it now. Let's call the police and have them look into him. They could search his house for clues. Question him. Maybe he'll get flustered. He's got so much money tied up in this estate, maybe he'll start panicking if he thinks he's going to lose it all. It's got to be worth a try, hasn't it?'

'No, it's not,' Theo replies firmly. 'Not unless you want to have your life blown up like mine has been. Look what happened to me and Hayley. We were ruined by this place. But we were just boyfriend and girlfriend. You have a husband, a son and a child on the way. If you start threatening Cesar, he might not be the one who loses everything. It could be you.'

It's a very ominous warning and it's more than enough to make me pause and not go running immediately to the police. Theo is right. Cesar always seems to be one step ahead, and unless I can be sure that the police will find something incriminating, I can't risk my family. One look at the man standing in front of me is proof of what it looks like to be left all alone and still with so many unanswered questions.

Though, if I'm not going to talk to the police, and I'm not going to talk to Cesar, I have to talk to somebody else and I know who that is.

As soon as Christian is home, I will ask him what his visit to Cesar's was all about.

Depending on the answers he gives me, it will determine whether I need to be worried about my own relationship being blown up like Theo's was.

I don't want to lose my husband.

But what if this place tears us apart too?

What if he is willing to lose me?

TWENTY-SEVEN

I've swapped the scenic view from the top of the hill for the less impressive view of my back garden through my kitchen window. What I've lost by altering my vantage point, I've gained by being home and in position for the moment Christian walks through the front door.

I'm ready for a make-or-break conversation with my husband, and it's not a leap to realise that what is said between us could determine the future of our marriage and our family. It's that pressure that is causing me to grip the edge of the kitchen countertop tightly with my two hands while the cup of coffee I made for myself half an hour ago sits untouched nearby, growing colder by the second. It's not a very comfortable position for me to maintain, but I have no plans to alter it. What else could I do? Watch TV? Have a shower? Fold the laundry? None of that domestic drudgery will occupy my mind. All I can think about is that whatever caused Theo and Hayley to split up might just cause us to separate too. But only if he knows what Hayley knows and won't tell me.

Only if he's forcing me to play the part of Theo, the helpless, clueless partner.

And only if he takes Cesar's side over mine.

By the time I hear Christian's car parking on the driveway, my knuckles are white, and my coffee is stone cold. It might be for the best that my drink is no longer hot because depending on how the next few minutes go, I might feel like throwing the contents of this cup all over my husband. Even though I am desperate to have a very long and serious talk with Christian, I first have to put on a brave face and welcome my son home along with him.

'How was your day at school?' I ask Kai as I go towards him in the hallway to give him a hug.

'Boring,' he replies, which is a fairly standard response from him. 'Can I watch TV?'

'Yeah, okay,' I say, figuring that's an easy way of getting him out of earshot, and as he slips away into the lounge, I turn my attention to the suited man walking through my door.

'In the kitchen. Now,' I say firmly before I head that way and expect Christian to follow me if he knows what's best for him. To his credit, he does, and as I close the kitchen door behind him, I notice him wearily lower himself down onto one of the stools by the countertop. He looks tired and fed up. He also looks like a man who knew he was coming home to a wife on the warpath.

'Start talking,' I say simply, figuring he must know what he is supposed to tell me.

'Well, as you already know, I went to see Cesar this morning,' he begins.

'Why?'

'Because I wanted to ask him a few questions.'

'What questions?'

'The same ones you have. Questions about this house. About all the things you're worrying about. I was there because I was hoping to get some answers that might put your mind at ease and as such, make things a little easier for all of us in this house.'

'Did you?' I ask, suddenly feeling a sense of relief that he has been taking my concerns seriously after all. I've feared a distance growing between us but maybe it's not as bad as I first thought.

'I got reassurances,' Christian replies. 'Reassurances that we have nothing to worry about and if we just focus on integrating ourselves into this community then we will be absolutely fine.'

'That's what he always says,' I lament. 'He wants us to be model citizens and live in our little domestic bubble. But he's controlling us, can't you see?'

'I'm so tired of this,' Christian admits.

'Me too,' I say.

He shakes his head. 'No, I mean I'm *really, really* tired of this. It can't carry on. You were right. We never should have moved here. It was a mistake and it's my fault. I brought us here. But I think we should leave.'

'What?'

This U-turn from Christian catches me by surprise, not just because he was so keen for us to buy this house in the first place but because up until now, he has never shown any sign of buyer's remorse.

'You're not happy here and I have a feeling you never will be, so I think it's best that we go before this gets worse,' Christian carries on. 'We still have a bit of time before our daughter is born. Hopefully we can find somewhere else before then. Even if we end up renting it would be better than all this stress.'

Despite what he's saying, Christian doesn't look like he wants to go through the hassle and upheaval of another house move, especially when we are really fighting against a ticking clock before our family size increases. That's why I get the feeling he is just saying what he thinks I want to hear, which I appreciate because it shows he is really trying.

'I can't believe this,' I reply as I try to process it. 'I thought you hated me. I thought you were thinking that I'm crazy and making all this stuff up.'

'No, I'd never think that,' Christian says, getting up and walking around the counter to try and reassure me. 'I want what's best for you and the kids. That's why I do everything I do. It's why I go to work. It's why I thought coming here was the right thing for us as a family. But I was wrong. We rushed into it. We should have spent more time looking elsewhere. We didn't need to come here.'

'I don't want to leave if you like it,' I say, feeling guilt over misreading Christian. I feel terrible that I had begun to suspect him of keeping secrets from me, but I don't want him to know that now. Not when he looks so cut up about all of this.

'It's okay. You were right. An older house has more charm. This place is missing something.'

'Missing. That sure is the right word to describe this estate,' I say.

'What do you mean?'

'I had a long conversation with Theo earlier,' I confess to Christian. 'His girlfriend, Hayley, is gone, and he doesn't know where she is. Cesar made her leave. It was some weird deal they all made. And then there's Rosie and Jordan. They lived here before us but where are they now? They're missing too. That's why I've been so stressed lately. I'm onto Cesar. I know he is hiding something. And the thing is...'

'What?'

'If we leave, I'll never know what it is.'

Christian frowns.

'Wait? You're saying you want to stay?'

'I feel like I'm getting closer to the truth,' I reply. 'But if we go, Cesar gets away with whatever he has done.'

'Why do you care? These are people you never met. We should be putting our children first, not some couple who may or may not have existed and not some woman next door who I didn't even get to meet.'

I naturally care for other people and I hate to say it, but Christian might be right. I can't take risks with Cesar. I've become so caught up in this that I've lost sight of what's important. My family is the most important thing and I have to put their safety ahead of my desire for the truth. Theo essentially said the same thing to me on that hill. Now Christian is giving me the green light for us to get out of here, I think I'd be a fool to ignore it.

'I can make the arrangements for us to move,' Christian says as he puts his arm around me. 'All you need to do is rest. Let me worry about everything else.'

It sounds good, but then I have a disturbing thought. What if it's too good?

Too good to be true?

As I watch Christian go over to the fridge and check inside for a snack, I try to push away the anxious feeling that rises up from my stomach.

I'm trusting my husband, as any good wife should.

But what if he has an ulterior motive here?

What if he has not divulged the full details of that conversation with Cesar?

What if he has made some sort of a deal with that man, just like Theo and Hayley made a deal too? If so, that would make me another pawn in Cesar's game and that would be exactly what that man wants.

Maybe Cesar wants me gone and he has convinced Christian to get me out of here.

But what do I want?

TWENTY-EIGHT

I've decided that there is only one thing I can do and that is to trust my husband. That's why I'm already planning the packing, so we can move out of this house as soon as possible. Christian has said he will deal with the sale of the property, just like he did when we moved here, so that's one less thing for me to worry about. I still have plenty to occupy my mind, the main thing being trying to answer the question of *where we are going to go next?*

There isn't time to sell this place, put in an offer on another property elsewhere and complete the move before I have the baby. That means we need another solution and there are a few options. We could go back to a hotel, but that is far from ideal when baby comes, so I'm ruling that one out. We could try and rent a place, and that is probably my preferred option, although our finances will be stretched if we do that while we are still paying the mortgage here until the sale completes. Or, the third option is I ask my parents if we can stay with them or at least move into one of the other properties they own.

As much as I hate to admit it, I know the third option is the most realistic one. Mum and Dad won't charge us rent to live with them or even in one of their other properties, plus we could literally leave here and move in with them as soon as the packing is done. Therefore, it's my quickest way out of this place and all the trouble it has brought. The problem is, I really, really don't want to be so dependent on my parents and especially not when I've just had a baby. Christian and I have worked hard to build our own life, and running to my parents in a time of struggle seems like a huge backwards step. I also know how difficult the first few months of motherhood are, having experienced it before, and I really don't want to make it more difficult by getting frustrated that my mum and dad are in control of my life again. But time is running out and I think I'm going to have to call my parents and explain to them what is happening. I'll delay it as long as I can, though, and focus on the packing for now, as we can't go anywhere until that is done.

As I open my wardrobe and stare at all the things inside it, I let out a deep sigh. I really don't have the energy for this. There's so much to pack and this is only my belongings. Christian can deal with his, but what about Kai? He won't be much help on packing, and that boy has a lot of stuff.

I think about my son, about how I haven't told him we're moving yet and about how disruptive this will be for him when we go through with it. A chaotic home life is hardly what he needs while he deals with both the early years of school and the fact that, very soon, he won't be the only one vying for his parents' attention when his sister gets here. I fear he may start acting out, be it at home or at school, as he deals with all the confusion and frustration that any kind of life change can cause at his tender age. Am I being selfish by deciding to get out of here? Is moving really the best thing for my family? According to both Christian, and Theo, it is, so I should just focus on putting some distance between ourselves and Cesar and get started on the packing. But before I can, I hear something troubling.

Christian is on the phone downstairs.

It sounds like he is having an argument.

I leave the bedroom and stand at the top of the stairs, trying to eavesdrop on his conversation in much the same way I was trying to eavesdrop on Theo's conversation with the police earlier. At least the danger of being caught is not as stark here, but I am still fearful as I try and hear what has got my husband so worked up. He really does sound frustrated.

'I've tried everything, I really have,' Christian says. 'It's getting too hard and I'm not sure this is best for us anymore.'

Who is he talking to and what is he talking about?

I lean over the staircase to try and hear better, but all I do detect is the sound of the back door being unlocked. I think he's going outside to continue this conversation and the only reason he would be doing that is because he doesn't want me to hear any more of it.

I think about the best way I can hear what is said next. I know I can't just run down the stairs and get closer that way because Christian might see me and go quiet. So what about hearing him from up here?

Knowing Christian has gone into the back garden, I think about which room upstairs will give me the best chance to continue eavesdropping and I realise it is Kai's.

Entering my son's bedroom, I find him lying on the bed with the television on, and I know he's going to want to know what I'm doing. I can't tell him, though, or he'll most likely ruin my chances of it being successful, so I come up with a better idea.

'We need to play a quick game. Can you be really quiet for a minute?' I ask him as I turn the volume down on his TV.

Kai frowns for a second before nodding, interested enough to humour me for now, at least.

'Okay, I'm going to open your window, and I need you to be silent, okay?' I say to him.

'Why?' Kai asks, but I just put my finger to my lips to let him know that the game has already begun.

Kai goes quiet, so I turn my attention to his window and now I need to open it as quietly as I can. If Christian hears the window above his head, he'll know someone is trying to overhear his phone conversation.

I grip the handle on the window tightly before slowly releasing it and allowing the window to open. It makes a slight noise, but I'm hoping it's not enough to alert Christian, and once the window is fully open, I realise I'm in the clear because he is still talking.

'I know that. I've tried to explain to her, but it's not working,' he is saying. 'You are welcome to talk to her about this, but it's not fair that I'm stuck in the middle having to keep all these secrets.'

I look down and see my husband pacing around a patch of grass directly below me. I can't see his face, only the crown of his scalp, but I can tell by his movements that he is agitated. I can also tell that by his words.

'I just need some help,' Christian says. 'Di is too clever. She'll figure out what I've done if we stay and then I'll be in trouble. She hates secrets, and this is a big one.'

My stomach churns as I realise Christian really is hiding something from me, and my paranoid worries about whether or not I can trust him are right.

'Mummy, what are you doing?' Kai asks me, and I wince as I turn around to see my son, as I fear Christian might have just heard his voice. I look down then to check if he has and that's when I see my husband looking up at me.

Caught.

I move back from the window, but I know it's already too late. Christian knows I have been eavesdropping. I close the window and turn to Kai, but it's not his fault. None of this is.

It's not mine either. From what I've just heard, a lot of the blame is my husband's.

'I need you to do me a favour,' I say to Kai as I kneel down and take hold of his hands. 'I need you to start packing. We're leaving.'

'What? Where are we going?'

'We're going to Grandma and Grandad's. Sound good?'

Kai nods, so at least that should get him moving. I do the same, heading for the door to resume my own packing, though when I do, I see Christian coming up the stairs.

'Di?' he says, trying to appear innocent even though he knows he was caught having that secret phone call, so I just ignore him and head for our bedroom.

'Hey, what's wrong? I don't know what you think you just heard but it's nothing,' Christian goes on as he follows me in.

'You've been lying to me,' I say as I start taking things out of the wardrobe. 'Either you tell me what it is right now, or we are leaving and you are not coming with us.'

'Di, seriously. Just stop. Slow down. You're overreacting. That was just a work call.'

'You expect me to believe that?' I hurl back at him. 'If it was a work call then why were you talking about me?'

I wait for Christian to give me a good answer to that, but unsurprisingly, he doesn't have one, so I resume the packing.

'I'm taking Kai and we're going to stay with my parents,' I tell him as I pull more of my clothes from my wardrobe. Except even this kind of physical exertion is draining me quickly and I realise I do not have the energy to properly pack all of our things. My bump is so big now that it just gets in the way, and as a few items of clothing fall onto the floor, I know bending down and picking them up will not be a simple process in my current state.

'You don't need to do that. There's no need for us to split up,' Christian says as he rather helpfully picks the clothes up from the floor, although he doesn't pass them to me so I can put them in a suitcase. He starts hanging them back up in the wardrobe again.

'This is not a discussion,' I say as I take the same clothes back out and this time, I don't drop them. 'We're leaving right now. Kai is packing too.'

I throw a big bundle of clothes into my suitcase before turning my attention to the bedside table where I keep all my underwear. Before I can start emptying those drawers out, Kai enters our bedroom.

'What's this?' he asks us, and I turn to see he is holding a small black object in his hand.

Christian is nearer to him than I am, so he gets a better look at the mystery item first, and as he takes it from Kai, I can see that he doesn't seem to know what it is either. That is until he has had a proper chance to inspect it. Then he tells us exactly what it is.

'It's a security camera,' Christian says, sounding confused before he looks back to Kai. 'It's capable of recording. Where did you find this?'

'It was in the kitchen on the bookshelf. I was trying to find my Blue Bear Book so I could pack it, and it fell off the shelf.'

'Let me see that,' I say as I step towards Christian before taking the item from him. But my husband is right. It is a camera. It's tiny, but there is the little viewing hole and according to my son, this was on a shelf in our kitchen.

'Is this yours?' I ask Christian, assuming it has to be, but he looks aghast.

'No, it's not,' he replies. 'Is it yours?'

'Why would it be mine?' I ask before looking at Kai. 'Does this belong to you? Is it one of your toys?'

'No,' Kai says, and I believe him. I always know when he's not telling the truth.

'Why is there a camera in our kitchen?' I ask my husband

then as my heart beats faster and faster, but he has no good answer for me, so I have to fill the silence with the only thing I can think to say next.

'I'm calling the police,' I say, choosing the option that I really don't want to because it ended so embarrassingly for me last time. But it's what I need to do. Unlike when I was mistaken and saw something that wasn't really there, this time is different.

There is zero doubt about what I'm looking at now.

There is zero doubt that the threat is real.

TWENTY-NINE

Aware that police responses aren't always prompt, I make sure to convey my distress clearly when the operator answers my emergency call.

'Please, you have to send help! Somebody has been stalking me and my family! We found a camera in our home that shouldn't be here. I have a young son. This is incredibly frightening, and we have no idea who put it here. So please, send help as soon as you can! I'm worried the person watching us might be nearby, and that we're in danger.'

Thankfully, my desperate pleas for urgent attention were met and the operator assured me officers would attend the scene as quickly as possible to ascertain if there was any ongoing threat to me and my family.

As I wait for the police to arrive, my mind races through all the people who have been in my house since we moved in. The camera on the kitchen bookshelf must have been placed there after all the books were put on the shelf. I would have noticed it if it was there before. It apparently fell out from its hiding place when Kai was moving books around to look for one of his own, so that tells me we were not supposed to find it. If I hadn't told Kai to pack, he wouldn't have been rummaging around on that shelf, and I still wouldn't know it was here. But I know about it now and that's why I'm trying to figure out who put it in my house.

According to my husband, a man I am already struggling to trust, it is not his. While I know Christian seems to have his secrets, I do believe him where this camera is concerned. If he had planted it there, he surely wouldn't have just stood by and allowed me to call the police. But he did. He made no attempt to stop me when I said I was calling them and instead he seems as horrified as I am that we have been watched all this time. We've probably been listened to as well if this camera has been recording sound as well as video.

It makes me sick to think that we have been spied on in the privacy of our own home. This is our personal space, but it has been invaded. Looking at this camera, it seems like a very expensive piece of technology. Rather than the bulky, traditional type of cameras I'm more familiar with having seen them in movies over the years, this is very modern and sleek, easily compact enough to be hidden. The quality of it makes me fear it is connected to some Bluetooth system somewhere from which the owner is able to monitor all we do in front of it. Whoever put this camera in my kitchen might have already seen that we have discovered it, but I'm hoping the police will be able to trace its origins and I'm more than willing to give them a list of suspects to start with.

That list contains the removals men, the phone line guy, Theo and, of course, suspect number one, Cesar.

Does he spy on his residents? Is this another way he controls what happens here? I wouldn't put anything past that man and that's why I'm prepared to make him my first target. I just need the police to hurry up and get here so I can do just that.

The operator I spoke to seemed like she took my call seriously and she assured me that officers would be dispatched promptly, so I have no reason to worry about this getting the attention I feel it deserves. But in the midst of calling the police, I haven't had time to make sure my son is okay.

'Am I in trouble?' Kai asks me in a meek voice, and I feel terrible when I see him coming towards me with worry etched all over his face.

'No, of course not,' I reply as I open my arms to take him in a hug. 'Why would you think that?'

'Because I found the camera,' he replies mournfully as he snuggles into me.

'That's not your fault. You didn't put it there, did you?'

Kai shakes his head.

'I'm glad you found it,' I go on. 'It's very helpful, thank you.'

Kai relaxes a little in my arms, though he still seems uncertain.

'Who put it there?' he asks then, which is a very good question.

'We will find out soon enough,' I reply, hoping I am right but aware that this may end up being another unsolved mystery to go with all the others.

I'm angry the discovery of this camera has caused my son distress, though he seems okay now as he leaves me to go and play with his toys. But one other thing it has done is delay my packing, as my suitcase is currently lying abandoned and the clothes that were due to go into it are still in my wardrobe. The camera also interrupted the conversation I was having with my husband, not that it seemed to be leading anywhere productive unless he was willing to tell me what that phone call in the garden was really about.

I could try asking him again, but Christian has not really given me the chance to do that since Kai found that camera.

Instead, he's been busy searching the house for any more hidden devices.

'I think the bathroom is clear,' my husband says as he comes down the stairs. 'And I've checked everywhere I can in ours and Kai's bedroom and didn't find anything in there. But there's so much clutter up there, maybe I missed it. Hopefully not, though.'

As frightening as it was to learn of a camera in our kitchen, I was soon afraid that there had been one planted in our son's bedroom. Thankfully, it seems not, just as it seems there are none in our bedroom either. Maybe the kitchen camera is the only one in the house, which would be bad enough, though it could be so much worse.

Imagine if someone had been watching my son in his own room? Or watching me and Christian? Or watching all three of us in the bathroom? It doesn't bear thinking about, except these are precisely the kinds of things I'm now forced into contemplating as I continue to wait for the police to arrive.

'I'll check in the lounge now,' Christian says as he goes that way, and I'm happy to leave him to conduct his search while I wait in the hallway so I can answer the door quickly when the officers get here.

As I watch my husband walk away, I wonder if he is genuinely trying to find any more cameras or if he is acting. If he put that camera there, he is doing a good job of trying to make out like he didn't. I tell myself that spying on his family is beyond my husband. He wouldn't do that, would he? He's not that devious, or desperate, surely. He wouldn't need to do it either because he lives here, and spying would be for somebody who does not have access to our home. Christian also wouldn't want the police involved if he was guilty because he'd know that if they did trace this to him, I'd react very badly. It means someone else must have hidden that camera on my shelf, and as

I hear movement on the other side of our front door, I am ready for the proper investigation to officially begin.

That's until I open the door and get a shock.

It's not a police officer staring back at me from my doorstep.

It's Cesar.

THIRTY

'What are you doing here?' I ask him as he maintains unbroken eye contact with me, but I fear I might already know the answer to that question. If he put the camera in our house, he'd have a very good reason to be here now.

'Can I come in?' Cesar asks me calmly, and while my first instinct is to say no, I think about how the police are going to arrive any second and hopefully this man does not know that. Maybe it would be better if Cesar were here when they arrived. I could then accuse him in front of the officers and see what his reaction is. He won't have time to come up with an excuse or prepare a lie. He'll just be trapped, and maybe that is the best way to catch him.

'Why do you want to come in?' I ask him, standing my ground while looking past Cesar for any sign of a police car.

'Because we have something to talk about and I'd like to get started so as not to waste too much of our evening,' Cesar replies.

That makes me laugh. 'Oh, I have a feeling you're going to be very busy tonight, whatever you do next,' I say to him, enjoying the idea of him being interrogated by the police about the camera.

'What is it that you think is going to happen?' Cesar asks me then, surprising me slightly.

Should I tell him? Or wait a little longer for the officers in uniform to get here?

Where are they?

I look past Cesar again but as I do, I catch him smiling and that unsettles me. What he says next only makes me feel worse.

'They're not coming,' he tells me gleefully. 'I know you called them but they're not coming here.'

'Why not?' I just about manage to mutter as I grip my front door anxiously.

'Let me inside and I'll tell you,' Cesar says. 'I'll tell you everything. But only if you let me in.'

I'm so desperate for answers that I am willing to allow this man into my home, but then I think about my son and worry that I might be putting him in danger if I do. Although Christian is here and whatever is going on with my husband, there's no way he would allow any harm to come to our child, so maybe I can take this risk.

I decide to step aside and, with that, Cesar walks in.

'What's going on?' Christian asks as he enters the hallway and sees our 'guest', but I keep my eyes on Cesar as he closes our door behind him.

'Tell me. Are you deliberately trying to make life difficult for me?' Cesar asks me with a heavy sigh.

'Excuse me?' I say venomously.

'Calling the police for the second time since you moved in. You know this creates problems for me. I made my feelings clear about this after the first time, yet you've done it again.'

'How do you know I called them?' I ask nervously before looking around and wondering if this place is bugged for sound as well as the camera being here.

'I have a friend who works in the local police force and after your antics the other night, I decided to ask that friend if he could let me know if any more emergency calls originated from here,' Cesar replies as if that's a perfectly normal thing to say. 'That way, I could come and check on the incident myself without the police having to be troubled and see if it really warrants their attention.'

'Why aren't they coming?' I ask desperately.

'Like I said, I have a friend there who is doing me a favour.'

'But that's illegal! You can't stop me calling the police if I want to!' I cry, not that Cesar looks like he cares about that. I presume the officer involved doesn't care either, probably because he is being paid handsomely to help with such information.

'I am not going to stand by and allow you to ruin this estate's reputation and all my hard work by continuously calling the police and making everybody here worried,' Cesar says simply, as if talking to a child. It's clear to me then, if it wasn't before, the incredible lengths he will go to, to make this place seem perfect.

'I called the police because we found a hidden camera in our home!' I fight back. 'Someone has been spying on us, and I think it's you!'

Cesar doesn't flinch at that accusation, which only strengthens my belief.

'Is it true?' Christian asks as he steps beside me, possibly to show he is on my side. 'Did you put a camera in our home?'

'No,' Cesar replies casually.

'Why should we believe you? You control everything here. You even monitor our phone calls to the police!' I cry, and while Christian puts a hand on my shoulder, I don't calm down because this is too important.

'You don't have to believe me,' Cesar replies bluntly. 'I don't care what you do as long as you don't cause any more trouble for me and this estate.'

'You're the one causing trouble by lying to us!' I tell Cesar. 'And there's no way I'm letting you get away with what you have done. I'll tell everyone who will listen about how you are manipulative and lie to your residents, and that you spy on them!'

'I haven't been spying on you,' Cesar says with a shake of the head. 'Just because you found a camera here, it doesn't mean I put it there.'

'Who else would do it?' I cry.

'I don't know. You have a young son. Perhaps it was one of his games.'

Is he serious? He's really going to try and deflect blame away from himself and onto an innocent five-year-old boy?

'You're disgraceful,' I spit back. 'My son is the one who told us about the camera!'

'A guilty conscience, perhaps,' Cesar says as if he knows my child better than me. 'Or maybe he got bored of his game and wanted to have a little fun making you think you were being spied on. Children are playful, aren't they?'

'My son did not do this,' Christian says, stepping up for me while I'm temporarily lost for words. 'I don't know how that camera got in this house, but it has nothing to do with the three of us.'

'Then I don't know how it got in here either,' Cesar replies. 'All I do know is that you need to put this behind you.'

'Excuse me?' I cry, aghast at what I just heard.

'You need to make your lives here as peaceful as possible, so I suggest you move on from this incident, and everything else that's happened, and focus on becoming a valuable part of this community.'

I could laugh if I wasn't angry. Instead, I launch into a tirade.

'We will never be a part of this community,' I cry. 'That's not even what it is. It's a dangerous place. No place for families, that's for sure. We are leaving!'

I wish I had said that last part triumphantly, but the truth is, I don't think we can leave. How can we? We can't afford to rent somewhere else, not while paying the mortgage here. The only option is to go back home to my parents. Cesar seems to know how trapped I feel too. Then he goes and makes it worse.

'If you try and sell this house, I will make sure the sale does not complete,' he says venomously.

'What?' Christian chips in with then, the concern in his voice clear.

'I will not have anybody bad mouthing this estate and ruining its reputation,' Cesar replies calmly. 'To ensure that, I will keep you here, where I can have an eye on you and know exactly what you are doing at all times.'

It's mortifying to hear, and terrifying, but Cesar looks like he means every word of it.

'Get out of our house,' Christian says then firmly.

At least as owners, we have the right to demand someone leave, and thankfully, Cesar turns towards the door. But before he can go, I have something else to say to him.

'Whatever is going on here, whatever it might be, I am going to be the one to put a stop to it,' I tell him before reaching past him and opening the door. 'Now get out of my house.'

Cesar looks like he is contemplating every possible option available to him as he holds my stare but rather wisely decides to do as I told him and retreat.

But as I watch him go, I doubt a man like him will retreat for long. He knows I'm his enemy now, and that means he'll be plotting how to silence me for good. But I'm already plotting how to do the same thing to him.

I know what I'm going to do.

I also know when I'm going to do it.

THIRTY-ONE

It's normal for people to count down to an event on their calendar. It just means they are excited they have something to look forward to and usually it's because they can't wait to socialise in a relaxed, carefree environment. But that's not why I have been counting down to the event that takes place this afternoon...

I'm not waiting for my chance to talk to people over drinks and food.

I'm waiting for my chance to find out what Cesar is hiding.

And today is hopefully the day I will do that.

It's time for the next community get-together on the estate, the one that Cesar organises and informs all his residents about, the one he insists they all attend and the one he mistakenly believes is the reason there is such a positive community culture here. He is wrong about that, just like he was wrong about us not causing any more trouble for him and this estate. That's because I haven't stopped thinking about how I can expose him ever since our confrontation in our home shortly after we discovered the hidden camera. Despite his threats to us, I'm still just as determined to find out more about Cesar and what he might be hiding about our house.

'Can you carry the lasagne? I'll take the cheesecake,' I say to Christian as he enters the kitchen and sees the various dishes I have prepared for today.

'You've gone to a lot of trouble,' he quite rightly notices.

I'm pleased that is his opinion because I want everyone else at the event to think the same too, particularly Cesar, who I know will be watching me closely when we arrive. But if I can distract him with food and fake smiles, I'm hoping he won't know why I'm really there.

'Kai? Are you ready? Have you got your football?' I call out to my son, and when I hear his ball bouncing in the hallway, I take it that he is prepared to leave.

'Let's go,' I say as I pick up a dish and head for the door. But Christian lingers.

'Are you sure about this?' he asks me. 'We don't have to go. We don't have to be around... him.'

'I want to go, and I want to see him,' I reply adamantly. 'We're not hiding away. At least not anymore.'

We've kept ourselves to ourselves since that argument with Cesar a few weeks ago, but that ends today. With that made clear to my husband, all three of us leave the house and set off in the direction of where the gathering is held on the estate. It's another fine day just like it was for the last one, but while I am reminded of how sunny it was back then, I'm also reminded of how Hayley came to me with a warning right before the alarm sounded and I haven't seen her since.

How will today end?

If things go wrong, it could be me who ends up mysteriously disappearing by the end of it.

But I hope not.

Christian and I carefully carry the food I've prepared while Kai kicks his ball down the street ahead of us, but he's sensible enough not to get too far ahead and is taking it slowly because he knows his mother isn't as quick on her feet as he is. My due date is looming large now, almost as large as my swollen stomach, and that's why I'm not able to walk as quickly as I once was. But even though I've had the best part of nine months to prepare for my daughter's arrival, I can't say I'm fully ready for when the day comes. That's because of all the recent distractions and the amount of things I've had to do that I frankly could have done without.

Like having the house searched for any more hidden devices.

The discovery of that camera, and my subsequent determination to find out what Cesar is hiding, prompted me to hire somebody to come to the house and search our property for anything else that shouldn't have been there. Cameras, listening devices, trackers, you name it, I had them look for it. They scoured all the rooms, as well as the garden, the garage and the car. Mercifully, they didn't find anything else.

That camera Kai found was the only thing there that shouldn't have been, though it was more than enough. At least it gave me the peace of mind to know that we could carry on living in our home without anyone watching or listening in. However, just to be on the safe side, I have made sure that when it comes to my plan for today, not a single soul knows about it other than me. I haven't articulated it to my husband, or written it down, or done anything that risks somebody else learning of it. Somebody like Cesar. If he finds out what I plan to do today, I'll lose my chance to do it and then I'll have to wait another month to get the chance again. By that time, my daughter will be here, and I won't have the energy or the opportunity.

It's now or never.

I see the large crowd of people on the grass up ahead, as well as hear music drifting towards us, and I smile because it looks like this event is well attended. That's just what I want.

The more people here, the less obvious it will be when I sneak away.

'Hey, I made a few things for today. Where shall I put them?' I ask one of the ladies who looks like she is abreast of all the culinary developments here, and she quickly points me in the direction of a large table where other delicious treats are laid out for the attendees.

Christian and I place the food down while Kai and his ball attract the attention of a few of the other children, and I briefly watch as my son plays with the local kids. Beyond the excitable youngsters, I spot Theo eating from a plate while talking to a woman his age. They seem to be flirting, and I wonder if this is Theo moving on from Hayley. I haven't talked to him properly in a while, mainly because I'm keeping the list of people I trust very short these days. He seems happy enough, though, and he doesn't notice me looking over at him. Nor does the man I start watching next.

I see him wandering through the crowd, dressed in a smart shirt and denim shorts, sunglasses resting on his head and a chilled bottle of beer in one of his hands. It's Cesar, and he looks like he is revelling in this sunshine-fuelled gathering. But when he notices me watching him, his enjoyment levels dip as he frowns and contemplates my appearance here before looking away and busying himself with somebody less challenging than me.

As Christian grabs a beer and I notice many of the other adults here enjoying some alcoholic liquid refreshment, I think about how it's only a matter of time until I can partake again. But staying sober and clear headed today is not just for the benefit of my unborn child. It's also for the benefit of my plan and after waiting another ten minutes and making sure Cesar has seen me a couple more times as he mingles with the other residents, I decide I'm ready to get things in motion.

'I've forgotten to cook the garlic breads I was going to bring,'

I say to Christian as he watches Kai run around. 'I'll just go back and prepare them. It won't take long. I'll be back in half an hour or so.'

'What? Just leave them. There's plenty of food here.'

'No, it's no trouble. You enjoy yourself. It'll be easier to get chatting to a few of the guys if I'm not with you. Go and make some friends. But keep an eye on Kai.'

I smile at my husband to let him know that everything is okay, and he has a pass to be free and drink beer with the other men on the estate while I leave him, and he doesn't argue too much after that.

I slip away from the gathering, making sure that Cesar doesn't notice me as I go. He doesn't – he has his back to me and is busy talking to a couple – and once I'm around the corner and the music quietens in the distance, I stop worrying about him and start worrying about my next task at hand. It's not cooking garlic bread, that's for sure. I'm not going to my house.

I'm going to Cesar's.

And I bet he'll be so busy playing host that he won't even notice I've left.

THIRTY-TWO

While it might seem daunting to be preparing to break into the biggest house on the estate, I try and find solace in the sheer size of this property.

The bigger it is, the more ways in there should be.

The music from the community gathering is barely audible from here as I approach Cesar's house and immediately head to the rear of the impressive building. While everybody on this estate is busy eating, drinking and engaging in small talk, I'm preparing to commit my second crime since I moved here. But I don't feel bad that I'm about to intrude on Cesar's privacy. If he was willing to make an enemy out of me, he has to know I will fight back at some point.

I enter the back garden and pause for a moment as I take in the sight of the perfectly manicured lawn that seems to stretch endlessly away from me all the way down to the back fence that is mostly obscured by a large oak tree. It's a lovely space, the perfect place to while away a summer's day like this one, but Cesar is not here enjoying it; he's too busy pretending to be a good guy elsewhere. That is to my advantage as I look around for a way inside. I broke the door handle at Theo's, so maybe I'll do the same here. But as I pick up a large rock and head to the door, the anger that I feel towards Cesar, mixed with the frustration of how long I've had to wait to get this chance, means I want to do something more dramatic.

Rather than hurl the rock at the handle on the door, I hurl it at the window just above it.

I wince at the loud crash as the glass shatters, as well as turn away in case any broken shards come flying in my direction. But nobody at the gathering could have heard that from here and no alarm has sounded, which is surprising until I remember how much Cesar wants to make this place appear crime free. If so, it wouldn't serve him well to have house alarms blaring and making the residents feel unsafe, But Cesar may have a silent alarm that alerts him on his phone, so I'll still have to move quickly. Once I'm sure I'm safe from the glass, I carefully reach through the gaping hole and unlock the door.

As I step inside and my feet crunch on the broken glass, my first thought is that Cesar has terrible taste. The décor in the kitchen is awful. Tawdry would be the best word to describe it and as I move on, it doesn't get much better. The lounge is a mess of bulky bronzed items and fur rugs and despite the wealth Cesar has, it seems it didn't stretch to hiring an interior designer. It's like he just filled this place with everything he's ever seen in his life, regardless of whether it suits the style in the room or not. But I'm not here to laugh at his bad taste. I'm here to see if there is anything that can tell me more about Cesar and what he might be hiding.

I move through the rooms until I reach what appears to be a study. There's a large desk with a computer on it, as well as two filing cabinets in the corner and a bookcase stuffed with all sorts of literature on finance, property and management. I bet Cesar credits his success in business to reading those books when really, it seems to have come down to him being selfish, secretive and controlling.

I touch the mouse connected to the computer, and while the screen lights up, it immediately asks me for a password to get any further and I know I don't have the time to try and guess that, so I move on to the filing cabinets. They're locked, so I begin the hunt for the key, hoping that Cesar keeps it in here rather than in his pocket.

I rummage around on a shelf full of framed photos ranging from one of him on a golf course to him standing in the middle of a building site with a spade. I wonder if that was him symbolically breaking ground on this new estate before the builders took over. I pick the photo up for a closer look and when I do, I feel something at the back of the frame. I turn it over and smile.

There is a key hanging on a small hook.

I take it and stick it into the nearest filing cabinet, and it instantly unlocks, giving me access to the contents in all these drawers.

I frantically start scouring through the organised files in each drawer, eager to find something that will explain everything that has happened since I moved here. I see that all these files are arranged in alphabetical order and as I take one out, I realise they are organised by surnames.

I open a file titled Sarah Hughes and very quickly learn that it contains a profile of this person. Their age, occupation, annual income. I also see a photo of who I presume is Sarah and as I stare at the brown-haired woman, I feel like I have seen her somewhere before. Then I figure it out. I saw her at the gathering today. She was the one talking to Theo.

'What is this?' I say out loud before I turn a page and get my answer. The second page shows a photo of a house with the address listed beneath it. It's a property on this estate, so I'm guessing Sarah lives in this house.

So Cesar keeps files on all his residents.

If Sarah is here then it must mean I am here too, so I start searching for my name, my fingers frantically flipping through files until...

I pull out the file with my name on it and open it to see my photo looking back at me, along with all my personal details. Sure enough, on the next page is a photo of our house. Right alongside my file are two more, those belonging to Christian and Kai, and my stomach turns as I see a photo of my son inside this secretive cabinet.

Why does Cesar have these?

It seems unnecessary, but very quickly I realise this trove of information may be helpful. If he documents everybody who lives here, what about the couple who I believe were in our house before us, the couple Cesar seems to claim did not exist?

Are Rosie and Jordan in here?

Without knowing their surnames, I can't narrow down the search, so I have to go through each individual file, a task that is time-consuming and as I glance up at a clock, I am aware that I've already been here too long. I should be getting out of here and going back to the gathering, because the longer I am away, the more chance there is that Cesar notices I have left. When he discovers his home has been broken into – and he will do so considering I wasn't exactly discreet at entering – he will very quickly suspect me of the crime. But I was at the gathering; I have been seen by people there. However, that alibi only works if I'm not away for too long, so I need to hurry.

I keep searching for Rosie's and Jordan's names, but their files are not in the first drawer or the second one. I crouch down to open the third and final drawer, and as I do, I'm already resigned to telling myself that even if they were here, Cesar would have got rid of the evidence by now, just in case. But I still have a glimmer of hope, as he presumably never would have thought anybody other than himself would gain access to these files, so maybe they are still here.

I keep looking but as I near the back of the third drawer, I'm losing hope.

Until I see the name *Jordan* staring back at me.

I pull out the file and when I do, I instantly see the one behind it. The one with the name *Rosie* written on it.

I lay the two files out on the desk and open them both at the same time, and I get my first glimpse of the mystery couple I have been trying to prove existed. They look young, late twenties, perhaps, and when I check their ages, I get confirmation that I am right with that guess. She is pretty, with short blonde hair and blue eyes, while he has a handsome, boyish look, clean-shaven, floppy hair and a polite smile. According to their files, their occupations are listed as 'Entrepreneurs'. That doesn't tell me too much about what they did for jobs, just like the blank space below their annual income tells me little either. What's their income? They must have made money to be able to afford a house here.

The house.

I turn the pages to see which property they are listed as living at, and I'm expecting to see my home address. But there are no other pages. The address is missing, which means this file differs from all the other ones here.

'Where is it?' I say out loud as I keep looking before returning to the drawer to see if any pages fell out in there. But they don't seem to have, so that tells me they were deliberately removed. Only the two names remain and without an address to link them to, I can't know for sure that they owned my home. I am convinced they did and now I have found proof of these people being connected to the estate, I at least have something I can use.

I close the drawers and lock the cabinet before returning the key to the hook. I have kept the two files out so I can take them with me and as I scoop them up from the desk, I'm ready to leave. In my rush, I drop the file belonging to Jordan and see the paper with his image on it fly out and land on the carpet under the desk.

I quickly drop to my hands and knees to retrieve it, and as I grab it, I lift my head up too quickly and bump it on the underside of the desk.

'Ouch,' I cry out, cursing my haste, but as I rub the back of my sore skull, I think about the noise it made when it connected with the desk. It didn't make a loud thud like I would expect when hitting wood.

I heard a rattle.

Peering under the desk, I see what caused the unusual noise. Another key is hidden here, this one taped to the underside of the desk. It's so well hidden that I would easily have missed it if I hadn't dropped the file and banged my head. But I know it exists now, so I take it out and then try to figure out what it will unlock.

I try a few more of the drawers and cupboards in here but it doesn't fit in any of those, so I leave the study and look elsewhere, moving through the home quickly because I really need to leave. I'm just about to give up when I notice a small door built into the underside of the staircase, and when I try the handle, I find it locked.

Will the key work?

I give it a go and, sure enough, it fits seamlessly.

As the door opens, I wonder why Cesar would go to the trouble of hiding the key to this door underneath his desk. When I step through the door and turn on the light, I get my answer.

The two files fall to the floor as my hands go over my mouth, covering my aghast expression as my eyes widen and my pulse quickens.

I can't believe what I'm seeing, but a second later, I can't believe what I'm hearing either.

It's the alarm I heard before. The one I'm sure went off at

just the worst time when Hayley was about to tell me something important.

It's going off again now and I have to believe Cesar has triggered it.

That means he must know I'm here.

But it's too late.

I've just discovered what he has been hiding.

THIRTY-THREE

I should be running already but I haven't moved, despite the alarm blaring and the belief that Cesar will be here at any moment.

That's because I know I can't leave.

Not until I have helped the prisoner escape too.

'Rosie?' I say tentatively as I stare at the pale woman's face through the darkness, a face that is only visible thanks to the light that is now filtering around this door that I just unlocked. I think the poor woman I am looking at is the same woman whose photo I saw in the file, but I have to check because there is some uncertainty on my part. While this woman does bear some resemblance to the Rosie in the photograph, she looks different too. She looks exhausted, and skinny, not to mention very, very afraid. She's also squinting her eyes as the light invades this dark, enclosed space under the stairs. And last but not least, there is a gag in her mouth, so she can't speak or shout for help or do anything that Cesar presumably doesn't want her doing.

But she can move and that's when I see her nod her head.

It's her.

I try my best to ignore the alarm, as well as every muscle

fibre in my body that is trying to pull me towards the exit, and instead, I step further into this small, dark space. When I do, I see that Rosie is not tied up, which seems like a risk on Cesar's part until I see how frail and weak she is. Maybe she was restrained at one point, but goodness knows how long she has been locked in here. She is emaciated now, so she doesn't seem like she could put up much of a fight to escape. As I get closer to her, I'm fearful she might not even have the energy to stand up and leave this room with me.

'I'm here to help you, but we need to get you out of here. Can you stand?' I ask her as I reach her and gently take hold of one of her skinny wrists.

Rosie instantly flinches at my touch, but I reassure her that I am a friend, not a foe and, to prove it, I untie the gag from around her mouth.

As I remove it, Rosie winces before putting a hand to her dry, cracked lips. I feel achingly sorry for the ordeal she must have been through. But it's not over yet.

'Can you get up?' I try again, and Rosie attempts to speak although no audible words come out. There's just the croak from a very dry throat, and it's obvious to me that Rosie is dehydrated as well as hungry.

'It's okay, you don't need to speak. But if you can stand, that will really help,' I say and, gradually, Rosie makes an attempt at getting to her feet. With my help, we are able to get her standing, although I can feel how fragile she is and realise that I will have to keep a firm hold of her as we go in case she takes a tumble and can't get back up again.

I have so many questions for her, ranging from how she ended up here, to how long it has been, but also queries about how much food and water her captor has given her. But now is not the time for all of that. The priority is getting her to a safe place before that captor returns and catches us.

As the alarm continues to sound, and I assume everybody at

the gathering is making their way to the evacuation point, I also assume Cesar is running back because he knows someone is inside his house. I must have triggered a silent alarm, whether it was in his study or out here somewhere, but wherever it was, it doesn't matter. All that matters is that he is onto me and if I'm not quick, I could find myself locked in the same room Rosie was in.

Keeping a tight hold of her arm, I escort her out of that room and head for the back door, the one I broke through when I arrived here. As we enter the kitchen, I see the rock lying on the floor on top of all the broken glass. But at least I don't see Cesar, so I think we still have time to get out before he catches us.

I regret not telling Christian what I was doing now. Even if I am caught, he would at least know I was here so he could send the police if I go missing. But he doesn't know because I kept this all to myself, which means if I am caught, nobody might ever know I was here. Nobody except Rosie and Cesar, and if he catches us, we'll be imprisoned together and I'll end up like her – scared, weak, afraid and totally dependent on somebody else to come and save me. Or maybe Cesar will decide that two prisoners is too much trouble, and he'll take more drastic action. He wouldn't have to worry about anybody finding us here if we were dead and buried elsewhere.

'It's okay, we're nearly there,' I say to Rosie as I continue to guide her towards the back door. But our progress is painfully slow, and I'm also well aware that we're not nearly there at all. Sure, we might make it through the door, but we'd still only be in Cesar's back garden and that means we'd still have a long way to go to get away from his house and off his street. But just as I'm worrying about all that, I hear something else to make me fearful, and as my panic levels rise rapidly, I fear this is about to be over.

There is a noise behind us, a noise I recognise all too well as a key turning in a lock.

I don't have to turn around because I know what I'll see when I do.

It'll be Cesar coming through the front door to check on his home and, more specifically, to check on his prisoner.

That's why I don't waste time.

Instead, I turn to Rosie and say one simple word.

'Hide.'

THIRTY-FOUR

I press a finger to my lips and hold it there as I stare at Rosie's frightened face and make sure she understands that she needs to be deadly silent now. It might not be necessary for me to make such a gesture because one, she can't actually talk at the moment and two, she's most likely well aware of the dangers of making any noise, but I do it anyway because I'm afraid.

Rosie does as I demand. She stays quiet, as do I. That means there are only two things we can hear as we stand in our hiding place between the fridge and the back of the kitchen door.

The alarm.

And Cesar rushing into the house.

I keep my finger to my lips as I listen to Cesar getting closer to making the discovery that I know will horrify him. Sure enough, it comes a moment later.

'No!' I hear him cry, and I guess he's seen that the door at the bottom of the stairs is unlocked and open and there is nobody trapped inside that secret room anymore.

I see Rosie flinch at the sound of that man's voice, but put a hand on her skinny shoulder to try and comfort her. But really, she must know the same thing I do. We're in big trouble if Cesar finds us hiding here, and while I will do my absolute best to fight back if he does discover us, he should be easily able to over-power me and not just because he looks stronger. He's not carrying a child like I am.

'Where are you?' I hear Cesar cry, the desperate, panicked call of a man who knows his carefully cultivated image in the outside world is now at threat of being blown apart and he will be exposed for the man he really is.

I have no doubt he set off that alarm that I can still hear in the background, and it is probably his plan to have the estate evacuated while he searches here. If he finds us, he can deal with us without anyone else seeing and that way, nobody else will know what happened. It's my job to make sure that doesn't happen, but to do that, I need to get myself and Rosie out of this house.

I cautiously peep around the kitchen door we're hiding behind and see the back door, broken and, thanks to me, now unlocked. But it might as well be miles away because I doubt we'll be able to make it there in time without Cesar seeing us, not when he's only a few yards away in the hallway. I'm also hampered by having Rosie with me, as she doesn't seem capable of moving quickly, so is it even possible for us to escape?

I stop worrying about that when I hear Cesar's breath on the other side of the door, and every muscle in my body tenses as I realise all he has to do is pull this door towards him and he will reveal the two of us hiding behind it. He's entered the kitchen, and I can hear how worked up he is. That only gets worse when he notices the broken glass of the back door.

'No!' he cries as he rushes towards the door and flings it open, and as I dare to peep out, I see him step into his garden and look for any sign of somebody escaping. Of course he doesn't see anyone. That's because we're still here. But he doesn't know that yet. What if he thinks we have got away and gives up looking for us? What if he just decides to run away himself, escape before the police come looking for him? If he does that, we might be okay. We might not have to try and run. We could stay here and hide until Cesar has gone and this is over.

Those wishful thoughts evaporate when I hear Cesar step back into the house, his shoes stepping over the broken glass on the floor before I listen to him pass the other side of the door and go back into the hallway.

'Where are you? I know you're still here!' he calls out then in a very menacing tone, and I silently curse him for seemingly knowing the impossible. How does he know we are still in the house? Why can't he just think that we have already fled?

I fear then that he has cameras in here. That would explain how he knows we're still on the premises. But if he had those, he would surely have seen us sneak into our hiding place, and he hasn't come and got us yet, so maybe not. Unless he's just toying with us both. Playing with us like a lion with its food. Not wanting to kill it yet because it's having too much fun scaring it first.

I don't know what to think.

Then I hear Cesar going upstairs.

'Come out, come out, wherever you are,' I hear him say and that gives me the hope that he is still genuinely trying to find us.

This is it. This is our chance. Possibly our only chance.

'We need to go,' I whisper to Rosie, who I notice is now visibly shaking as she stands beside me. 'I'll help you as much as I can, and I promise I won't leave you, but I need you to try and move as quickly as possible. Okay?'

Rosie continues to shake but doesn't offer me any other form of communication.

'Rosie, please. We need to go. Can you move?'

My hushed but urgent tone snaps Rosie back into the moment and she stops shaking before nodding her head.

With that, as I hear Cesar's feet stomping around above us, we move out of our hiding place and go towards the back door.

The broken glass makes it impossible to tread quietly but we can't slow down now and as we open the door and step outside, the fresh air is momentarily soothing. But it'll be of little relief if Cesar rushes downstairs and catches us, so we have to keep going.

'This way,' I whisper to Rosie as I guide her to the side of the house, and I'm glad that she is moving quicker than she was when I first discovered her. Perhaps adrenaline has kicked in and is helping mask all the pain she would otherwise be in from the treatment she has endured. When the adrenaline wears off, she'll most likely either pass out or have a complete breakdown, but I need to make sure that doesn't happen until we are in a safe environment where I can get her the best medical assistance.

We move along the side of the house before we reach the front of Cesar's property, where we've no chance but to move out into the open if we are going to get away from here.

'We can do this. Come on,' I say to Rosie by way of final encouragement before we take the leap of faith and move away from the house and along the driveway, passing Cesar's expensive car and heading to the street beyond it.

I look at the street and all the houses on it and wish this were a normal community. If it were, I could simply run to the nearest neighbour, bang on the door and when they opened it, fall into their arms and tell them to call the police because Cesar is dangerous. Then they would look after us until the police got here, and this would all be over. But this is not a normal community. Cesar has seen to that. Everybody here seems to think he is wonderful which means they are less likely to help me. But more than that, so many of these homes are still unoccupied so my odds of knocking on the right door are reduced due to that. Even the ones that are occupied are all empty because the residents are at that gathering and will now have evacuated due to the alarm that is still sounding loudly.

Rosie suddenly stumbles and I have to grip her thin left arm tightly to prevent her from tumbling to the tarmac. Fortunately, I keep her on her feet because her breaking a bone is the last thing we need; it would make our escape totally impossible.

'It's okay, I've got you,' I say to her by way of reassurance. 'Come on, let's keep going. We're almost there.'

That last part is a massive exaggeration because I know we are not almost there at all. We are only at the top of Cesar's driveway, still well within view of his property and we have a long way to go just to make it off his street. That's even before we find somewhere safe to hide.

As I anxiously process all of that, I instinctively take a look behind me at the house we have just escaped from. I want to make sure Cesar isn't running towards us and, for a brief second, I'm relieved to see that he is not. But that relief evaporates when I do see something disturbing. It's Cesar and while he isn't running, he has seen us.

He's standing at an upstairs window looking down at the two of us trying to get away, and now he has spotted us, he seems confident that he can catch us.

His ominous smile tells me that.

THIRTY-FIVE

'We have to run. Now!' I cry to Rosie once I realise Cesar has seen us, and I instantly increase the pace.

For a second, Rosie struggles to keep up and almost falls over again, but I keep her upright and my momentum gets her moving again, though it's still slow progress due to her frailty and my pregnant condition.

We're out of time and the chance of a sneaky escape has gone, so the outcome of this comes down to sheer desperation now.

Do we want to escape more?

Or does Cesar want to stop us more?

I'll get the answer in the next few moments.

Without daring to look back again, Rosie and I move as quickly as we can along the street, and we make it to the end without Cesar catching us. But I can hear him calling out to us in the background and his voice sounds like he's getting closer.

I see more houses, and I'm contemplating trying to run into one of them and hide with Rosie in the hopes that Cesar won't catch us there. But just before I can make a call that may or may not be the right one, I hear something amazing.

'Di! There you are! I've been looking everywhere for you!'

I spin around and see Christian rushing towards me. Kai is with him too, his football under his arm, and the sight of my family is most welcome. At least it is until I quickly remember the danger I'm in and, by association, they are now in danger too.

'What's going on?' Christian asks as he looks at Rosie, and it must be very confusing for him to see me with my arm interlinked with a woman who looks like she has been locked away in a room for a long time. *Because she has.*

'It's Cesar! He's coming!' I cry as I turn around and, sure enough, there he is, that evil man running towards us with dangerous desperation on his face.

Christian sees him coming too, and as Rosie instinctively moves herself closer to me and away from the advancing danger, I have no idea what is going to happen next.

'We need to go!' I urge Christian, praying he really understands the danger we are in, but there simply isn't enough time for me to explain all of this to him before Cesar gets here. But maybe I don't need to because as Cesar is just about to reach us, I see Christian has squared up his shoulders and shielded us from him, and I also notice his fists are clenched, as if he's ready to go into battle for us.

The problem is, Cesar looks ready to fight too.

While it's Rosie's instinct to look to me for safety, it's also Kai's instinct to look to me and as my son cowers beside me, I already know I am prepared to fight to the death to protect him. But Christian is ahead of me, so he gets to have the first go at doing just that.

'Get out of the way!' Cesar calls as he reaches us, but Christian doesn't budge and when Cesar doesn't stop advancing, my husband does what he has to do.

He punches Cesar in the face and sends the man toppling backwards before he falls to the pavement, groaning as he goes.

I had no idea the man I married had something like that in him, but he has succeeded in stopping Cesar, so he's certainly done what needed to be done.

'Let's go,' Christian says then as Cesar remains on the ground, blood pouring from his nose, dazed and disorientated and showing no signs of wanting to get back up in case he is struck again.

The four of us take off then, rushing down the street away from the injured man, but we're quicker now that Christian interlinks his arm with Rosie too so the pair of us can help her move faster. Kai has the energy of youth on his side, so he has no trouble keeping up the pace and very quickly we have made it back onto our street. But we're still a fair distance away from the evacuation point, which might be why Christian suggests what he does.

'Let's get her inside our house. She needs to rest,' he says to me, talking about the ailing woman we are both helping to support.

'What if he comes after us there?' I ask, my fearful voice referring to Cesar, who is not behind us again yet but might be once he recovers from my husband's punch. 'Should we not take the car and try and get out of here?'

'The keys are inside but she's too weak to move. I'll deal with Cesar if he comes here,' Christian says boldly, and my confidence is boosted by how he already dealt with him so well a few moments ago, so I agree that getting Rosie into our home is the best thing to do.

We reach our house and as we burst through the door and into the hallway, I feel Rosie slipping from my grasp. I know she needs to lie down, and the sofa would be the easiest place for her to do that, but it feels too close to the door if Cesar comes back, so I need to get her upstairs.

'Let's put her on our bed,' I say to Christian, and after our son has helpfully closed and locked the front door, my husband and I help Rosie up the stairs.

When we reach our bedroom, we help lower her onto our bed and as she lies before us, my heart breaks for how broken she is. She needs rest, but she also clearly needs fluids and food, so we can't just leave her lying here and hope she'll get better. She needs urgent medical attention, so I grab the landline phone and prepare to call for help, wishing I could use a mobile but knowing there is still no signal here.

'I'll do it,' Christian says, taking the phone from me. 'You look after her.'

As he speaks to the emergency services and requests both an ambulance and the police, I sit beside Rosie and make sure she isn't going into shock. Meanwhile, Kai stands in our bedroom doorway, looking worried for all of us.

'It's going to be okay,' I say out loud, speaking for both my son's benefit and Rosie's while Christian continues to talk to the operator, urging them to send help because there is a dangerous man out there who is trying to hurt us.

I hope the operator is taking him seriously, but if not, what happens next might help with that.

We hear loud banging on the front door.

Cesar is here.

'Oh my god, he's outside,' I say to Christian, instantly wishing I hadn't just panicked because my getting so worked up won't help Kai or Rosie keep calm, but I couldn't help it. The banging on the door is loud, frantic, and it doesn't sound like it is going to stop.

'He's going to break the door down,' I say to Christian as if he hadn't realised that, but the serious look on his face tells me he's already thought this.

'He's outside our house. He's not going to stop until he gets in,' my husband says to the operator as he grips the phone tightly. 'You need to send help now, but it might not be in time, so I'm going to have to do whatever it takes to keep my family safe.'

Christian puts the phone down then and before the operator, or myself, can ask him what he meant by that, he heads to the bedroom door.

'Stay in here and don't come out unless I open this door again,' Christian tells Kai. But our son doesn't want to just watch his father walk away into danger, so he rushes to Christian and clings to him because he wants us all to be together.

'Do as I say,' Christian tells him urgently, and while Kai has tears in his eyes and the banging gets louder, our son does as he is told and rushes to me by the bed. I take him in my arms, and we hold each other as we watch Christian take one last look at us cowering in the bedroom. Then he leaves the room and closes the door.

Everything goes quiet for a moment before I hear the sound of glass smashing downstairs, and I gasp as I fear Cesar has just found his way in. Just like I broke into his house by breaking a window, it sounds like he has done the same thing here, so now all I want to do is rush outside this room and make sure Christian is okay. But he told us all to stay in here and not come out unless he reopened the door, and I know he has done that because it is the best way to ensure our safety, so we have to try and stick to the plan.

'Daddy,' Kai says quietly through heavy sobs, and I give him a tight squeeze. I feel a hand on my arm then and presume it belongs to my son, until it keeps tapping me and when I look down, I see it's Rosie who is touching me.

She wants to tell me something. Her mouth is open, but her throat is still too dry, and she can't get the words out.

'What is it?' I ask her, but she still can't muster up the words, so I look around for something that might help her communicate with us. But there's no pen and paper in here, so she can't simply write whatever it is she's trying to say, and I don't think she'll be able to tell me.

'Use your phone,' Kai suddenly says, and I realise my boy has just had a brainwave. He's right. We don't need pen and paper because we have more modern ways for people to write things.

I take my phone from my pocket and while it's mostly useless here due to the lack of signal, it can still be used for what I need it for now, so I open the Notes app and hand the device to Rosie.

She takes it before initially dropping it on the bed and I fear she might be too weak to do this. But then she picks it back up and her fingers start tapping the screen. As I wait for her to complete her message, I listen out for any indication of what might be going on out there. But it's all quiet. Then Rosie turns the phone screen to me so I can read what she has written on it.

I have been here before

'I know,' I tell her as tears form in my eyes. 'You used to live in this house, didn't you?'

Rosie nods and she is on the verge of tears too. I appreciate her trying to give me this information, but it's info I already had. What I don't know is why she left here.

'What happened?' I ask her. 'How did you end up locked in that room?'

Rosie starts typing again, and as I look back to the closed bedroom door, I worry we might not have time for her to tell me. But she has to because the more of us who know the truth, the more chance there is of it being told, as long as at least one of us can survive this.

It's still dreadfully quiet out there as Rosie shows me the phone screen again.

*I was looking for my boyfriend and Cesar said he could tell me
where he was, so I went to his house. But he tricked me.*

For such a short statement, it's harrowing. She must be
talking about Jordan, and as I look at Rosie, I see that she fears
her boyfriend is dead and that Cesar killed him. It would be
hard for me to argue with that assumption based on the fact he
locked her away, presumably to try and keep his deadly secret.
Before either of us can do anything more, or before Kai can ask
me if everything is going to be all right, we hear the sounds of
shouting outside the bedroom, followed by what sounds like a
scuffle. Then I hear the distinctive noise of somebody falling
down the stairs.

Everything goes quiet then.

Until I hear footsteps.

Then the bedroom door opens.

THIRTY-SIX

'Oh my god,' I say as I stare at the man who enters my bedroom, the man with a bloodied nose and a cold expression.

'Daddy!' Kai cries as he leaps off my lap and rushes towards his father, and as I watch my two most loved ones embrace, I wonder what happened. If Christian is here, it must mean Cesar is...

'He's gone,' Christian says to me and Rosie, but while that could mean that Cesar has literally left the premises, the blank stare on my husband's face tells me he is just choosing his words carefully in front of Kai.

By gone, I fear he means he's *really gone*.

'Stay in here until the police arrive,' Christian tells Kai, and with him not wanting our son to step outside the bedroom, that only reinforces my feeling that there is a grim sight waiting for us beyond these four walls. He doesn't want Kai to see what has happened to Cesar. He probably doesn't want anybody except the trained professionals to have to see it. But he has seen it himself.

Christian should not have to deal with death in his daily life.

But I think he just has.

As Christian brings Kai back to the bedside, I take one of Rosie's hands and grip it tightly.

'You don't have to worry anymore,' I tell her, forcing a smile onto my face. 'It's over.'

My words don't seem to give her the comfort I intended them to because she still looks upset, and I realise that for her, this isn't over. Not if the whereabouts of her boyfriend, Jordan, remain a mystery.

I hear sirens then, and Christian noticeably stiffens at the sound of them, suggesting to me that he is wary about what is going to happen when the respondents get here and start asking questions. I realise then that I need to see exactly what has happened so we can support each other through this next part.

I go to leave the bedroom and while Christian calls out for me to stay, I ignore him and reach the top of the stairs. When I do, I look down and see that Cesar is still in our house. But our husband is right. He has gone. I can tell that as I look at him lying at the bottom of the stairs and see his eyes are staring life-lessly up at the ceiling; there's a twisted grimace on his face and he is not moving.

Based on what I heard, there must have been a scuffle on this staircase, and during it, Christian got the better of Cesar and pushed him back down. Cesar fell and now he's dead. I don't blame my husband. He was just protecting his family.

But it's not me who he has to convince of that.

It's the police coming through the front door.

As our home is infiltrated by the people we desperately called to help us, I rush back to the bedroom and find Christian and Kai standing beside Rosie.

'What's happening?' Kai wants to know, and with time limited, I make sure to explain this to him the best way I can.

'The police are here and we're all safe now,' I tell him. 'Mummy and Daddy are going to have to talk to them, but we're not in trouble so we'll be finished soon, and then everything will go back to normal. In the meantime, I need you to be a good boy and help us, okay? If the police want to ask you anything, just tell them the truth. That's all you have to do. But if you don't want to talk to them, that's okay as well. You don't have to. Just be well behaved and this will be over quickly, I promise.'

My beautiful boy hears what I just said and nods his head to tell me he understands, and that gives me one less thing to worry about as the police officers call up the stairs.

'We're up here!' Christian calls in response before he leaves the room. I stay back with Kai and Rosie until an officer comes in and finds us. When he does, I start talking.

'I found this woman locked up in a room in Cesar's house. He's the man at the bottom of the stairs. He had imprisoned her, but I helped her escape!' I cry, breathlessly trying to get all the information out as quickly as I can. 'Cesar chased us here and broke into our home, so my husband defended us. Now you need to help get this woman to a hospital and give her the medical care she needs. You also need to begin an immediate search for her partner. His name is Jordan, and he has been missing for some time. There is a photo of him in the files I...'

I realise that in all the commotion, I lost the files I found in Cesar's office. Maybe I dropped them at his house or on the street while we were running here. Damn it, it would have been good to hand them over to the police. Surely Rosie can help with the description, and when I look at her, I see that she is no longer crying. The sight of the police seems to have emboldened her. I guess she realises this really is over now. As such, she seems less afraid and more determined to find out where her boyfriend is.

Did he suffer the same fate as her? Is he currently locked up somewhere needing to be released? Or did something different happen to him? Something worse? And what about Hayley?

Could she be locked up somewhere too? It's certainly conceivable.

Has Hayley suffered the same fate as Rosie?

And has Jordan suffered the same fate as Cesar?

'I don't want you harassing my wife. She's heavily pregnant and she needs rest,' I hear Christian say out in the hallway. 'Leave my son alone too. He's only five. I'll tell you everything you need to know, but leave them alone. Leave that poor woman on the bed alone too.'

By the sound of my husband's voice, he is in some distress, and when I rush out of the bedroom to find out why, I get my answer.

Two police officers are standing beside Christian, looking very stern and serious.

I guess he has just told them he is the reason Cesar is lying dead at the bottom of the stairs.

That must be why my husband is now in handcuffs.

THIRTY-SEVEN

Nobody wants to see their husband taken away for police questioning. And nobody wants to spend two days frantically worrying about their partner while also caring for an upset child who wants to know why their father can't tuck him into bed at night. Recent events have been incredibly tough on all of us, but when I got to see Christian again after a tense forty-eight hours away, he said he had some good news for me.

'They've let me come home,' he told me with exhaustion all over his face, presumably from an anxious time spent being questioned. 'And I'm hopeful that once they have searched Cesar's house and corroborated what we told them about him keeping Rosie a prisoner there, they will fully believe me and drop any further investigation.'

Being out on bail didn't mean this was over, far from it, and the fear of charges being pressed and a potential need for a trial still loomed scarily large in our future. But it was certainly preferable to him being kept in custody and away from me and Kai in the short term. That's why I'd hugged Christian tightly then, squeezing his strong arms, the same arms that had pushed

Cesar down the stairs when that man was threatening to hurt all of us if he had been left unchecked.

As I'd embraced my husband, all the fears I'd had about him being locked away for several long years for murder washed away, just like the fears that I would be forced to raise Kai and our unborn daughter by myself until Christian was eventually released back into society. He was a free man, as he should be, not completely but surely it was only a matter of time, and as such, he was able to continue to provide the support that he needed to for his family.

That support now means helping me with the house move.

Unsurprisingly, once Cesar's body had been removed and Rosie had been taken to hospital and the forensic investigators had completed their work, I had decided that we were selling this house and getting as far away from here as possible. Once Christian had been released, he quickly agreed that was the best course of action, so he told me he would deal with the sale while I got started on the packing. But he advised he would have to keep the police updated on his whereabouts at all times in case this house sale looked like him preparing to flee. That was an extra irritant, but understandable, and I knew Christian was still stressed about not being fully in the clear yet. That's why I wanted to give him as little to do as possible. But as my due date nears, packing is a task that takes a lot of energy I no longer possess, which is why my parents have been here to help too.

Mum and Dad are currently helping me put everything in this house back into the boxes it all came out of, while Christian has gone to work to speak to his boss and request an extended leave of absence and also to explain why exactly it is he needs such a thing. I'm sure his boss will be understanding and, if so, Christian won't have to worry about work for a while. But there is a chance his boss panics at the idea of having an employee under police investigation and potentially opts to suspend him. I guess we won't know until Christian walks into that office and drops the bombshell about what he has been getting up to outside of office hours. But if he does get a break, hopefully one that is on full pay, he can help with the house move and then focus on being a dad to our daughter who we could meet any day now. As for our daughter's big brother, Kai is back to his usual energetic self, kicking a ball around the house, and while he isn't helping us get the packing done any quicker, it's just a relief to see that the recent events don't seem to have traumatised him too much. It helps that he didn't see Cesar's body. Only Christian, myself and the responding officers and paramedics have to process that grim sight for the rest of our lives.

'Which box do you want me to put this in?' Dad asks me while holding a lampshade, and I point out where to put it until we move to our new place.

Where is that next place?

It's going to be a little closer to here than I had anticipated.

'You're more than welcome to stay with us,' Mum had said to me when I had told her we were leaving here and looking to start again elsewhere, and once she had, I was anticipating moving in with them. It would be a little bizarre to be back with my parents especially when I welcomed a new baby, but I suppose there might have been some kind of sentimental 'full circle' aspect to it all for our family. The main thing that mattered was we all had a safe roof over our heads for the foreseeable future until Christian and I had had the time to go house-hunting again.

But that was when Mum had dropped her bombshell.

'The thing is, your father and I decided to sell our main residence,' Mum had gone on to explain, using the title she always used when discussing the family home, simply because she and my father owned rental properties all over the place.

'What? You've sold our house?' I'd cried, calling it that because it was ours. It was where I had my first bedroom, it was where the garden was where I learnt how to ride a bike, and it had the kitchen where I sneakily scoffed snacks after school. 'Can I not see it again?'

'I didn't realise you'd be so upset, darling,' Mum said. 'You've hardly been a regular visitor there in recent years.'

That's true, but still, it felt sudden.

'We decided it was time for a change. We wanted somewhere more modern,' Mum had gone on. 'And we found the perfect place. Well, at least we thought we had.'

'What are you talking about?' I'd asked then before my face had dropped when I recalled an earlier conversation I'd had with my parents. It was during the dinner party I hosted when we had first moved in here. I'd cooked for them when they wanted to come and see our new home. It was during that dinner when they had suggested they might be tempted to buy a house on this estate too.

'No, you haven't,' I'd cried then. 'Please tell me you haven't bought a house here.'

Mum had winced as the startling reality had dawned on me.

'You bought a house from Cesar? What were you thinking? That man was evil!' I cried.

'We didn't know that at the time,' Mum had replied in her defence.

'You have to cancel it,' I'd tried then, but I was told it was too late, and the sale had already gone through.

'We just wanted to be closer to you and our grandchildren. We feel like we've missed out on a lot in the past and we don't want to make the same mistake again,' Mum had said, which made me feel a little guilty for being against this idea, even if it was their fault they had missed out on things.

'But you can't live here. Not after what has happened. I doubt anyone wants to live here anymore.'

'What that despicable man did shouldn't ruin this place,' Mum had said then. 'It's still a lovely neighbourhood and the houses are beautiful. You should see the place we have bought.

It's huge and there's more than enough room for all of you to stay with us until you get somewhere else sorted. And look on the bright side, at least you haven't got far to move.'

I suppose Mum had been right about that last part. It would be quite convenient for the removals teams to only have to take our belongings a few streets away rather than across town. But if we agreed to moving in with Mum and Dad, it meant staying here, in this place, on this estate. Why did they have to sell the family home?

Christian had wearily shrugged when he had learnt of the news before saying we didn't really have any other option, and because he was right, I'd begrudgingly accepted that we were going to be moving into another house on this estate. But at least we'll be away from this particular house, and as I look out of the window and see the removals van parking on the driveway, I know we'll be gone from here soon.

Beyond that van, I see a police car driving past and that has become a very familiar sight on this estate ever since Cesar died. I expect that particular police car is on its way to join all the others that are currently parked either in or around the section of the estate that is still being built. That large building site is now the main focus of the search for Jordan, or rather, for Jordan's body. Rosie's boyfriend is still classed as missing and because there was nothing discovered in a search of Cesar's home to suggest otherwise, he is now sadly presumed dead.

Is his body buried somewhere here? Like the police, I am inclined to agree that a huge building site that will eventually have dozens of homes on top of it is a perfect place to hide a body. But now Cesar's secrets are out, will it stay hidden? Or is the body elsewhere?

I feel terrible for Rosie, that poor woman who not only has to try to recover from the traumatic ordeal she has been through but has to worry whether her boyfriend's body is going to be discovered at any moment.

I'm about to go and continue helping guide my parents with the packing when I notice the police car I just saw has reversed and is now parked outside our house. I keep watching as I see a uniformed officer get out along with a man in a suit whom I recognise as Detective Wilkins, the detective who has been leading the investigation into Cesar and his various crimes ever since they were exposed.

Realising they intend to come in here, I head downstairs and, as I do, I see my mother opening the door to the two visitors.

'What's going on?' I ask as I walk down the stairs, one hand on the banister, the other on my bump.

'We'd like to speak to Christian,' Detective Wilkins says as he looks around. But all he sees are myself, as well as my parents holding a box each and Kai rushing in with his football. 'We've tried reaching him on the mobile number he gave us, but there's been no answer.'

'He's not here,' I reply. 'He's at work.'

'Please can you call him and ask him to come home,' the detective replies calmly, looking like he's ready to settle in and stay as long as this takes. But what is this exactly?

'Why do you need to speak to him?' I ask. 'I thought he'd answered everything he needed to, and you were satisfied that he had been acting in self-defence.'

'There's been a new development,' the detective tells me then as the officer he came here with looks out of the window as if to check if Christian is coming back.

'What development?'

'Like I said, we just need to speak with Christian about this.'

'Why? Why can't you talk to me?'

'Because he's the homeowner,' Wilkins replies.

'I'm the homeowner too,' I say. 'I live here like he does, so you can tell me whatever it is you need to say. Have you found out something else about this place? Is it to do with Jordan?

Have you found him? Or is there something else? Whatever it is, you can tell me because I have as much right to this place as Christian does.'

My mind is racing with possibilities, but as the detective continues speaking, he says something that had definitely not occurred to me. That's because it's so ludicrous.

'I'm not disputing who owns this house today. I'm talking about who owned it when Rosie and Jordan lived here.'

'What? They must have owned it. If they were living here, it must have been theirs, surely?'

Detective Wilkins shakes his head and, as he does, I have the feeling my whole life is about to be turned upside down.

Sure enough, it is.

'According to the property records, neither Rosie nor Jordan owned this house when they lived here,' Wilkins tells me. 'Christian did.'

THIRTY-EIGHT

'There must be a mistake,' I say because that's the only possible explanation. 'Christian didn't own this house when Rosie and Jordan lived here. We had never been here before. We only bought this place after them.'

I glare at Detective Wilkins, not in anger but more in desperation that he will double-check something in his notepad before apologising for the confusion. I just need him to tell me that he has been mistaken, or that he is joking. Anything other than what he is telling me.

'There's no mistake,' Wilkins replies. 'This came to light during our interviews with Rosie in hospital. She told us that she and Jordan did not actually own this house, but they were renting it. They never met the owner, and always dealt with an estate agent, so we decided to try and track down the owner to see what they might have known from that time. When we checked the property records, it was Christian's name listed as the owner.'

This makes no sense.

'I don't care what you think you know, you are wrong!' I cry, losing control. 'Christian did not buy this house before we moved in. We bought it as a family, and we moved in together. How would he have owned it before that? That's impossible!'

I wish that were true, but Wilkins seems sure that he is the one who is right, not me. I also think about how Christian dealt with the purchase of this place himself, telling me he would deal with it all and leave me free to focus on other things. I thought he was doing that so I didn't have the extra stress while pregnant. It almost made sense for him to do it all as he has such an extensive background in finance that he understands big transactions and money movements a lot more than I do. But what if that was just a ruse to keep me in the dark? What if taking full control of our financial affairs gave him the opportunity to keep a secret like this? A secret as big as owning a house I didn't even know about?

Surely not. It's impossible, isn't it?

Not according to the detective.

'This is why we really need to speak to Christian,' Wilkins says.

'You're not the only one!' I blurt back, and the detective is going to have to wait his turn. I want the first go at my husband when he reappears.

'Look, this may all be perfectly okay,' Wilkins goes on. 'We're not saying your husband is in trouble or in any way connected to what happened to Rosie or what might have happened to Jordan. But he might have some more information from that time that could help us shed some light on Jordan's whereabouts or how Rosie came to be imprisoned at Cesar's.'

'Oh, he is in trouble,' I reply, correcting the detective. 'He's in trouble if he has lied to me about this house just like everybody else has lied to me about it.'

As well as being confused, I'm furious that Christian could have led me here under false pretences. He made out like he had discovered this place and thought it was the perfect setting for us to raise our family. But if he owned this house before, then it wasn't that at all, was it? Instead, he deliberately misled me, making us move into a house he apparently already owned.

How could he have bought this house months before I even knew it existed?

If this is all true, I won't just be angry at my husband. I'll be angry at myself for being so stupid.

'I need to speak to him right now!' I cry as I turn to go for the phone, but I'm on the warpath and Dad expertly intervenes before I make this worse.

'Just try and calm down. This isn't good for you and the baby. I'll phone him and get him to come home,' Dad says as he puts his hands on my shoulders and does his best job of calming his erratic daughter. I suppose he had plenty of practice at that when I was younger.

'Fine, just tell him to get here and explain himself!' I tell my father before suddenly feeling like I need to sit down. Is the room spinning or is it me?

I collapse onto one of our sofas and put a hand to my head, struggling to understand that even after all the crazy happenings recently, things seem to be getting even worse now. But as Mum goes to make me a cup of tea, while Kai sits anxiously beside me to check I'm okay, and as the detective and his colleague take a seat on the sofa opposite us, I know that this can't be a misunderstanding. The police don't get things like this wrong, so they wouldn't be here saying all this if it wasn't true.

That means it's not just Cesar's past with this house that needs fully explaining, or Rosie and Jordan's.

It's my husband's.

And what if his past is worse than all of theirs combined?

THIRTY-NINE

It's been two hours since the detective arrived and a similar time since Dad tried reaching Christian on his phone. But my husband has not answered any calls, nor has he arrived home from work, and the longer he stays away, the worse I am beginning to feel.

I'm becoming alarmed by his absence and therefore, more suspicious of him by the second. The hopes I harbour that there is some mistake are dwindling, and I'm starting to fear what everybody else is fearing.

Christian knows something about Rosie and Jordan and Cesar, something he hasn't told anybody else. But considering one of them is dead, one is in hospital and the other is missing, my husband is the only one who might be able to fill in the final jigsaw piece about what really happened before we moved in.

I notice Wilkins talking quietly to his colleague before the detective stands up and looks like he's preparing to excuse himself.

'I'm going to go back to the station, but this officer will stay here, just in case Christian comes back,' Wilkins says.

'Why are you leaving? I thought you wanted to wait to talk

to him?' I ask fearfully. Unless this is a good sign that they're not actually as interested in my husband as they initially seemed. But I'm wrong.

'I'm going to go back to the station and help coordinate the search,' Wilkins replies grimly.

'The search? For what?'

'For your husband,' he replies. 'He might still return home and, if so, we can conduct our interview with him and hopefully get all of this resolved quickly.'

'But if he doesn't?'

'Then we need to find him rather than waiting for him to come to us, and our best way to do that is to actively start looking. We'll start at his workplace where we believe he is and expand out from there if we have no luck locating him. I'm sure we'll find him soon. Now, if you'll please excuse me.'

Wilkins leaves the room and a moment later, the house. As I hear him drive away, I think about how he is going to spring into action when he gets back to the station. Gathering all the police officers, pinning a photo of Christian to a noticeboard and then telling them all that this man needs to be found as soon as possible because he has links to serious crimes that as of yet have not been fully resolved.

Then I think about Rosie and about how it was her interview with the police that led them to check the property records on this house and discover that Christian was the original owner. Apparently, she never met the owner, she just dealt with an estate agent. There's no reason not to believe her, not after what she has been through and not now when she is clearly desperate to find out what happened to Jordan. But I wouldn't mind talking to her myself, if only to try and make some more sense of this. I feel I would have a better time hearing things from her, a woman who I helped rescue, rather than a surly detective who is simply trying to do his job and cares less about me and my family.

'What do you want to do, darling?' Mum asks me after she has cleared away the first cup of tea she made me and brought me another one that will also remain untouched. Considering how little effort I have been making with my appearance lately, my mother looks positively glamorous alongside me, even if she isn't intending to be. But then again, she always did like to make an effort and, despite the upheaval in my life, she found the time this morning to apply a little make-up.

'What do you mean? I want to find Christian and ask him what the hell is going on,' I snap back at her, which I instantly feel bad for doing because she is only trying to help. But it's okay for her. It's not her husband who is apparently hiding from the police and his family. It's mine.

'Yes, I know that, darling, but this might take some time, and I want to make sure that you, Kai, and the baby are okay until this is sorted out,' Mum replies, keeping her cool with me just like Dad kept his cool earlier. 'You're in the middle of a house move and Christian isn't here to help you, but we are, so let us help you.'

'How can you help?' I cry, throwing my hands up in frustration at my life and how it seems to lurch from one problem to the next with no end in sight.

'You and Kai come and stay at ours tonight,' Mum says as I watch my son doodling with a crayon in his drawing book. He's been very well behaved since the police came and as there is an officer still here, he continues to be quieter than usual.

'I need to stay. I want to be here when Christian gets home,' I reply.

'Our new house isn't far away, it's only round the corner,' Mum tells me. 'You can be back here in minutes if he does come home. Plus the police will keep you informed, as they might find him first.'

'I want to be here when he gets back,' I repeat myself before Mum takes a deep breath.

'He might not come back,' she says.

'What? Why are you saying that? Of course he'll come back!'

Kai looks up from his colouring then, and I realise we are probably worrying him and should have this conversation elsewhere. But it's too late now.

'Yes, he will come back,' Mum says, seemingly to put Kai's mind at ease even if she doesn't believe it. 'But just think practically. Most of your things here are in boxes, so how will you prepare food or get yourself ready for bed? Come to ours. You'll both be much more comfortable there.'

Mum turns her attention to Kai.

'Would you like a sleepover at your grandparents' house?' she asks him, and he thinks about it for a little longer than usual before saying yes. I can tell he is worried about his dad, just like I'm worried too, although for different reasons, I imagine.

Kai wants his father home so he can give him a hug.

I want him home so I can decide if we need to separate again.

'I can stay outside your home and watch to see if Christian comes back,' the police officer who has remained behind Detective Wilkins says then. 'I'll call you with any news as soon as we have it.'

That's reassuring, if still a little scary that I'm relying on police information to know my husband's whereabouts. But feeling more relaxed, I decide that Mum is right. Kai and I will be better off in their house than here, surrounded by all these boxes as well as all these unanswered questions.

As Dad offers to stay back and help the removals men get the van loaded, I take Kai and follow Mum to their new house.

It's weird to be walking through the estate to get to their house rather than leaving here and having to drive further afield, but Mum was right. It's really not far at all. They are around the corner from us and when I see their new house, I am not surprised to see that it is a bigger version of ours. Of course it is; not only do they have more money, but I doubt they would have wanted to buy something as 'small' as I had.

'Cool,' Kai says as we enter their house and he sees how much more spacious it is in here. I imagine he's already visualising all these rooms being his new 'football pitch' when he kicks his ball around indoors, although when I see the expansive garden at the rear, I see he has ample space out there to play as well.

'I still can't believe you bought a place here,' I say to Mum as we watch Kai running from room to room.

'I thought it would be nice,' Mum says as I catch her looking at my bump and probably imagining lots of future playtimes with her granddaughter. 'I'm just sorry all of this has happened.'

Mum looks upset then so now it's my turn to try and comfort her, which feels awkward because it's not usually the child comforting the parent, and this is certainly not the normal way my relationship with my mother has ever been.

'You have nothing to be sorry about,' I say to her. 'You're not the one who needs to apologise or explain yourself.'

I don't need to state who that person is because it's obvious.

My husband better come home soon and tell me what is going on.

Or there won't be a home left for him to return to.

FORTY

It's six o'clock in the evening and there is still no sign of my husband anywhere. I've spent most of the afternoon at Mum and Dad's new place, but did walk back around to my old house a couple of times just to check if there had been any developments. All I saw was Dad helping the removals men carry boxes from the house, while the police officer who was remaining there on watch told me he hadn't seen Christian, nor had any of his colleagues called him to say they had seen him either.

The sun isn't due to set for a few hours yet, but I feel like it might as well just go down and get this day over with. That's because I have come to the very sorry realisation that Christian is not going to show his face on this estate today.

And maybe ever again.

I can hear Mum in the kitchen cooking dinner for us while Kai and my father are in the lounge watching TV. As for me, I'm lingering in this house that doesn't feel comforting, because it's new and I'd never been here until today And how am I supposed to relax when my husband is missing?

At least Kai hasn't asked where his daddy is for half an hour or so, a question that always prompts me to give him a hug of reassurance. But I know my son's questions will only increase the later it gets, and by bedtime, if Christian isn't here to tuck him in, Kai will really start getting upset.

I wish there was something else I could do, something that feels more productive than simply hugging my son and hanging around here waiting to hear some news. Soon, Kai will be in bed and I won't even have him to distract me, meaning I'm likely to drive myself mad with my worries. If only I knew where Christian was, I could go to him and make him talk, tell me everything and then this would all be over. But I don't, so it feels like there is no one else to talk to. At least no one else who might have any information that could help me.

Then I think of Rosie again.

I know she's still in the local hospital, and she's obviously well enough to talk now because Detective Wilkins gained a lot of information from her which has led to the search for Christian. What if I was to go and talk to her myself? See if there is anything else she might have to offer? Something she perhaps didn't tell the police? But she might tell me. I did save her life, after all.

I do a quick Google search to find out the visiting hours for the local hospital this evening, and I see that they begin in half an hour, so that means I just need to get there and, preferably, without Mum or Dad or the police knowing what I'm doing. That's because they'll most likely either try and talk me out of it or in the police's case, tell me to stop interfering. But I have to do something. Even though I am technically living back with my parents again, I am not the reliant child I was when I was younger.

'I'm going to go for a walk,' I tell Mum. 'Can you look after Kai? I'll be back in an hour or so.'

'But the meal will be ready soon,' Mum replies, looking up from a boiling pan of potatoes.

'I'll have mine when I get back. I'm not really hungry

anyway,' I say, and it's hardly a stretch to assume I don't have much of an appetite at the moment.

'Is it a good idea? You should be resting,' Mum says as she eyes my bump again, and I'm already feeling the frustration of being under her watchful eye now that I'm living here.

'Exercise is always beneficial,' I reply quickly before heading out. 'See you later.'

I leave the house then and start walking, but I take a bit of a detour around the estate, so the police officer stationed outside my old house doesn't see me and wonder where I'm going. I don't need him radioing one of his colleagues and having them follow me to the hospital.

It takes ten minutes longer than it usually would due to the detour, but I make it off the estate and no sooner have I done that than I have a phone signal, so I call for a taxi. It takes another ten minutes for it to arrive so by the time I'm getting into the backseat and telling the driver where to go, the visiting hours at the hospital have already commenced. But they are open for two hours, so I have plenty of time to get there, talk to Rosie and get back without my parents thinking it is too late.

It's like I'm a naughty teenager sneaking out and hoping I don't get caught.

I hate this feeling, but it could be worse.

I could be my husband.

Wherever he is, he must really be afraid of being caught.

I'm conflicted because on one hand, I'm angry at him for what he might have done, as well as afraid to learn the full extent of it. But he's still the man I married and the father of our children, so I am worried too that he's not okay. Whatever he's done, I want him to be safe and well, but I don't know if he is. Is he worrying about me as much as I am worrying about him?

Another thing I don't know the answer to and as I recognise that fact, I move back into the anger realm again.

I try not to feel too down about Christian and his apparent lack of caring for me and Kai and focus on the task at hand, and by the time the hospital comes into view, I am thinking about Rosie again.

I pay the driver and leave the taxi before walking through the sliding doors, thinking about how I presumed I wouldn't be here again until my baby was born. But here I am attending on different business, and I look around the busy entrance area for a receptionist before spotting one behind their desk.

'Hi. I'm here to visit Rosie Driscoll but I've forgotten which ward she is on,' I say with a smile and one hand on my bump. I know hospitals wouldn't normally give out patient information and location so freely but I'm hoping that a heavily pregnant woman does not appear to be a threat, and I get lucky when I'm told that Ward F is where I need to go.

I make my way to the ward, passing the maternity ward as I go and wondering how long it will be until I'm having to go there. But for now, I'm in a different section of the hospital and as I reach Rosie's ward, I tell the nurse on the desk who I am here to see.

'She's in bed four,' the nurse tells me with a smile, so I move on and then I eventually lay eyes on the woman I have come here to speak to.

Rosie is lying in her bed with a tray of untouched food on the table beside her. She is awake but not moving, her eyes simply staring out of the window. She looks incredibly sad. I wonder if she has had many visitors other than the police. If not, hopefully I might brighten up her day a little. Although considering what I'm here to talk about, I doubt that very much.

'Rosie? Are you okay?' I say as I tentatively approach the bed, and she quickly turns her head to see who has just walked in. Maybe she was expecting to see another nurse or another detective but it's just me, the woman she has met once before in the most dramatic of circumstances.

'What are you doing here?' Rosie asks me, and I realise this is the first time I have heard her speak.

'I wanted to come and see you,' I say. 'Can I take a seat?'

I look at the vacant chair beside her bed before Rosie nods.

As I sit down, I'm trying to think of a way in which I don't cause this poor woman any more distress than she has already been through. The last thing I want is to make her relive a painful past. Before I can come up with the best thing to say to get this conversation started, Rosie speaks again.

'They still haven't found him,' she says sadly, and I realise she must be talking about Jordan, which only makes me feel even guiltier about being here. She has enough to worry about without me giving her more problems.

'I'm sure they will,' I reply. 'And I'm sure he's okay, wherever he is.'

Rosie might still be in recovery, but she's well enough to know that I'm simply saying what she wants to hear rather than what I think is actually true.

'I'm looking for somebody too,' I admit then. 'Christian. He's not come home today and now the police are trying to find him.'

I wonder if Rosie is going to tell me that she doesn't care and then I might have to leave, but thankfully, she keeps engaging with me.

'It's about the house, isn't it?' Rosie replies. 'About him owning it when Jordan and I lived there.'

'Yes,' I say, sitting forward slightly. 'I had no idea my husband had bought that house before we actually went to view it, but apparently he did and I'm just as surprised about that as the police are. I wish I knew where he was so I could ask him about it.'

'But you don't know, so you've come to see me,' Rosie rather astutely says. 'You want to see if I know anything else I might not have told the police.'

'I just want to know how it's possible that my husband could have bought that house and rented it out to you and Jordan without me ever knowing about it,' I reply. 'Because I swear, I didn't know. You have to believe me.'

'I do,' Rosie replies. 'I can see why your husband was good at keeping it a secret. He kept himself a secret from us too. Like I told the police, we never met your husband when we lived there. We just came for a viewing with an estate agent, who I have to assume was working closely with Cesar and had some sort of commission arrangement. That agent told us the rent price and then we agreed to live there. The first time I ever saw Christian was when we escaped from Cesar's.'

'The records say he is the owner,' I reply. 'I just wish I could make some sense of all this.'

The tables turn then as Rosie suddenly becomes the one who is looking after me.

'I'll tell you everything that happened because I'm guessing the police would have withheld a lot of it from you,' she says. 'Maybe something I say can help you figure out where your husband is now. I do owe my life to you, so it's the least I can do.'

I look at this brave, remarkable woman with interest, grateful and ready for her to divulge as much as she knows. I'm also in admiration of her for how strong she looks, because despite her ordeal and the fact she lost a lot of weight, she is looking much better than I thought she would be at this stage. Then again, she is hooked up to an intravenous drip and has medical aid twenty-four-seven, so it's hardly like she's anywhere near ready to thrive on her own again yet.

'Jordan and I had only been living in the house for a couple of months when we had trouble making our rent payment,' she admits. 'We run our own business, or at least we did. But we had a few cashflow problems. The estate agent warned us we were in breach of contract and could be removed, and I'm sure he was prompted to do that by Cesar, but we asked for more time. Then, a couple of nights later, I came home and found Cesar in my house.'

'Had you met him before?' I ask, but Rosie shakes her head.

'That was the first time. I was obviously shocked that he had just let himself into my house. I didn't know how he could have the key, but then he told me that he was the owner of the estate and as such, he had an interest in every property on it and what the residents did while they were there.'

'That sounds like Cesar,' I say with a shake of my head. 'So controlling.'

'He told me that he wanted a meeting with us regarding the unpaid rent and that Jordan was already at his house. Cesar asked me to go and join them.'

I fear that was a lie and sure enough, Rosie tells me it was.

'It was stupid. I should have tried calling Jordan to check it was true but there was no phone signal. So I believed Cesar. He seemed like he was being honest, so I went to his house thinking that Jordan was going to be there waiting for us.'

'He wasn't?'

Rosie shakes her head as tears form in her eyes.

'No. I got there and then Cesar attacked me before he locked me in that room. I was in there until you found me.'

It's an awful story, but it does give me more of an insight into that time and it's valuable.

'You said you owed money on the rent,' I say, going back over the facts. 'That must have meant you owed money to my husband, right? If he owned the house, he's the landlord.'

'I guess so,' Rosie replies. 'But like I said, I never saw him. Maybe he was getting Cesar to do his dirty work for him.'

That's a horrifying thought, the idea that Christian tasked

Cesar with scaring Rosie and Jordan and abusing them simply because they missed one rent payment.

'My husband defended us from Cesar and pushed him down the stairs to his death,' I remind Rosie, not that she needs it. 'It doesn't make sense that they were friends or working together. There has to be something else that happened.'

'I don't know what it is,' Rosie says sadly. 'Only your husband would know that.'

There's a long moment of silence then as the pair of us realise that without the two missing men in our lives, we are never going to fully understand what happened and why each of us has had to suffer so much. But that silence threatens to be broken when I turn around and I see Detective Wilkins walk in.

He appears as surprised to see me as I am to see him, and I worry that I'm going to get in trouble for being here. But Rosie speaks up quickly.

'It's okay, I asked her to visit me,' she says. 'I wanted to thank her for helping me.'

That was incredibly kind of Rosie to do that, but Wilkins still doesn't look happy that I'm here and then he asks me to leave.

'Okay,' I say, figuring I should be getting back to Kai anyway, but Rosie holds out a hand to stop me.

'No, it's okay. It's nice to have a visitor,' she says. 'Whatever it is you have to say, you can say it with her here.'

I realise Rosie really trusts me, and while it could just be down to the fact that I saved her, it might also be because she doesn't have many other people in the world who care enough about her to visit.

'I'd rather have this conversation in private,' Wilkins says, which sounds very ominous, but Rosie insists that he go on so he reluctantly does, but not before clearing his throat and making sure the door is closed.

'We found him,' Wilkins says then.

'Christian?' I ask, but the detective shakes his head.

'Jordan?' Rosie asks, and I feel her hand squeezing my arm tightly as she prepares herself for this news.

'Yes,' Wilkins confirms. 'I'm afraid it's bad news.'

'Oh no,' Rosie says and she suddenly lets go of my arm, her hand limply falling back onto the bed. I quickly take hold of it myself and now I'm the one squeezing her hand because I have an awful feeling that I know what is coming. When it does, it's as if all the air is sucked out of this stuffy hospital room.

'We found Jordan's body just over an hour ago,' the detective tells us. 'He was buried in the building site on the estate. I'm terribly sorry.'

FORTY-ONE

I'm reeling from the awful news that Detective Wilkins just delivered to Rosie, but obviously nowhere near as much as she is. Her boyfriend has just been found, dead and discarded, his body in a building site where it was intended to be covered up by the new homes that were being built all around it. But it has been discovered and, now it has, a full-scale murder investigation is underway. All of this comes after Rosie told me that she and Jordan had been struggling to pay their rent. If Christian was the landlord, that means they owed him money. Considering what has happened since then, it's difficult not to think my husband had a motive to potentially punish the pair.

But did he? Or was it all Cesar?

I don't know and at this stage, neither do the police. Cesar can't tell us for obvious reasons, so that just leaves my husband. But we won't know any more until Christian comes out of hiding and explains himself.

If he ever does.

I've left the hospital and I'm in the taxi back to my parents' place, in the process leaving behind the grieving Rosie, who was still sobbing. I stayed as long as I could and offered as much support to her as possible, but in the end, trained support staff who help victims of serious crime stepped in. I really hope they can give Rosie the professional help she needs because there's no doubt she is in a huge state of shock. And she's not the only one. As my taxi reaches the estate and I see numerous police cars and blue flashing lights as well as several media vans, I realise that everyone here must know by now that something terrible has been discovered close to their homes.

I leave the taxi and rush inside, ignoring the police car that is now stationed at the front of my parents' property, and as I go in, I see my mum and dad in front of the television. They're watching a news bulletin, and I quickly realise that the reporter on screen is broadcasting from a nearby location on the estate.

He's at the building site where Jordan's body was found.

'Where have you been? We've been worried,' Mum says when she sees me walk in. 'We've been trying to call you to make sure you were okay.'

'Sorry, I haven't looked at my phone,' I reply honestly as I stare at the screen where the reporter is telling the viewer that the search for the missing man has now reached a grisly end.

'Have you heard the news?' Dad asks me from his armchair, his arms crossed and a newspaper folded on the table beside him.

I nod in grim confirmation.

'I was with Rosie at the hospital when they told her,' I admit then, much to my parents' shock.

'What?' Mum cries. 'I thought you went for a walk.'

'I knew you were gone for too long,' Dad says then, shifting slightly in his seat.

I can imagine the pair of them were clock-watching while I was gone and the later it got, the more they realised I wasn't simply out walking at all.

'Is Kai okay?' I ask, guessing he must be in bed at this time of night.

'He went straight to sleep. He was tired,' Dad tells me. 'I think he's asleep, but he might still be awake. He's been very quiet.'

'I'll go and check on him,' I decide, but before I can leave the room, Dad turns off the TV and looks like he has something important to say.

'We need to talk about this. About what it means for Christian and—'

'I don't want to talk about it,' I cut him off quickly. 'This will all be sorted out when he gets home.'

'Dionne, we need to try and prepare ourselves for—'

'I said I don't want to talk about it!' I snap back, not ready to hear any worst-case scenarios yet, before leaving the room and not giving my father the chance to keep pushing the subject.

I go upstairs and hope he doesn't follow me, and thankfully he doesn't, so I'm free to quietly check on my son as I find him in one of the spare bedrooms. He is asleep, snoring gently, and looking far more peaceful than I feel, so I am grateful that at least one of us is at rest tonight. It's lucky that he's young and I hope that most of what is happening will go over his head.

I carefully close the bedroom door again before picking a room for myself this evening. It's weird being here in what is technically my mum and dad's house, yet it feels totally alien to me because I've never spent a night here before. As I flop down onto a bed and feel like crying into this soft pillow, I take out my phone and check it. When I do, I see the missed calls from Mum that she told me about when I got back here a few minutes ago. I also see something else. There is another missed call and it's not from Mum's number. It's from one I don't recognise. They have tried calling me three times this evening, but I missed them all while at the hospital.

Who is this?

There's only one way to find out.

The fact I have a signal tells me Dad must have got a signal booster installed here like he suggested Christian and I got in our house. That allows me to make the call and as I press my phone to my ear, I hold my breath as I wait to find out who will pick up.

'Di?'

The short and simple word is like a dagger to my heart because it's him. The man everyone is looking for. The man who has kept so much from me. The man who may be responsible for some terrible crimes. I have a direct line to my husband and nobody else knows about it but us two.

'Where are you?' I ask as tears fill my eyes.

'Are the police listening in?' he asks me then like some scared criminal on the run in the movies, terrified that the phone line is tapped and paranoid that even their closest family members have been compromised.

'No, they're not,' I reply, but I'm not sure if he'll even believe me. I don't think I would believe anything he could say right now either.

'Oh, Di. I'm so sorry,' he goes on then. 'I didn't want to leave, but things have got crazy and—'

'What have you done?' I ask nervously, stifling sobs as I speak.

My hand is trembling as I wait to hear what my husband has to say. Will he have a plausible explanation? Or will he give me the worst news I've ever heard in my life?

'It's not as it seems. I haven't done anything wrong, I swear!' Christian pleads, and while his voice is loud, it sounds very quiet in the background. Where is he hiding?

'The police are looking for you,' I tell him without needing to. 'You need to come home. If not for me, do it for Kai. The longer this goes on, the harder it will be to shield him from all of this. How do you think he will feel if he sees on the news that his father is wanted or hears about it from some kid he knows at school.'

'I want to come home, I really do. But I can't. Not yet. Not until I've figured out a way to sort all of this out.'

'Sort what out? What have you done? Just tell me, please,' I say, keeping my voice low as tears stream down my cheeks. 'Is that not why you've been trying to call me on this secret number? Aren't you going to tell me what you've done?'

'I want to,' Christian replies. 'But that's not only why I've called.'

'Why else would you call?'

'Because I need to warn you.'

'Warn me?' I repeat, my tears ceasing momentarily as I try to assess how I could be at risk of something bad other than news. 'Warn me about what?'

Christian pauses then but I don't speak either, and for several heart-stopping seconds, it's as if we both want silence because we know that once it's broken, things will never be the same again.

Then my husband speaks.

'It's not just Cesar that you need to be worried about. And it's certainly not me because I'm innocent in all of this,' he says.

'Then who do I need to be worried about?' I cry, desperate to know and I'm already getting off the bed to go and get closer to Kai because this sounds bad. *And it is.*

'Your parents,' Christian replies firmly.

I freeze just inches from the closed bedroom door.

'It's them I'm trying to warn you about. It's them you need to be worried about. You have to believe me.'

Before I can ask what that is supposed to mean, I hear a

footstep on the other side of the door before a voice speaks. It's a voice that should be comforting considering who it comes from, but instead, it causes me nothing but fear.

'Is everything okay in there, darling?' Mum asks me as I stand with the phone in my hand and Christian's warning still ringing in my ears.

FORTY-TWO

I don't know what to say. I don't know what to do. Should I answer my mum? Or should I be wary of her now that my husband has just told me to be?

I stand as still as I can with the phone to my ear as I try and figure out what to do. I don't want Mum to know I'm on the phone to Christian, though, so I guess that tells me who I trust at this moment in time.

There was something so fearful in Christian's voice when he gave me that warning. It was that fear that is now making me trust my husband over my parents.

'I'm okay,' I call out to my mother. 'I'm just trying to get some rest.'

'Are you sure? I thought I heard voices,' Mum replies.

I wonder if they're already onto me. Were they eavesdropping or did they just innocently hear me on the phone?

'No, I'm just resting,' I reply. 'Everything's okay.'

I pray that will work.

'Okay, well, if you need anything, you know where me and your father are,' Mum says then.

'Thank you,' I reply, figuring Christian will be able to hear this exchange, as our call is still connected. Sure enough, he has.

'Where are you right now?' he asks me, but I dare not try and say another word to him until I know that Mum has gone back downstairs, so I stay quiet until I hear her footsteps descending. Even then, I have to double-check, so I cautiously open the bedroom door and peep out. She has gone, so I assume it's safe to talk again.

'Di?' I hear Christian say, but I wait until I have closed the door again and gone as far into the bedroom as I can before I speak. I even get under the duvet on the bed because I figure that will muffle the sound a little better. Then I start whispering.

'I'm at my mum and dad's new house,' I finally answer him, and while I assume he'd be surprised to learn my parents have a new place, I'm not prepared for the reaction he does give me.

'Is Kai with you?'

'Of course. Where else would he be?'

'You need to get out of there right now,' Christian urges me. 'Both of you. You need to leave and get somewhere safe.'

'What are you talking about? What has this got to do with my parents?' I ask him in hushed tones. *Why the hell does he sound so afraid of them?*

'They came to me with a proposition,' Christian says, talking more quietly himself now even though he's not the one trapped in the house with the people he seems so worried about. 'They said they wanted to do something, and they felt it could be good not just for them but for us too. For you and Kai and our daughter. For everyone.'

'What was it?'

'They wanted to buy a house. Another investment property. You know how they like those. Except this time, it was different. Your father said he would be heavily taxed if he bought any more properties, so he was looking for a different way to do it.

That's when he suggested that he give me the money so we could buy the house in my name.'

My thoughts are all over the place as I try to piece this together.

'I don't get it,' I say from my dark duvet bubble. 'What are you talking about?'

'The house we moved into, the one you thought we were buying as a couple. We'd already bought it before we moved in. Your parents sent me the money and I completed on the sale.'

'So it is true?' I gasp as I think about what Detective Wilkins told me. 'When the police told me you owned the house before, I thought there had to be some mistake. But there's not? You lied to me.'

'I'm sorry, but you have to believe that I genuinely thought this was the best thing for our family,' Christian goes on. 'Your parents told me that in exchange for helping them buy this investment property, they would give us a cut of the money they made on the rent. It sounded good. Easy money. I mean they were paying for everything, including the house itself. They were sending me the funds. All I had to do was put my name to the sale.'

'How could you not tell me about this?'

'Because your parents asked me not to. They knew you'd say no to the idea. They knew you hate taking their money, so they knew you'd never agree to being a part of one of their financial schemes. They insisted that it could be a great investment for our children's future. The kids could have the house one day. We could all make money on this, not just your parents, but everyone. I agreed. For the kids.'

'How could you do such a thing without talking to me about it first?' I reply, breaking from a whisper into a low cry.

'I thought it was a good idea,' Christian says lamely. 'And your parents can be very convincing.'

'You were blinded by money,' I say, reading him like a book. 'You got greedy. Just like they are.'

'It was supposed to be easy money,' my husband goes on. 'They sent me the cash, I bought the house then they put me in contact with a rental agency who could get some tenants in. I didn't have to do anything after that, the agency just dealt with it all. Your parents told me that two tenants had been found, a young couple, and that the money would start rolling in now.'

'A young couple,' I say. 'You mean Rosie and Jordan?'

'I guess so. I never met them, though. Like I said, the agency dealt with it all, and your parents seemed to know what they were doing with things like this. They have rental properties everywhere. They told me it was simple. I thought it was. I guess something went wrong.'

That might just be the understatement of the year considering that one of those tenants is dead and the other was imprisoned and almost died herself.

'Your parents called me not long after the house sale and said there had been an issue with the first tenants and that they had already moved out. Then they suggested something. They said that rather than just find two more people to move in and rent the house, what about if I moved into it with you and Kai?'

'It was my parents' idea for us to move in there?' I ask, and Christian confirms.

'Yeah, they knew we were looking for a bigger place and considering I technically already owned the house, we could just move in. Of course, you didn't know about it, so I had to go through the motions and make it look like we were buying it for the first time. But really, it was all for show. The house was already in my name. We just had to move in.'

I'm disgusted by everyone's part in this, from Mum to Dad to Christian. But I'm also disgusted at myself because how could I not know something like this had happened right underneath my nose?

'I should never have left you to do it all yourself,' I say, realising some of the blame for this falls on me because I didn't get involved in the financial transactions. I left that all up to the man I thought I could trust.

'I thought it was a good idea,' Christian laments. 'We could never have afforded to live in a house like that otherwise. But your parents had paid for it, and it was in my name, and we did need a bigger space. It seemed to make sense.'

'It doesn't make sense,' I reply firmly. 'None of this does. How can it when Jordan is dead, and Rosie is in hospital? Didn't you ask my parents what happened to them? Didn't you want to know why it hadn't worked out with the first tenants?'

'They just said they'd left. How would I have known something bad had happened? But...'

'But what?'

'But something bad has happened and I guess your parents must have had something to do with it. Them and Cesar. That's why I'm trying to warn you and that's why I'm currently hiding. I don't want to come back, but it's not the police I'm worried about. It's them. Seriously, Di, you're not safe there. Take Kai and leave.'

It's impossible to try and visualise my parents as dangerous people, especially on Cesar's level, but Christian certainly sounds afraid of them. It's also impossible to imagine how I could just take my son and get out of here without my parents asking why.

'They have to have known what happened with Rosie and Jordan. They're so controlling that there's no way they didn't play a part in it,' Christian goes on. 'Even if there was a chance they were innocent, that all went away when your father phoned me yesterday.'

'What?' I ask. As I sit up, the duvet falls off me and onto the floor, but I don't pick it up and try and muffle my voice anymore. I just grip the phone and wait.

'He called me and said the police were at our house,' Christian tells me; and I realise this was when my father offered to call my husband and ask him to come home. He made out like he was doing it because I was too upset or angry to do it myself. But it seems there was another motive.

'He didn't tell me to come home and explain what had happened to the police,' Christian says. 'Instead, he offered me a lot of money to disappear.'

'Disappear?'

'Yes. He said he would send me money, more than enough for me to start a new life elsewhere under a false name, but it meant I could not come back and see you again or tell anybody about what had happened.'

I shake my head and almost look at my phone as if it's some alien object that is deliberately trying to confuse me. None of this can be real, can it?

'Why would my father want to pay you to stay away from us?'

'Don't you get it? If I disappear, I'm the one who looks guilty. That means the police will figure that it's only Cesar and me who had anything to do with what happened to Rosie and Jordan, and if they're only looking for me, they aren't looking for the real culprits.'

I don't need to ask because I know who he is referring to. He thinks my mum and dad are the ones who the police should be looking at.

'What did you say to him?' I ask.

'I told him I couldn't do that. I couldn't leave behind you and Kai and our baby. No way. But then your father made it clear that it wasn't so much a suggestion than it was an order. And I got the sense that if I didn't follow his wishes, I was going to end up disappearing in a different way. In a way like Jordan did.'

No. Surely not. Christian can't think that my parents would hurt him. Can he?

'I told your father that I would go, but only because I needed to buy myself some time to make a plan,' he goes on. 'I also felt it was too risky to come home in case he did something to me. I'm calling to let you know that I could never leave you or the kids, and I'm explaining this all to you just in case something terrible happens to me. If I die, I need you to know the truth. I need you to know that I'm not a bad guy like the police think I am. I would never hurt anyone, you know that, don't you? I only hurt Cesar to save you all. And now I'm trying to save you from *them*.'

Before I can say anything more, Christian carries on, his troubled thoughts pouring out of his mouth and down the line.

'Maybe it's best if you don't try and leave,' he says, thinking out loud. 'I'll get you out of there, I promise. I just need to figure out a way to do it.'

He's trying to sound confident, but I can tell he is not. My poor husband sounds so afraid. He's afraid of the two people who brought me into this world. The two people I am stuck inside this house with.

And now I'm afraid too.

There is still so much to say, but I have no choice but to lower the phone when I hear more movement outside the bedroom door. Is it Mum again? Or is it Dad this time?

'Are they there?' I hear Christian ask me through the phone. 'If they are, you need to stay calm, Di. Don't let them know what I've told you. You have to act like everything is okay. You have to—'

I don't hear the rest because there's a loud knock on the door.

Then I have no choice but to quickly end the call.

That's because the door opens.

FORTY-THREE

'Mummy?'

Initially, it's a relief to see that it's my son and not my parents coming through the door, but that relief quickly evaporates when I think about how Kai is in just as much danger as I am.

'I thought you were asleep,' I say as I rush towards him. He rubs his eyes, indicating that he is still drowsy. I close the bedroom door as quickly but as quietly as I can behind him.

'I heard you talking,' he mumbles, which worries me – if he heard me then maybe my parents did too. 'Is Daddy home?'

'Not yet,' I reply, giving Kai a kiss before thinking about how I abruptly ended the call with Christian when I feared I was about to be caught talking to him. What will he be thinking now? Will he be worried that my parents have caught on to us? Maybe I should try and call him back. Before I can even attempt to do that...

'Dionne? Kai?'

I hear Mum's voice calling out to us from the hallway. She must have heard our voices, or our footsteps, and now she's coming to see us. I don't want to see them, although I sense Kai does because he looks excited to hear his granny approaching. That's only because he doesn't know that she shouldn't be trusted now. Not her or my father.

Before I can stop him, Kai has reopened the bedroom door, and I see Mum reaching the top of the stairs. This is the first time I have laid eyes on her since I found out she might be dangerous and it's a very sobering moment. No longer is she just the woman who raised me, the one who annoyed me and was never truly emotionally close to me, but she was still my mother. Now, it's as if she is a total stranger to me. I know that when I next see Dad, the feeling is going to be exactly the same.

'Is everyone okay?' Mum asks.

'Yeah, fine,' I reply feebly, but I'm wary of saying anything else in case my voice cracks and gives away how nervous I suddenly am.

'I didn't realise you weren't asleep, darling,' Mum says to Kai as she approaches. 'Would you like a milky drink and a biscuit to help you get back to sleep?'

'Yeah!' Kai cries, innocently following the whims of his appetite, but I'm aware that Mum knows the fastest way to get my son to do something, so I wonder if it is a tactic on her part to get us to go downstairs. I'd much rather stay in here. I want to close the door and hide away with Kai. Then I want to plan how I can get out of this house without having to deal with whatever my parents might have done.

I can leave that for the police to find out.

But I can't do that if we're stuck with my parents downstairs.

'It's getting very late, I think we should all go to bed,' I suggest, knowing Mum will check the time and surely agree that it's way past her grandson's bedtime. Then we can all retire to our bedrooms. That would give me and Kai the opportunity to sneak out if so. But Mum doesn't go for it.

'It's never too late for milk and biscuits, is it, darling?' Mum says as she takes Kai's hand. My son has no idea that he shouldn't just skip away with his grandma and go downstairs to the kitchen.

I follow them out of the bedroom and immediately descend the staircase behind them, as it's the only way to keep watch on my son. Then I hear Mum's voice in the kitchen as she talks through her process of preparing the snacks, telling Kai that she is getting the biscuits from the cupboard and asking him which plate he wants to eat them off. But where's Dad?

'Hi, darling. Are you okay? You look a little pale.'

I spin around at the sound of my father's voice and see him lurking behind me in the hallway. He must have just emerged from one of the other rooms, but he's caught me by surprise. Maybe it was intentional. It was certainly his intention to point out how pale I'm looking.

Does he know what I know?

'I'm fine. Just tired. It's been a very long day,' I explain, and he seems to accept that.

'It sure has. But it's nearly over now,' he says, which sounds somewhat ominous, especially when he gives me what is clearly a false smile before heading into the kitchen.

I slowly follow him in and see Kai is already seated at the table with his biscuit and milk in front of him and he is hungrily tucking into the snacks. As for Mum, she is making herself and Dad a cup of tea, and she asks me if I want one.

'No, thank you,' I reply quietly, struggling to keep up the act. This might look like a normal domestic scene; it is anything but, not when I've just been told my husband has essentially been forced into hiding by my father based on something terrible that he and Mum may have done.

Steam seeps out of the boiling kettle and the louder the device gets as the water bubbles, the faster my heart beats in my chest. I feel a kick from my baby then too, as if she's trying to warn me to take Kai and get out of here before it's too late. But what can I do? I can't just take him and leave while my parents are here. They'll know something is wrong then, and if they are desperately trying to hide something, how far are they willing to go to keep it hidden?

'I've been thinking,' Mum says as she sets out three cups on the countertop, and I realise she is making a drink for me even though I just turned it down. 'How about we all take a trip? A family holiday. I think we all need one with everything that's been going on. We could get away somewhere warm. Doesn't that sound nice?'

'Yeah, I think a change of scene could do us all some good,' Dad agrees. 'We could go tonight. It wouldn't take long to throw a few things into a suitcase.'

'No time like the present,' Mum goes on as she picks up the kettle and starts to pour the boiling water into the cups. As the hot water hits the teabags, I feel like I'm being hit by something harsh myself.

My parents are talking about us going away.

Are they running?

If so, they want us to go with them.

'A holiday? No, it's not the right time,' I reply with a shake of the head.

'Why not?' Mum asks as she finishes pouring and places the kettle back down. I feel Dad's eyes burning into me as much as that water would do if it were poured onto my skin.

'Because Christian isn't back yet,' I say, staring intently at my parents to gauge their reaction to his name. But they both remain calm and give nothing away.

'He can join us when he's back,' Mum replies casually, as if she really thinks that could happen.

I need another excuse.

'I can't be travelling this close to giving birth,' I say, and I'm glad I actually have a card to play because it's a great one.

'I'm sure it'll be fine,' Mum says, which does not sound very caring and nurturing of her, as if she is actually worried about me and my unborn child. 'I doubt the baby will come while we're away.'

'It might do,' I reply firmly, refusing to be talked into this, whatever *this* is. 'I'm not risking it. I want to be here, near the hospital, just in case.'

I see Mum and Dad share a look then before they take their drinks and place them on the table near to where Kai is still eating. Then Mum approaches me with my drink, the one I refused, and as she hands it to me, she looks sterner than I ever remember seeing her.

'I really think you need a break from here,' she tries again. 'You look stressed and that's not good for the baby. A trip away might be just what you need.'

'There's a flight to Spain tonight that still has a few seats on it,' Dad says, and I notice him looking at his phone. 'How about I call a taxi, and we can get going right away?'

'No time like the present,' Mum says again as she walks away from me, and I feel the heat from the hot drink in my hand starting to burn me. I need to put this cup down before it does, but more urgently, I need to get myself, Kai and my baby out of this very last-minute trip that is being prepared.

'Sorry, but I've already said that we're not going,' I repeat. 'I am due to give birth soon and Kai has to go to school. We can't go to Spain or anywhere else. You two can go if you like.'

I'm hopeful they might just take that last part of what I said and run with it. If Mum and Dad leave for the airport, at least Kai and I will be safe. I can call the police and have them caught there. But then Dad lowers his phone and looks at me, and as I see a darkness in his eyes, I realise that between us, there's only one person who is going to get what they want. *And it isn't me.*

'We're not asking you, darling, we're telling you,' Dad says sincerely. 'Why don't you want to come with us?'

Then he adds the kicker.

'Is it because of what Christian just told you on the phone?'

FORTY-FOUR

I want to grab my son and get us both out of this house. But based on what my father has said, it sounds like it's too late.

'I don't know what you're talking about,' I try unconvincingly. 'I haven't spoken to Christian.'

'Don't lie to us, darling,' Mum says. 'We're your parents. We know you better than anyone. We certainly know when you're hiding something.'

I realise the game is up then, but if it is, I have to start fighting back immediately.

'I'm hiding something?' I repeat, getting agitated. Kai senses it because he stops eating. 'You're the ones hiding things! You persuaded Christian to buy that house, and you kept it quiet from me. Then you told him to leave us behind and offered him money to never come back. What else have you done? Did you tell Cesar to lock Rosie away? And did you tell him to kill Jordan too?'

The things I'm saying are shocking and shouldn't be said in front of my son, but I have no choice. The fear has risen up out of me faster than I can keep it in.

'Wow, Christian did say an awful lot on that phone call,

didn't he,' Dad replies calmly. 'I was eavesdropping on you outside the bedroom door, so I could only hear your side of the conversation, but I guess you've filled in a few of the blanks for me and, as I suspected, Christian has filled your head with all sorts of nonsense.'

'Is it nonsense? Or is it the truth?' I cry, taking a step towards the table, but Mum puts an arm around Kai as if knowing that the only reason I'm getting closer is because I want to get my son away from them.

'Okay, you want the truth?' Dad asks as he sits back in his seat and takes a deep breath. 'I guess you can hear it and then you can make an informed decision on what to do next. You need all the facts and now I'll give them to you. First, I think Kai should go and finish his biscuit in the other room.'

'That's a good idea,' Mum says, and she picks up my son's plate with his half-eaten biscuit on it before standing. But Kai doesn't move. He's looking at me. He senses something is wrong and he wants to know what he should do.

My heart is telling me that he should stay here where I can see him.

But my head is telling me that I won't get the full truth if he remains in the room.

'It's okay, go with Grandma and I'll come and join you in a minute,' I say as I smile at my son, figuring they will only be in the next room, and I'll still be able to hear them and get in there quickly should I need to.

Kai decides to follow my mother and as the pair of them leave the kitchen, I watch my son go, feeling heartbroken for him that his grandparents aren't the amazing people he thinks they are. But he's not the only one who will have to deal with that realisation. As I look back at my father, I prepare to hear some very hurtful things. Not that he seems worried about that. He looks surprisingly calm given the circumstances. Like he's fully in control of this situation – and maybe he is. This is his house, after all, plus he knows I'm not going to go anywhere without Kai.

If he keeps my son here, he keeps me here and that might be all he wants at this moment in time.

'When this estate was first being developed, your mother and I realised it offered a fantastic investment opportunity,' Dad begins from his seat at the table while I continue to stand several feet away from him. 'We decided we wanted to buy a property here and rent it out, just the same as we have done elsewhere. Except there was a difference this time. Our accountant advised us that there had been some changes in the law regarding taxes on additional properties and how things weren't quite so easy for landlords anymore and all those sorts of boring, frustrating things. Considering how many homes we already owned and how high our tax bills already were, that did not sound appealing, and we realised that if we did buy a house here, it wouldn't make us quite as much profit as we had hoped.'

I could say something nasty here about how the only thing he and my mother have ever cared about is that 'P' word, but I don't because I need to hear the rest of this story.

'That's when I had the idea of lending the money to somebody else so they could buy the house for us,' Dad goes on after he has taken a sip of his tea. 'That way, we'd save money in the long term but still make great profits in the short term.'

'So you told Christian to do it,' I say, filling in the blank.

'I didn't tell him. I asked him and he agreed.'

'You knew he would. You knew he was always nervous around you and Mum and all your money. He's your son-in-law, he would have done anything to appease you and avoid any awkwardness.'

'You think that's the only reason he said yes?' Dad says with a snigger. 'Or did it have something to do with the fact that he would make some money out of this deal, and he could spend that to make his life easier too.'

I hesitate to answer so Dad carries on.

'See, it's not just your parents who like making money, your husband does too. So we sent him the cash, and he bought the house in his name and then we agreed to use a rental agency to find a couple of suitable tenants. We figured once the rent money started rolling in, everything would be easy.'

'But it went wrong,' I say, and Dad actually agrees with me for once because he nods.

'The tenants they found for us were no good.'

'Rosie and Jordan,' I say, and Dad nods again.

'They missed their first month's rent payment and showed no signs of being able to get it anytime soon. The agency contacted Christian and told him there was an issue, and he passed that information on to me.'

'What did you do?' I ask, my question dripping in anxiety.

'I told Christian to get the agency to do their job,' Dad replies. 'The tenants were contractually obliged to pay their rent. I figured once a bit of pressure was applied, they would pay what they owed and if they couldn't pay anymore, they would leave and new tenants would be found. But that's not what happened. Rosie and Jordan did not pay any more money. It was excuse after excuse. Cashflow problems with their business. Unexpected unemployment. Waiting to hear back about a new job. Blah blah blah. The bottom line was they owed us money and refused to pay it.'

'What did you do?' I ask again.

'I realised that either the agency or Christian wasn't resolving the issue,' Dad says. 'So your mother and I got involved. We decided to get a spare key from Christian and go and pay Rosie and Jordan a visit.'

'To threaten them?'

'No, of course not. Just to remind them that they had to pay the money they owed or they were breaking the law.'

'Did it make you proud? Going around to people who were

struggling and telling them to pay you money while you just got richer and they got poorer?' I say, realising my parents were even more obsessed with money than I had thought.

'I'm not going to apologise for being wealthy and neither should your mother,' Dad replies curtly. 'And I'm certainly not going to apologise for trying to extract money out of two people who owed it. Especially not when we got to the house and saw the state of it. It was obvious to us that Rosie and Jordan were not taking care of the place and that only made me angrier.'

'So what did you do?'

'It was only Jordan who was there when we arrived, so your mother and I made an attempt to talk to him reasonably. We explained the situation and that he needed to pay the money he owed by the end of the week, or he would have to leave and we would seek to get the money back at a later date while the police were notified.'

'And what did he say to that?' I ask nervously.

'He didn't like it,' Dad scoffs. 'He asked for more time and said he didn't have the money. Then he said he had rights and he told us to go away. Can you believe that? We were standing in a house that we had paid for, and we were being told to get out by a man who owed us money. That just wasn't going to happen, so I took out my phone and told Jordan that I was calling the police right there and then. I expected he would fall for my bluff and agree to pay us the money as soon as he could.'

'But he didn't?'

Dad shakes his head and now he is wearing a slightly vacant stare, as if currently transported back to that time in his mind as he describes it to me.

'He tried to take the phone from my hand,' Dad tells me. 'He begged me not to call the police. He said he was trying his best. But I knew it was just excuses. I'd heard it all before. I pushed him away from me. That's when he fell backwards...'

FORTY-FIVE

'What happened?' I ask, needing to know the rest.

'He banged his head as he fell down,' Dad replies, but he looks more irritated by that fact than worried.

'You hurt him!' I cry, aghast that the man who used to care for me when I was a little girl is capable of causing physical harm to another person.

'No, it was an accident,' Dad replies defiantly as he gets up from his chair. 'I didn't mean to push him, but you have to understand, I was frustrated. He was the one in the wrong, not me or your mother. Him!'

'What happened?' I ask. Dad starts pacing around the kitchen, but I maintain my distance from him.

'He didn't get up. He just lay there on the ground. I told him to stop messing around but he didn't move. That was when your mother checked on him and told me she thought he was dead.'

'Oh my god!' I cry, horrified and disgusted in equal measure.

'I guess we went into survival mode,' Dad goes on, still pacing. 'I knew we couldn't call the police and try to explain it.

It was too complicated. The house was in Christian's name, not ours, so technically, we didn't have a right to be there. I couldn't risk the police classing us as intruders and not believing me when I said the push was accidental. I couldn't risk going down for murder, certainly not for a loser like Jordan.'

I can't even speak as I hear all of this. I have to sit down before I pass out, so I take an empty seat at the table, the one Dad just left as he continues wandering around the room in a distracted daze.

'We knew we had to do something about the body, but we didn't want to risk being seen. That's when I had the idea of going to see Cesar.'

I bristle at the mention of that awful man's name. I guess this is where he comes into the story.

'I'd never met him, but I'd read numerous articles about him in the local news,' Dad explains. 'About how he had grand visions for this new estate he had developed. About how it was going to become home to the most sought-after properties in town. Most importantly, about how it was going to be a totally crime-free neighbourhood with an outstanding reputation. I figured that if he wanted to maintain that idea, he was not going to like the fact there was now a dead body on the estate. So maybe he would help us cover it up.'

I am so glad Kai is not in the room. It means I'm the only one who has to hear this terrifying tale.

'Your mother and I went to the estate office and asked to see Cesar. We initially pretended like we were interested in buying here. We figured that would make him want to see us quickly. But when he did, we told him the truth and, more specifically, we told him that if he wanted to sell the rest of the houses here, as well as the new ones being built, all while maintaining the "crime-free" status, he would have to help us deal with Jordan.'

'So he did,' I say quietly, and Dad stops walking and looks at me, which I take as a yes. 'Who buried him? You or Cesar?'

'We did it together,' Dad replies.

I feel nauseous again.

'We did that while your mother cleaned the house and removed our fingerprints. She was also waiting for Rosie to return.'

I think about that poor woman who was out while her boyfriend was killed and buried. What shocking scene did she come home to?

'By the time we'd buried Jordan and cleaned the house, there was no sign of Rosie returning. That was when Cesar told us to leave and that he would take care of her when she got back.'

'What did he mean by that?' I ask, and Dad doesn't reply, but I don't let him off the hook that easily. 'Did you think he was going to kill her? Were you happy to let him do that?'

'I was just trying to keep your mother safe,' Dad replies. 'We left and we didn't hear anything again. Not from Cesar or the police or anyone, so it seemed like it was all going to go away. To ensure that, we suggested to Christian that he move into the house with you and Kai rather than rent it out again. I pitched it to him as a gift from me and your mother ahead of you having the baby. A big new house for you to all live in and, of course, Christian thought that sounded good. He didn't know the truth of what had happened. He just thought Rosie and Jordan had left after being kicked out by the agency. As for me, I thought it was safest to have family living there rather than two more strangers who might cause problems because I obviously wanted the house's true history hidden forever.'

I think about how my poor, stupid, naïve husband really was an innocent pawn in this awful, deadly game that my parents played with Cesar. A game that had more life in it based on what my father says next.

'Cesar came to us one day and told us that based on the help he had provided to us by getting rid of Rosie and Jordan, he wanted something in return. He said that we had to buy a house here. An investment to pay for the crimes he had helped us commit.'

'So that was another lie,' I say, losing track of them all now. 'You didn't buy this house here to be closer to me and the new baby. You bought it as part of your sordid deal with Cesar.'

Dad can't argue with that, and he knows better than to try.

'I just wanted all of this to go away. For things to go back to normal again. And I thought they had,' Dad laments. 'But Cesar had lied. He hadn't held up his end of the bargain. He hadn't got rid of Rosie. Not properly. Unbeknownst to us, Cesar hadn't properly dealt with her. He had just locked her up in his house and then you went and found her. How could he have been so stupid? He left a loose end and look what's happened. Cesar's dead. Rosie's been talking, and now Christian is suspected of being Jordan's killer.'

'He a suspect because you told him to leave!' I cry, and again my father can't dispute that. While he's quiet, I think about some of the other things that haven't been answered yet.

'Who put the camera in my house?' I ask him, expecting him to say it was either him or Mum.

'That must have been Cesar,' Dad replies. 'We didn't do that. He must have been wanting to keep an eye on you and make sure you weren't getting close to the truth.'

That's one thing they didn't do, but it hardly makes up for everything else. Then I think about the phone call I got that day from the person who was asking for Rosie and Jordan. More specifically, I think about how the line got cut at the most inopportune time. I had figured it must have been Cesar's doing too, but now with what I know, I realise who was actually in my house that day.

'You ended that call, didn't you?' I say as I think back to how my father had called around to visit me shortly before he told me to go upstairs and get some rest. I was upstairs when the phone rang and while I thought Dad had left the house, he must have lingered back and heard me talking to somebody. He must have picked up the phone and heard what was being said on the call. *So he ended it.*

Dad confirms it was him.

'I took the socket off the wall and cut the cable inside before covering it up again,' he sheepishly admits.

'All this time! All the stress and anxiety I've had over this! All the paranoia and sleepless nights, worrying I was losing my mind when the whole time, I was right. Something was being covered up and it was being covered up by you and Mum!'

I've totally lost it now, shouting and screaming and crying, and it's no surprise when Kai comes running into the room to check if I'm okay. Dad takes a step towards him, but I reach out and pull my son close. I'm not going to let go of him while my parents are around.

Mum rushes into the kitchen and then joins her husband as they stand and stare at me and Kai, the pair of us cowering by the table, and there's a very long silence which I'm not sure how to fill. I want to ask to be allowed to leave, but I know my parents won't give me the chance. Then, after all Dad has had to say, it's Mum who speaks next.

'I'm guessing you've heard about everything that happened,' she says calmly as I stifle my sobs and Kai snuggles into my shoulder. 'So, the only question now is, what are you going to do about it?'

FORTY-SIX

As I hold my son and stare at my parents, I know there is only one thing I can do.

I have to do the safest thing for me, Kai and my unborn daughter.

'I'm not going to try and stop you from getting away,' I tell Mum and Dad. 'Just go. Leave us. You can get out of here tonight. Go to Spain like you wanted to. Maybe you'll never get caught. Maybe all this will go away.'

I hope they'll accept that. I really want them to pack their things and leave this house. Once they have, I can call the police and explain everything and then Christian can come home and be reunited with his family. I just want the four of us to be safe. Right now, I don't care what happens to my parents. Nor do I want them to feel like they have to hurt me to protect their secret.

'We're not leaving without our family,' Dad replies. 'We want you all to come with us. You, Kai, and of course, we want to meet our granddaughter when she is born. So we all have to leave together tonight.'

'Where are we going?' Kai asks.

'On a holiday,' Mum tells him. 'Would you like that?'

Kai thinks about it for a second before answering. 'Only if Daddy can come.'

'I'm afraid he can't come tonight,' my mother replies. 'But he can meet us when we get there.'

They know full well that Christian wouldn't be able to come and find us, because if we board a plane, my parents will be doing so with the intention that we never get found and we never come back.

'I can't leave,' I tell them. 'You have to understand. I can't take the kids away from Christian. It's not fair on him.'

'You have to understand that we can't just walk out of here and not expect you to call the police the second we are gone,' Dad replies, and I'm feeling less and less like their daughter by the second and more like another one of their business transactions.

'Please, don't make me do this,' I say, feeling the tears returning, and now Kai is getting upset because he can see that his grandparents are not behaving the way they usually would around him. Gone are the warm smiles and the offers of snacks and in their place are threats and warnings.

'It doesn't have to be difficult,' Dad tells me. 'Just come with us and we can all be together. Like we said, maybe Christian can join us afterwards.'

'You know he can't!' I cry. 'Not when you've forced him to go on the run. But he won't stay away forever. He could be talking to the police right now. They could be on their way over here to arrest you and then you'll be screwed.'

'That's why we need to leave right away,' Dad says as Mum nervously glances out of the window. I can see she is afraid of the police coming here like I just said. 'Come on. It's time to go.'

Dad sends Mum upstairs to pack some things while he stays and watches us. I really hope that Christian is in contact with the police. If so, maybe they can be stopped but, in the meantime, I fear I might have to go along with Mum and Dad's plan. If I at least pretend to be prepared to leave the country with them, they won't do anything drastic. I just have to hope that they are caught before we get too far away.

'Kai, listen to me,' I say, looking at my son's worried face. 'We're going to go with Grandma and Grandad, okay?'

'What about Daddy?'

'We'll see him soon,' I reply, praying that I'm right so it's not a lie.

'You'll see that this is the best thing for everyone,' my father interjects, but I just ignore him and keep staring at my brave boy.

He agrees to do what I'm telling him, and we reluctantly go and get a few things so it appears as if we're actually going along with this. I'm taking my time, hopeful that the police will appear before we have walked outside. I'm also hoping to get a chance to contact them or Christian, but Dad asks me to hand my phone over, 'just to be on the safe side'.

As horrible as this whole thing is, one of the hardest parts of it is seeing how my parents are more worried about saving themselves than they are about what they are doing to me and Kai, not to mention their unborn grandchild.

'Time to go,' Dad says after I've stalled as long as I can, and he carries the small bag I packed along with the one Kai has to the car.

While he's outside, I consider trying running with Kai out the back door, or hitting Mum so she can't stop us, but I really don't want to do anything to scare my son. So I just stand in the hallway and watch as Mum turns off the lights in the house before she tells us it's time to leave.

I step outside while holding my son's hand before looking up and down the street for any sign of help being on the way. But I don't see any help, and while I can hear noise in the distance which I assume is coming from the building site where

Jordan's body was found earlier, there is nobody outside on this street now except us.

Dad has got the bags in the car and now he is standing with one hand on an open door, waiting for Kai and myself to get inside.

I guess we're really leaving.

Until I decide I cannot risk this any longer…

'Run!' I say to my son, giving him a push in a direction away from my parents and their car. I have no idea how I'm supposed to outrun them in my physical state, but I know our lives might depend on me trying.

Then I start running too.

FORTY-SEVEN

It might have been a stupid thing to do but we've done it and now Kai and I are moving as fast as we can to get away from the two people behind us.

I expect my son will be able to move quicker than I can considering he is young and light on his feet while I am older and carrying another person. I'm also expecting that if my parents do try and chase us, they will make do with trying to catch me, so at least Kai will get away. Although as I see my father run past me, I realise he is going for his grandson rather than his daughter.

'Get off him!' I cry out as I watch Dad grab Kai and pick him up before turning back to his car.

I run over to him now, abandoning my own chance of escape because I obviously am not leaving Kai behind, but as Dad bundles Kai onto the backseat of the car, Mum moves in front of me to block me.

'What are you doing? Let him out of the car!' I try as Mum puts her hands on my shoulders.

'Calm down. Think of the baby,' she says, but I'm too hysterical to listen and my parents must realise that because they make no attempt to try and get me in the car as well. Instead, Dad just closes the back door so Kai can't get out before getting in behind the wheel and calling for Mum to join him.

'No!' I cry as Mum suddenly leaves me and dashes into the car. I realise they are prepared to leave me behind if it means they can at least get away with one of their family members.

As Mum closes her door and Dad starts the engine, I lunge towards the vehicle, but it speeds away and it's as if what happens next is in slow motion.

My parents are genuinely taking my son away from me.

'No!' I cry as I realise I'll never be able to catch the car. 'Kai!'

I watch them driving away and hope that this is all just some sick joke and my parents will stop and turn around. They have to, don't they? They can't genuinely be doing this to me, no matter how desperate they are. Can they?

But the car isn't stopping and, in a few seconds, it will turn off the street and be totally out of sight.

I try to run again.

I already know it's futile. I'll never catch them, even if I wasn't heavily pregnant, because no human can catch a speeding car, but I can't give up. I run as fast as my legs will carry me, but the car leaves the street that I'm still on, so I know they're getting further away.

As the gap between us widens, I try to see through the tears in my eyes and as I reach the corner of the street and look down it, the car is quickly disappearing from view again already.

'Somebody help me! Please! They're taking my boy!'

My desperate cries pierce the suburban stillness and if anybody is out here, they will have no doubt heard me. But can they help me?

The car continues to get further away and I'm expecting that it will be gone in a matter of seconds, leaving me here alone and with my only hope being to call the police and pray they can catch up with them before they board that plane and leave the country.

Then I see the lights belonging to another car turn on and suddenly, that car starts reversing off its driveway at high speed.

It's right in front of where Dad is about to drive by, and he can't slow down in time which means the impending collision is inevitable.

When it comes, there is a loud crunch as my parents' vehicle crashes into the car that just blocked them and now they have been stopped. I start running again, my odds of catching up to them having greatly improved. But Kai was inside that car, and I have no idea if he is okay or if he just got hurt, so the closer I get, the more afraid I grow.

I see a door open and somebody gets out, but it's the person who was driving the other car. When I get a proper look at who it is, I gasp.

It's Theo.

But he doesn't stop to look at me. Instead, he opens the back door of the car he just caused the impact with and, a moment later, I see him taking Kai from the backseat.

My son is okay.

I reach Kai and pull him into my arms and hug him tightly while Theo checks on my parents before telling me that they are groggy but conscious. Then he asks me if I am all right, but I don't answer him because there is far too much adrenaline coursing through my body for me to be able to string a sentence together at this moment. But I also don't answer him because I hear something in the distance.

Sirens.

The police are on their way, so Christian must have called them.

That means I can save my talking for when they get here.

I also hope it means I am about to see my husband again very soon.

EPILOGUE

I'm overwhelmed. I'm exhausted. And I don't know if I can do this.

I guess I feel like every mother of two young children.

I am holding my six-month-old daughter in my arms while my six-year-old son runs around my legs trying to get me to play football with him, and it's taking all my effort not to drop the baby and fall over. Add in the fact that I'm running on just three hours' sleep and I could use another pair of hands to help out around here. Fortunately, I have them.

'Kai. Come with me. We're going outside,' Christian says, scooping up the football and heading for the door when he sees I'm struggling and, mercifully, our son follows his father in leaving the house.

There is a moment of temporary calm once Kai is out of the way, although that is broken when the child I'm carrying starts to cry.

'Oh, darling, what's wrong? Are you getting hungry again?' I ask Sophia, my gorgeous girl, who thankfully, since her birth, has not had to witness any of the drama I experienced while I was pregnant with her.

I grab a bottle from the fridge before taking a seat and giving Sophia a feed, and her screams for nourishment are replaced by soft, sucking sounds on the teat. Peace at last, or at least it's mostly peace because I can hear the football being kicked around in the back garden before Kai lets out a big cheer, suggesting he has just scored a goal against his father.

As Sophia's eyes start to close and she looks like she could drift off, I wish I could do the same. A knock at the door forces me out of my comfortable chair, and while Sophia is still asleep in my arms, I am intrigued as to who has come to visit us.

I really hope it's not a detective or a police officer or anybody like that.

It's not.

It's Theo.

And he has somebody with him.

'Hayley?' I say as I look at the woman standing beside Theo, the woman I haven't seen since that day she came to my house and tried to tell me something important, the same woman I feared had been killed and silenced.

'Hi,' she says with a warm smile before noticing Sophia. 'Oh, wow. Congratulations!'

'Yeah, congrats. She's beautiful,' Theo says before he puts an arm around Hayley, suggesting these two are very much a couple again. It's more just a relief to see that she is actually okay and as she clearly is, it proves that Theo was telling me the truth about her reasons for leaving. But I'd already figured he was a good guy who was on my side based on the fact that he drove his car into my parents as they were trying to flee with Kai. I've already thanked him for doing that several times, but that was many months ago now and I hadn't expected to see him again. Certainly not considering Christian and I left the estate and bought a house elsewhere, far away from that place where so many things went wrong. But here he is again now, and he has brought company.

'Can we come in?' Hayley asks me. 'It's just there's a few things I want to tell you that might clear up any remaining questions you had about what happened.'

'Of course,' I say as I step aside and allow the couple in, and I consider letting Christian know they are here. But he's occupying Kai and if my son comes in, there is little chance we'll get to talk in peace, so I decide to leave my male family members outside the house for now.

Neither Theo nor Hayley accept my offer of a drink so we all take a seat, and while Sophia continues to snuggle and snooze on my chest, I wait to hear what Hayley has come to tell me.

Let's just hope there is no alarm to interrupt us this time.

'First of all, I want to apologise,' Hayley says, surprising me.

'You have nothing to apologise for. Neither of you do,' I say adamantly. 'You tried to warn me about Cesar, which I appreciate, and Theo, you stopped my son from being taken from me. As far as I'm concerned, I owe you two a lot.'

Theo seems appreciative of those remarks, but Hayley still looks conflicted.

'Thank you for saying that,' she replies. 'But the truth is, I wasn't as much help as I should have been to you back then. I let my emotions get the better of me and I was drinking too much. That made it harder for me to do what I really needed to do. I should have spoken to you as soon as you moved in. More than that, I should have spoken to the police as soon as I knew something was wrong next door. If I had, you and your family would not have had to go through what you did.'

Hayley does look genuinely upset, but she doesn't seem as in distress as she did that day she showed up on my doorstep. I could tell she was drunk then, as well as extremely sleep deprived, but while she feels bad now, it's obvious to me she is in a much better place. I am too, so that's why I try and tell her again that she is not to blame. But she has more to say.

'I was at home alone the evening Jordan must have died,' she tells me. 'I suspected something was wrong because I heard shouting from next door. I wasn't sure what to do, though. I wondered if it was just a domestic dispute between Rosie and Jordan, although I never heard her voice, I just heard his. He sounded upset. Angry. Then afraid.'

Theo reaches out and takes Hayley's hand and it seems to give her the strength to carry on.

'I didn't tell anyone that night. Theo had been away on business for a while. So long, in fact, that he had never met Rosie and Jordan. I always slept badly while he was away, but I slept terribly when worrying what might have happened next door, and I thought about going there to check everyone was okay. Before I could, I got a visit from Cesar.'

I bristle as I hear that man's name again, while Theo continues to hold Hayley's hand.

'He asked me if I heard anything the night before and I told him I had before asking him what had happened. But he didn't tell me. He just said it was a minor incident, and it had all been resolved, but that Rosie and Jordan had left the property, and we would be getting new neighbours instead.'

'I can't believe he would come to you with those lies,' I say as I shake my head, but there's more.

'That's not all he said. He told me that he wanted to make up for any inconvenience or distress I might have experienced, so to do that, he was offering to reduce the mortgage term on our house, which would save us quite a lot of money over the next few years. I was shocked. It seemed like a very generous offer. We certainly could have done with the financial help too as we'd overstretched ourselves a little on the house when we bought it.'

'It seemed like such a great area to buy in,' Theo says sadly before Hayley carries on.

'I was tempted to take the offer, but said I'd need to discuss it with Theo when he got home. Cesar didn't like that. He said I had to keep this between ourselves, and that the offer had to be accepted immediately or it was no longer on the table. So I took it. But I wish I hadn't.'

Now it's Hayley who is shaking her head.

'I was so stupid. I should have known he was trying to cover something up. Why else would he suddenly come to my house and do such a big favour for me? He was hiding something that happened next door, but because I accepted his offer, I wasn't able to find out what it was. The deal was, I told no one. Not Theo. Not anybody else. And certainly not the next people who moved into that house.'

I think about how Hayley had only done what she thought was right for herself and Theo by saving them money, yet in the process, she allowed Cesar to keep getting away with the horrors that had unfolded next door. The horrors that my parents were also a part of.

'As time went by, despite saving money on the house, I felt guiltier and guiltier,' Hayley goes on. 'I wondered what had happened to Rosie and Jordan and feared it was something bad. I was afraid Cesar had a dark secret, but I was scared of angering him in case he really was dangerous. So I kept quiet. I became distant from Theo. And I started drinking too much to try and alleviate the guilt. But it didn't work. I knew I had to do something and when I saw you move in, I felt I had to try and warn you that something bad might have happened there. Something more than just the note I left.'

I recall the note, the thing that first started all this for me. 'How did you leave it there for me to find?' I ask her, trying to complete this little piece of the jigsaw puzzle.

'I was able to get in while the house was unoccupied. It was easy because the estate agent came and went a few times but he rarely, if ever, locked up. There was hardly anyone on the estate then and Cesar always talked about how it would be crime free, so I guess he believed that, or he was just lazy. Either way, I was able to get inside, and I put the note where I thought a new resident might find it, but crucially, somewhere Cesar and the estate agent would miss it.'

She certainly did that well, not that she looks too proud of it.

'It's okay,' I say again, not wanting her to feel any worse than she does.

'Nobody blames you,' Theo says then, backing up my point as he continues to squeeze Hayley's hand. 'Cesar put you in a very awkward position, and you weren't to know what had really happened. How could you? Nobody could have predicted what he would do.'

'Or what my parents would do,' I say sadly.

I think about Mum and Dad, the things they did in desperation, in pursuit of money, in a desire to protect themselves and the comfortable life they had. Jordan's death. The plan with Cesar. How they thought Rosie had been killed to protect their secret. How they tried to put it all on Christian and then, when the plan was unravelling, they tried to get me to flee with them before they kidnapped their grandson. It's not the kind of story I want Kai or Sophia to grow up and read about, though I fear they will because it was obviously all over the news. There are plenty of articles online talking about what happened, just like there are articles detailing how my parents were sentenced to at least twenty years behind bars each for their part in the crimes, which ranged from murder, perverting the course of justice and the attempted abduction of their grandchild. I wish I could delete those articles. I wish I could delete the entire internet just to be sure. Some nights, I wish I could delete my parents' presence in this family too.

But I can't do any of that.

All I can do is be the best parent to my children and that's Christian's vow too.

This family will not repeat the mistakes of those who came before us.

'It's great to see that you two are back together and supporting one another,' I say after Theo has suggested he and Hayley leave now that she has said what she came to say. 'I wish you both all the best and if you're ever in the area again, feel free to call by and say hello.'

'We'll do that,' Theo says with a smile before he departs, though I suspect it might just be one of those agreements made out of politeness rather than a real desire to ever see me again. I wouldn't blame them if they stayed away forever now. Why be reminded of the awful past?

As I watch them both go, I think about how, if things had been different on that estate, we could have become best friends as we spent many happy years living next door to each other. They might have had children one day too and they could have grown up with my kids, all of them playing outside in our garden while we four adults barbequed and drank wine in the summer sunshine.

Alas, it was not meant to be.

———

But there is some sunshine showing itself today, so I place the sleepy Sophia carefully in her pram before suggesting to Christian and Kai that we all go for a family walk.

As we leave our new house and head along our street, I think about how we haven't had much of a chance to explore this estate since we moved here. It's all been so hectic, what with the house move, the new baby and, of course, the regular updates from the police about what was happening with my parents. Today is a good opportunity to find out more about our surroundings and the people in it.

'I love you,' Christian says to me as he takes over the

pushing of the pram while Kai runs ahead of us with his ball like he usually does.

'I love you too,' I reply with a smile, feeling like all is well in the world again, or at least as well as it can be.

'I hate you!' comes the curt cry from a female to our left then, shattering the serene moment between myself and my husband, and as we both turn, we see a woman storming out of a house followed by her husband who is trying to catch her up.

They both look angry, distressed and still very much in the heat of an argument and, for a second, Christian and I stop and aren't sure what to do about what we are witnessing. Then we both quickly resume walking, and as we turn the street corner, we don't look back.

I guess every estate has its dramas, secrets and lies, but we're not getting involved in any of that around here.

I'm just going to focus on my family.

There's enough drama to deal with there.

A LETTER FROM DANIEL

Dear reader,

I want to say a huge thank you for choosing to read *The Couple Before Us*. If you did enjoy it and would like to keep up to date with all my latest Bookouture releases, please sign up at the following link. Your email address will never be shared and you can unsubscribe at any time.

www.bookouture.com/daniel-hurst

I hope you loved *The Couple Before Us*, and if you did, I would be very grateful if you could write an honest review. I'd love to hear what you think!

You can read my free short story, *The Killer Wife*, by signing up to my Bookouture mailing list.

You can also visit my website where you can download a free psychological thriller called *Just One Second* and join my personal weekly newsletter, where you can hear all about my future writing as well as my adventures with my wife, Harriet, and daughter, Penny.

Thank you,

Daniel

KEEP IN TOUCH WITH DANIEL

Get in touch with me directly at my email address
daniel@danielhurstbooks.com. I reply to every message!

www.danielhurstbooks.com

 facebook.com/danielhurstbooks
 instagram.com/danielhurstbooks

PUBLISHING TEAM

Turning a manuscript into a book requires the efforts of many people. The publishing team at Bookouture would like to acknowledge everyone who contributed to this publication.

Audio
Alba Proko
Melissa Tran
Sinead O'Connor

Commercial
Lauren Morrissette
Hannah Richmond
Imogen Allport

Cover design
Lisa Horton

Data and analysis
Mark Alder
Mohamed Bussuri

Editorial
Natasha Harding
Melissa Tran

RAISING READERS
Books Build Bright Futures

Dear Reader,

We'd love your attention for one more page to tell you about the crisis in children's reading, and what we can all do.

Studies have shown that reading for fun is the **single biggest predictor of a child's future success** – more than family circumstance, parents' educational background or income. It improves academic results, mental health, wealth, communication skills, and ambition.

The number of children reading for fun is in rapid decline. Young people have a lot of competition for their time, and a worryingly high number do not have a single book at home.

Our business works extensively with schools, libraries and literacy charities, but here are some ways we can all raise more readers:

- Reading to children for just 10 minutes a day makes a difference
- Don't give up if children aren't regular readers – there will be books for them!

- Visit bookshops and libraries to get recommendations
- Encourage them to listen to audiobooks
- Support school libraries
- Give books as gifts

Thank you for reading: there's a lot more information about how to encourage children to read on our website.

www.JoinRaisingReaders.com

www.ingramcontent.com/pod-product-compliance
Lightning Source LLC
LaVergne TN
LVHW042242280725
817309LV00006B/83